"I know how you feel," Howard said. "This isn't a nice job, so let's get it over with."

They dug in silence. When they struck the top of the tiny casket, they continued digging along one side until there was room to stand beside it. The hinges were rusty and the lock was badly corroded. With a sickish dread of what he was about to see, Martin helped Howard lift the cover.

"My God," Martin breathed. "It's empty."

Howard said quietly, "I thought it would be. But I had to be sure."

A CHILD IS MISSING

CHARLOTTE PAUL

A CHILD IS MISSING

Charlotte Paul

A Bernard Geis Associates Book
Published by G.P. Putnam's Sons
Distributed by Berkley Publishing Corporation

G. P. Putnam's Sons
200 Madison Avenue
New York, New York 10016

SBN 425-03833-5

BERKLEY MEDALLION BOOKS are published by
Berkley Publishing Corporation
200 Madison Avenue
New York, N. Y. 10016

BERKLEY MEDALLION BOOK ® TM 757,375

Printed in the United States of America

Berkley Edition, July, 1978

A Bernard Geis Associates Book

A CHILD IS MISSING

Prologue

AT THE EDGE of the woods the man paused and lowered the heavy ladder to the ground. The dark, dripping forest and the dense undergrowth had sheltered him. Now, in the open, the bitter wind struck him full force and the cold rain lashed his face. He rested for a moment, panting.

Before him, only fifty feet away, the Dahlquist mansion was silhouetted against the stormy sky. Windows. There were many windows. At the far end of the house, light spilled out onto the driveway. But his goal was the second-floor window nearest him, and that was dark.

He was sweating now in spite of the cold. Drawing damp air deep into his lungs, he renewed his grip on the ladder, lifted it, and slid cautiously out of the woods. Half blinded by rain, he stumbled across the driveway and stopped in the freshly dug flower bed at the corner of the house, gasping for breath but more from tension than exertion.

His boots sank into the soft clay. With every labored

breath he sucked in the mildewed odor of mud. Though it was black all around, the darkness seemed even thicker against the house, as if, even at night, the great white house cast a shadow.

The man's arm muscles knotted with the effort to control the weight of the ladder as he let it tip forward and come to rest against the house. Heart pounding, he lifted his right foot and tested the lower rung. "Gott, Gott in Himmel!" he whispered frantically as, rung by rung, his mud-caked boots found a firm footing. The shrill voice of the wind cried through the eaves. A dagger of lightning split the sky. But now the man was almost smiling as he reached the top of the ladder. He steadied himself against the windowsill with one hand, and with the other he reached into his pocket and drew out a screwdriver and a chisel.

Inside Leif Dahlquist's house, the sounds of the storm were reduced to a muted obbligato blending with the snug creaking of old floors and walls and the comfortable murmurs of a household preparing for the night.

In the servants' wing, the middle-aged couple had already gone to bed. The wailing wind and the pelting rain did not disturb them, for they had drunk their nightly cups of hot Ovaltine and they always slept soundly after that. The only other servant was the nursemaid. She was leaning over a small oak desk in the servants' sitting room just off the kitchen. As soon as she finished this letter to her sister in Ireland, she would go upstairs and check on the baby.

In the spacious master suite, Leif Dahlquist's wife Elizabeth was running a hot tub. The noisy splash of water filled the steamy bathroom, a barricade against all outside sounds. With a contented sigh, she turned off the taps and slipped into the pine-scented water. She had been suffering from a head cold. A long soak would prepare her for a good night's sleep.

In the library on the ground floor, Leif Dahlquist was listening to the last news broadcast of the day. The fire in the hearth had burned down to a few embers. From the radio at his elbow, the news droned on, tinny and monotonous. The Soviet Union announces the beginning of the second Five-Year Plan.... Franklin D. Roosevelt is gathering support for his campaign to unseat President Hoover.... America's superior technology has finally produced balloon tires for tractors.... Tomorrow the new London Philharmonic plays its first concert under the direction of Sir Thomas Beecham, while in the cultural centers of the United States, music lovers are humming "Minnie the Moocher," "Mood Indigo," and "Goodnight, Sweetheart." The number of unemployed in the United States has risen to fourteen million.... In Los Angeles, preparations for the Olympic Games are nearing completion.... Mussolini, continuing his record of heroic achievement, is now draining the Pontine marshes southeast of Rome....

Leif rested his head against the back of his armchair and wearily closed his eyes. Benito Mussolini, Italy's hero.... Leif had been proclaimed "Hero" so often in the past five years that the word embarrassed him. The hero is the lonely quarry, pursued relentlessly by hungry packs of hero worshippers. But in Italy? No, Leif thought. Il Duce's privacy is insured by an army of palace guards. No Italian newspaper photographer would dare pursue Il Duce's car. No tourists would dare to sneak into Il Duce's private home or sit with picnic lunches in his front yard....

Leif Dahlquist's eyes flew open. What was that sound? A snapping, muffled by the storm. A branch, broken off by the wind? He sank back into his chair, his attention once more focused on the news. "... Engineers report progress on construction of the Golden Gate bridge.... Jack Sharkey training hard for the match he hopes will take the world heavyweight boxing crown away from Germany's pride, Max Schmeling.... Gandhi fasting in his prison cell.... A candidate for the Nobel Prize.... Matrix theory of quantum mechanics...."

In his basket by the fireplace, the cocker spaniel snored softly. He had been a present to baby Leif on his first birthday. The quilt he slept on was almost a twin to the one that covered the baby in his crib upstairs. Leif looked at the dog and smiled. What a watchdog! It was a family joke that the pretty curly-haired spaniel had never protected them from anything but the family cats.

Many miles to the east of the Dahlquist estate, a modest frame building called the Cascade Inn was stolidly accepting its share of lashing wind and driving rain. Officer Jack Howard was in his one-room bachelor apartment on the ground floor, where a window he could neither open nor completely close looked out on a meadow and a few scattered fruit trees.

Tonight, the view from that window was swallowed by the dark, but Howard wasn't interested in it anyway. He was seated in his one and only easy chair, trying with less and less success to finish one chapter in a particularly boring textbook on police science. "One chapter a day, and on your own time!" That was the captain's edict to all rookie cops, but tonight Howard was too tired to be intimidated. It had been a rough week for the Green Hill precinct, and being the newest man on the force, Howard had drawn the roughest hours. He wanted to sleep, he needed sleep. But for some reason he felt too tense, too keyed up. He knew it would be useless to go to bed in such an uneasy frame of mind.

Eyes closed, he listened to the storm. The wind drove the rain so that it rattled against the windowpanes, as demanding as a knock on the door. Somewhere between waking and sleeping, Howard answered, inexplicably, "Come and get me...."

The storm grew louder. The rhythmic beat of the rain slowed to an insistent rapping. *One,* two, three... *one,* two, three... Sharp knuckles seemed to strike the glass. Someone at the window? Someone calling his name?

Now he was across the room, seemingly without effort. He raised the shade and peered through the rain-washed glass.

There was no one there.

Howard shivered uncontrollably, for suddenly the window glass had shattered and the storm had burst into the room. Rain pelted his face and blurred his vision. And then, miraculously, he could see. Out of the opaque blackness, a vivid picture emerged. It was a three-story mansion in the center of sloping lawns completely encircled by woods. In spite of the trees, the great white house was visible, and he recognized it. It was the Dahlquist house, The Aerie. Though the estate lay within the boundaries of his precinct, Howard had seen it only once, on a peaceful sunlit day when he was touring the area. It was miles away! He couldn't possibly see it. And yet the image was as clear as if it were at the end of the meadow.

As suddenly as the scene had come to life, it changed. At first there had been light in only three or four windows. Now there was light in all of them, streams of gold pouring into the night. Staring at the blazing windows, Howard felt inexplicably fearful. He tried to call out, to shout a warning.

Officer Howard sat bolt upright, awakened from his nightmare by the sound of his own voice. The agonized cry richocheted in his head. He was in his easy chair... But hadn't he been standing at the open window, with rain stinging his face and soaking his clothing? How, then, had he come back to his chair?

He jumped up and hurried to the window. The glass was intact. He looked out but there was nothing to see. No house, no lights. Only the tap, tap, tap, the rapping at his window caused by a broken branch of the shade tree outside, swinging against the glass in rhythm with the gusting wind.

He tried to raise the window, but as usual, he couldn't. It was the one with the rusty lock. It hadn't been broken and he couldn't have opened it. He couldn't have been standing in the rain. . . . For several minutes, he remained at the window, looking out. Then he drew the blind. He was bone-weary now, ready to sleep.

His last ritualistic act before going to bed was to mark the calendar tacked to the wall. March 1, 1932. He drew a large X through the date, and noted below: "Bad storm tonight, but I slept through the worst of it." Minutes later, he was sound asleep.

In the servants' sitting room, the Dahlquist baby nurse had finished her letter. She rose, pulled her wrapper around her, and hurried to the second floor. Ordinarily, there was no necessity for a late evening visit to the nursery. But tonight she was concerned because the baby had caught his mother's cold. She wanted to make sure he was warm and secure inside the cocoon of blankets she had fashioned with the help of two large safety pins.

She opened the nursery door cautiously, not wanting to awaken him. For the same reason, she did not turn on the light. Crossing the room in the dark, she sensed a strange stillness. A kind of vacuum she could not identify.

A terrible premonition gripped her as she reached down into the crib. Her frightened mind begged to hear the soft sound of a baby's breathing. Her fingers groped through the blankets, searching for the form of a sleeping child. The crib was empty.

Fighting for control, she told herself that the baby must be with his mother. Or his father had carried him downstairs. But even as she ran down the long corridor to the master suite and rapped urgently on the bedroom door, even as she tried to believe the mother's reply, "Isn't he with his father?"—*she knew*. The beautiful little boy, the Dahlquists' firstborn, whom she had fed, bathed, and watched over since his birth, had been taken from his bed and carried off into the night. To millions of Americans, Leif Dahlquist was adored as the greatest hero of all time. Who could be so greedy for money—or worse, who could hate him so savagely as to kidnap his only child?

MARCH

S	M	T	W	T	F	S
		1	2	3	4	5
6	7	8	9	10	11	12
13	14	15	16	17	18	19
20	21	22	23	24	25	26
27	28	29	30	31		

One

ON FRIDAY, MARCH 4, the news flashed around the world. The Great American hero Leif Dahlquist was dead at seventy-two.

It had been many years since the name of Dahlquist had made headlines, for his aversion to any kind of publicity was almost as famous as his deeds. What started as a trickle of last-minute spots in television news shows quickly grew into a flood. In the following days his life was covered in detail, the emphasis always on two early events.

First, his legendary feat in 1927, a feat that endeared him forever to a youthful and romantic nation whose citizens would remember him best as the tall, slight twenty-five-year-old who smiled out at the cameras with hands tucked shyly into his pockets.

Second, the tragic kidnapping and murder of his firstborn son in 1932. This part of the story was usually illustrated by a photograph of a child in a white romper, seated in a small chair with a toy sand bucket and shovel at his feet. In the three months prior to the discovery of a tiny, mutilated corpse, this picture of Leif Dahlquist II, the photo given to the police, had been circulated all over the world. It had appeared a thousand times during the trial, conviction and execution of an Austrian immigrant named Klaus Ochsner.

Now, over forty years later, Ochsner's son, who had taken the protective name of Ricky Cummins, was waiting to read the last installment of the story—"The Hero Dies—End of an Age"—that had been running for six days in the Seattle *News-Record*. No other newspaper had given the Dahlquist story the full treatment it received in the *News-Record*.

Leif and Elizabeth Dahlquist, as well as their only living son, Martin, lived in the Seattle area. In spite of the family's fanatic zeal in avoiding the public eye, Elizabeth's watercolors had been exhibited in Seattle galleries, which, at least in the eyes of local residents, made her a "Seattle artist," and Martin had been glimpsed from time to time in connection with his work in the preservation of wildlife. The managing editor of the *News-Record* shrewdly guessed that a good percentage of his readers had a proprietary interest in the Dahlquists and that now was the time to reinforce Seattle's claim to being the hero's hometown. It was also one of the few papers able to obtain a photo of the funeral—a clear picture of the widow, son, and daughter-in-law, who carried in her arms a small curly-haired child, a boy bearing a startling remembrance to his late grandfather.

With every installment of the article Ricky's tension had mounted. For the last segment was to be about the kidnapping itself. There would be pictures, the old pictures he had first seen as a boy of twelve in the reading room of the public library, a scared, puzzled child in search of his own identity. Pictures of the kidnapped baby, the bereaved parents, the ransom notes, the crude ladder. And, of course, there would be the only picture of his father that Ricky Cummins had ever seen—a man with a long narrow face and deep-set pale blue eyes, wearing a wide-brimmed felt hat— Klaus Ochsner, convicted kidnapper and murderer, executed when Ricky was too young to understand, or even to ask, what had happened to his father.

Part of Ricky's tension was due to worry about his mother's reaction to the sensational articles on the kidnapping. It had been almost four years since her last "bad spell." For Lisa Cummins, old ghosts had finally been exorcised. Her sudden rages, her hysterical accusations against the Dahlquists, seemed consigned to the past. Now, once more, he feared for her. All week, he had begged fate to leave her the degree of forgetfulness she needed to be sane.

His morning coffee had grown cold, and left a bitter taste. Ricky poured it into the kitchen sink, rinsed the mug in hot water, and put it carefully back in the cupboard. The moment had come. With anxiety rising in his throat like bile, he went to pick up the Sunday paper lying outside in the hall.

He had just closed the door and dropped the paper on the table when the telephone rang. The sound hit him like an electric shock. After four rings he picked up the receiver.

A matronly voice told him that Mrs. Lisa Cummins of 122 West Hurley had set fire to her apartment. Her screams had been heard by the people in the next apartment. Unable to reach her themselves, they had called the fire department. The emergency squad had arrived very quickly and entered by way of the fire escape. Mrs. Cummins was taken to the psychiatric ward of the county hospital, where she was sedated and treated for burns and then transferred to a nursing home with special psychiatric facilities.

Now the voice from Sylvan Home West was pitched

somewhere between sympathy and the speaker's need to indicate that she had been having a very trying time. It said she would have called earlier if Mrs. Cummins had been able to tell them where Ricky could be reached. By questioning her neighbors, the hospital had finally learned she had a son and that he lived in the Wendell Arms. If Mr. Cummins would please come to Sylvan Home West as quickly as possible, and bring information about Mrs. Cummins's hospital and medical insurance.... Being Sunday, the regular registrar was not at work but they really did need to have some forms filled out. "You are the next of kin, Mr. Cummins?"

"Yes."

"The senior Mr. Cummins—that is, her husband? She keeps talking about him. The people in the apartment were so very vague. Has he been living at 122 West Hurley? He really should be notified."

Ricky closed his eyes. The tick of the mantel clock seemed very loud as he tried to control his voice. At last he said, "My father died in 1936," and dropped the receiver into its cradle. He would visit his mother, of course. He had seen her in a straightjacket before. He had heard her screams and watched the intelligence drain from her large, unhappy eyes. It would be no worse now.

And this time he had his own plan of striking back at the Dahlquists. Now, after all these years, he had found the instrument of revenge, an idea triggered by a blurry picture of a curly-haired boy smiling unknowingly at his famous grandfather's funeral.

Sunday, March 13

Two

MARTIN DAHLQUIST FINISHED reading the *Record*'s last story about his father and dropped it into the box at his feet, where it settled softly on the untidy pile of clippings his mother had just received from her service.

They were in the library, his father's sanctum. Elizabeth Newton Dahlquist, diminished behind her husband's massive desk, had been trying to read the paper, but her expressive brown eyes were focused on something beyond the page. Of course, Martin thought with a twinge of the old familiar sadness. The picture.

To be fair, four pictures, in heavy silver frames stationed in a military lineup across the corner of his father's desk. Three Leif Dahlquists—Martin's father, Martin's older brother, Martin's infant son, all with fair curly hair and blue eyes. And Martin himself with the dark eyes and small neat body of the Newtons. Martin repressed a sigh. He had never lost the childish notion that it was somehow "better" to be tall and blond than short and dark.

"Mother..."

Elizabeth started. Both small hands flew to her forehead; fingertips massaged the frown lines between her dark eyebrows. "Yes, Martin. Sorry, I was daydreaming."

"You're leaving in the morning. I don't like the idea of your coming home after two months in Europe and having to face boxes of unhappy reminders. I'm sure Father would have advised us to start a roaring fire with all these clippings."

Elizabeth's eyes filled with tears, but she managed a smile. "Yes, indeed he would. He would hate all this."

"And he would be angry."

"Only out of fear."

"Exactly." Martin picked up the *News-Record* feature and frowned at the bold five-column headline. "All this rehash of the kidnapping. But to me the worst aspect of all this publicity is the new pictures taken at the funeral. Of you and me, Laurie and the baby, complete with our addresses."

She sighed. "Yes, I know. I didn't see a cameraman, did you?"

"No. But there was one, obviously. Someone with a powerful telescopic lens."

"It's a little bit blurred, isn't it?"

"Not blurred enough. All our efforts to keep out of the papers ruined by an unscrupulous photographer. A grand announcement that there is now another Dahlquist infant, who even looks like the kidnapped child, and that his grandmother, being a Newton, is an extremely wealthy woman."

"Oh, my God..." Elizabeth's voice was an anguished whisper. "You're afraid, too."

Martin nodded. "Yes, Mother, I'm afraid."

"But you have no cause."

"Don't I?" Martin asked. "Maybe it *is* an irrational fear. You and Father suffered it while I was growing up, but I survived. Nevertheless..." He broke off. His mother's dark eyes were bright with alarm. He got to his feet, walked across the room, and smiling down on her, gently patted her hand.

It was as cruel as it was useless to tell her that for the past week he had been haunted by the fear that somewhere, among all those thousands and thousands of people who had been reading accounts of the famous kidnapping, there might be another Klaus Ochsner, another man cruel enough to kidnap a child and mad enough to think he could get away with it.

"Let's talk of other things." Elizabeth Dahlquist got up and crossed the room to a carved teak cabinet where a decanter of sherry and two glasses stood on a silver tray. She filled both glasses and handed one to Martin.

"To your trip," Martin said, raising his glass. "To a happy flight, and a long rest on the beautiful shores of the Lago di Como."

"Thank you." She sighed. "I'm *so* relieved about the baby. I wouldn't have considered going abroad if you hadn't had such encouraging reports from the doctor."

"Leif is fine," Martin reassured her. "No problems, no symptoms, as long as he gets his medication. Neostigmine. Sounds more like a minor Greek god than something you'd give to a baby."

"And the milk allergy?"

"Yes, that, too. The poor little guy got more than his share, didn't he? But the allergy's relatively simple compared to the myasthenia. It's dormant, you might say, as long as we give him soybean milk instead of cow's milk. And he will probably outgrow it."

"That's comforting. But, Martin, do write me, please. I worry about him."

"I know you do, Mother. Honestly, Leif is in excellent health. And I *will* write." He picked up the decanter and refilled their glasses. "By the way, if your plane leaves at eight o'clock, I suppose you want to be at the airport by seven. That means I should pick you up about six."

"It's terribly early, isn't it?" she said with a rueful

smile. "I'm sorry, Martin. I should have taken a later flight."

"No problem. Together we'll watch the dawn come up like thunder, or whatever it does."

"But there's really no point in your going home tonight, is there? Stay here. Then you won't have the long drive to Black River, only to drive all the way back in the morning."

Martin shook his head vigorously. "No, Mother. I don't leave Laurie alone overnight. Not since all this..." He paused. "Besides, I thought I'd bring Laurie and the baby with us to the airport."

"Oh, lovely!"

Martin put down his glass and placed both hands on his mother's shoulders. "I'd better be going now. But before I leave, I'd like very much to get rid of these damned clippings. If you won't let me burn them, please let me put them someplace, out of sight."

"Oh, Marty..."

Looking down into his mother's delicate face, Martin said urgently, "*Please*, Mother..."

Elizabeth sighed. "I suppose you're right. I'll put them away."

"*I'll* put them away," Martin said firmly. "Right now, before I leave. Where do you keep such things? In the attic?"

Elizabeth's troubled eyes looked away in an obvious attempt to avoid his gaze. "I'll do it," she said evasively. "I'll put them... somewhere."

Martin's hands tightened their grip on her shoulders. "I said where shall I put them, Mother?"

"I'll..."

"Mother, *where*?"

Elizabeth pulled free and moved soundlessly across the thick Chinese carpet to her husband's desk and from an inner recess to the top drawer produced a large brass key. For a moment she looked puzzled, as if the object in her hand were strange to her and she hadn't decided what to do with it. Then, with a small shrug, she seemed to reach a decision. She turned to the big cabinet behind the desk, fitted the key into the lock, and opened the door. But only an inch or two. "Bring the box, please." Her voice was almost inaudible.

Martin crossed the room quickly. His mother faced him with her back against the cabinet. But before she managed to block his view, he caught a glimpse of the contents. Boxes, bulging manila envelopes, file folders. A commonplace horde of old papers, except for a small package on the bottom shelf. It caught Martin's eye because it was not only tied heavily with twine, but the knots had been covered with red sealing wax.

"What are you guarding, Mother? You look like a Spartan at Thermopylae."

"It's your father's. Your father's private... collection."

"Collection? What sort of collection?"

"Letters, notebooks, pictures."

"I'd like to take a look," Martin said casually, but before he could move his mother whirled around, slammed the cabinet door, and turned the key.

Martin began to protest, but his mother's expression startled him so that the words died in his throat. Her face was ashen.

"Mother," he said gently, "why are you acting so strangely? Here, give me that key. I don't know what you're hiding, but it's obvious that it upsets you very badly. I think you ought to get rid of it."

"No," she whispered. "*No.*"

"Then let me take it home. Get it out of here."

"NO!" Martin sensed that the violence of her reaction was caused by his nearness to the secret contents of those shelves. Like the age-old game, he was getting warm, warmer, warmest...

"Mother," he said again. "I'm no longer a child. You don't have to protect me."

Suddenly her body sagged against the cabinet. He

reached for the key and she let him take it from her. "Please, Martin. Please don't prod old wounds. Don't bring it all back, not now. All these new stories—they hurt, but the old clippings are much worse. And it's no use. It's all in the past, and that's where I want to leave it."

He put his arms around her and she wept against his shoulder. When she was quiet, he kissed her cheek and said goodbye. She didn't ask for it, but before he left, he offered her the key. She accepted it in silence. She was still standing with her back to the cabinet and the key in her hand when he closed the outside door and hurried along the driveway to his car.

Elizabeth Dahlquist stood at the library window and watched the bright red taillights of Martin's car grow smaller and dimmer and finally disappear over the brow of the hill. Even then, she remained motionless, fearing her sensitive and loyal son would turn around and come back, not so much to apologize as to heal an imagined breach. At last certain that Martin was not going to return, she left the window and for the second time that night opened the thick oak door of the cabinet.

She had told Martin the truth when she said that it contained his father's souvenirs and that her reason for preventing him from going through them was to spare him the pain of digging through the past. For there were no real secrets among Leif's papers, only bitter reminders. But there was a secret in the cabinet, as Martin suspected, only it was her own, not Leif's. She had guarded it for more than forty years, even from Leif—or, she thought guiltily, especially from Leif. Earlier in the week she had retrieved the small carefully wrapped package from the niche under the attic floor where she had hidden it so long ago, meaning to burn it.

More than once she had stood in front of the hearth fire with the dreadful packet in her hand, and found she could not throw it into the flames. It was her albatross, the secret guilt she could neither confess nor cast away. So she had hidden it again, this time among Leif's papers, and locked it up in a cabinet for which there was only one key. Now she would have to do more, for she had seen too much understanding in Martin's thoughtful brown eyes.

Kneeling, she picked up the parcel, bitterly remembering the day she had first received it, young, grieving, and terrified of what had fallen into her possession. She had never been able to hide from the knowledge of what the packet contained, but at least she could conceal its secrets from others who would suffer, as she had, from knowing what she had done.

She closed the cabinet, locked the door, and hurried up the wide stairway to the master bedroom where she rearranged the contents of her suitcase to make room for the small dusty package.

As Martin turned the car into the narrow lane leading to his home, the headlights illuminated the mailbox in which the rural carrier stuffed the evening newspaper. The rolled-up paper was still there and this surprised him. The carrier was religious about his schedule. He passed the Dahlquists at 5:15 P.M., never more than a few minutes early or late. Laurie was just as faithful to routine; she always walked up the lane for the paper at 5:30 P.M., right after the baby's evening meal. Martin braked the car, shifted in reverse, and lifted the *News-Record* through the open window. A curious feeling that something was out of place prodded him, like an odor too faint to be identified.

He was surprised again when his car reached the crest of the hill and the comfortable old farmhouse came into view—all the lights were out.

He slammed the accelerator almost to the floor. The car plunged down the hill and turned into the circular driveway leading to the front entrance. He was out of the car in seconds, leaping up the steps, into a dark house. He began to run—up the circular staircase to the second floor, down the wide hallway to the bedroom where Laurie should be reading and the baby sleeping. He flung the door wide and flipped the switch. The ceiling light burst over an empty room.

He paused for only an instant before racing down to the playroom that opened off the kitchen. He heard Laurie's soft moan before his frantic fingers could locate the light. Then he was plunging across the room, stumbling over the baby's toys in his haste to get to the chair in which she was tied. She sat limp and motionless as he took the gag out of her mouth and cut the rope that bound her hands and feet, her eyes staring in mute terror at the far wall. Martin turned slowly, knowing even before he did that the playpen on the other side of the room would be empty.

Three

A STORM HAD been gathering all afternoon. When Ricky Cummins ran out of the farmhouse with the baby in his arms, the sky was a savage gray and thunder rolled angrily in the distance. He had driven only a few miles before the black clouds caught up with him and rain laced with icy sleet began pelting the windshield.

Night came, closing down as suddenly as if the sky had fallen. At the intersection between the county road and the state highway, Cummins braked the car, pulled over to the graveled shoulder, and stopped. He was shivering, more from fear than cold. He hadn't thought of bringing a jacket and the chill air was seeping through his sweater. But he had taken warm covering for the baby. He reached into the back seat and brought forward a soft terrycloth robe, freshly laundered and smelling faintly of lemon detergent.

The baby was still groggy from his interrupted nap. As Cummins lifted him out of the cardboard box, he opened his eyes and uttered a small whimper of protest. The large hands that turned him and wrapped him in the robe were gentle but awkward. His tiny mouth puckered and his eyes squeezed closed and the whimper became an indignant wail.

"Sshh, sshh`...`" Cummins lowered the child back into the box and tucked the robe around him. With a quick glance through the rear-view mirror, he reentered the county road and turned left at the state highway.

He must not run, or hide. He must act each day as he would normally, or if that was impossible, he must offer plausible excuses. Stealing the baby had been easier than he expected. No one had seen him entering or leaving the driveway, he was sure of that, and the woods where he left the old Plymouth were hidden both from the road and from the house. Though he had seen Mrs. Dahlquist through the kitchen window when he was unscrewing the backyard spotlight, he felt sure that if she had seen him, she wouldn't have left the house to investigate. And even when he had been tying her up he doubted that she had glimpsed his face. So far, he had been lucky.

The car swayed under the impact of the gusting wind and the downpour became heavier than the rubber wipers could sweep away. With great effort Cummins forced himself to slow down. It was thirty miles to his apartment in the city and he would have to drive cautiously. Despite an instinctive desire to put as many miles as possible between him and the Dahlquist farm he could not risk being stopped by a traffic cop, or skidding into an accident. His hands gripped the wheel furiously, relaxed, then contracted again.

Ollie White had just begun to read the Sunday *News-Record* when the call came from the warden's office. A guard in a badly fitted uniform and visored cap strode into the A Block rec room and screened the occupants with a cold, deliberate, look.

Custodial officer, Ollie thought contemptuously. As if you could change a guard into a friendly human being by calling him something else. His thin-lipped mouth twisted disdainfully until he observed over the top of the newspaper that the guard was signaling to him.

The grin dropped from Ollie's thin, sallow face. He had been enduring rehabilitation for almost five years. He knew what kind of an act this moment called for. "Yes, sir? Were you looking for me, sir?"

"The super wants you. Get the hell down to his office."

It had to be good news to bring the super into the joint on Sunday. Ollie made a shrewd guess that he was about to hear the report he had been anticipating ever since his parole hearing three weeks earlier. "Thank you, officer," he offered politely as he jumped to his feet.

The warden looked up as Ollie entered his office and grunted, "Come in, White. This won't take long but have a seat if you want to." With one sweep of the hand he spread a heap of correspondence out on the desk like a magician beginning a card trick. With another wordless grunt he pulled one sheet out, frowned at it, and said, "The report's back from the parole board. Damn their eyes! Why do they have to pick Monday for a release date? Can't they get it through their heads that a Monday date means doing the paperwork on Sunday?"

"I've been anxious about the report, sir."

The warden's shrewd eyes rested on him. "I kind of doubt that. But let's get on with the show. You've got your parole, all right. You'll get a ride to the city tomorrow morning. Pick up your suit of clothes this afternoon. The clerk will give you forty dollars gate money just before you leave. After you get home, you've got forty-eight hours to report to your parole officer. . . ." He hesitated, looking at the sheet in his hand, and read "Lew Backstrom. Room 347 Pratt Building, corner of Terrace and Bellevue. No, no, you don't have to write it down. This copy is for you." He flipped the paper across his desk and leaned back in the outsize armchair that barely accommodated his bulk. "Just one word of warning, White. I know your history. You've never done time before, but your name has popped up more than once when it looked like everybody got caught but you. You like guns. So do I. I collect them. The difference is, *you* can't own one. *You* can't be caught with one in your possession, which means in your home or your car, no matter how much you claim it belonged to a friend and you didn't even know it was there."

"Yes, sir. I understand. Thanks for your advice."

"Bullshit," the warden said, waving a big hand in dismissal.

At the door, Ollie looked back. The warden was still watching him as if his narrowed eyes were making a photograph for future use. "Good luck, White," he muttered without conviction as Ollie closed the door.

Ollie winked at the clerk and proceeded jauntily toward A Block. He still had a half hour before his final appointment with his caseworker and he wanted to get back to the Sunday paper.

The rec room was empty. Without his privileged status as a man awaiting parole, Ollie, too, would have been on the job or in his cell. The Sunday *News-Record* was scattered all over the room. He gathered it and, grunting contentedly, dropped into the nearest chair.

When the guard had summoned him to the warden's office, he had just spotted a headline that reminded him of an old score he was going to settle when he got back on the street. It was more than a grudge. It was revenge, and it had been festering for five years. When he found the story, it gushed through him like a narcotic high. "The Hero Dies—End of an Age," the top line said, and below it, in smaller type, "The Dahlquist Kidnapping—Klaus Ochsner's Brutal Crime."

As he read, Ollie's mind skipped from Leif Dahlquist to the famous Dahlquist kidnapping to the name of the kidnapper to the name of the kidnapper's son—his old classmate. "Ricky Cummins," Ollie said out loud, like a bailiff calling on the accused to stand while the verdict is read. His narrow face twisted into an ugly grin, because suddenly it seemed funny, that little speech of the warden's about how he wasn't allowed to own a gun.

Four

THEY RACED FROM room to room in a last desperate hope that the baby would be somewhere in the house. They examined the wet ground between the kitchen and the garage, where muddy footprints showed that the man who caught Laurie when she went outside to check the floodlight had hidden in the garage. They retraced the course of the kidnapper's flight, from the crib to the central hallway to the unlocked front door and stood on the verandah, cold rain soaking their clothes, before going back to the downstairs nursery. Through it all they had hardly spoken, and Laurie hadn't cried.

When Martin broke the long silence, his voice was almost toneless. "There's a note."

"Yes, I see." Laurie's voice was as flat as his.

"Don't touch it."

"I know. There might be fingerprints. But we've got to see what it says."

"Yes, of course. I suppose...if I put on a glove...God, I don't know. I might smear his fingerprints, even wearing a glove."

31

"If we picked it up with tweezers? Just by the corner?"

Martin nodded. "That ought to work."

"I'll get them..."

In the two or three minutes Laurie spent running to and from her dressing table, Martin's eyes remained fixed on the paper, as if even blinking would sever their only line of communication with the kidnapper. Oh, my God... Oh, my God, he thought. It's happening again. It's all happening again.... When Laurie returned, he was standing just as she had left him.

Martin said hoarsely, "Okay?" and reached into the playpen. As he pinched the corner of the note between the tweezers, the old childhood chant was racing crazily through his mind. One for the money, two for the show, three to get ready, and four to go...

He lifted the paper and laid it on the breakfast table. In silence they read the beautifully formed script, black ink on heavy white paper.

My father was a kind man. He was hungry for money—of that he was guilty. But it was hard for an immigrant, living in poverty, while all around he saw great wealth. He deserved punishment. *He did not deserve to die.* If the rich and famous Leif Dahlquist had been a poor unknown, Klaus Ochsner would never have been executed. You lost a brother. I lost my father, and my mother has been dying for many years, a little bit at a time. Think about it, while you pray for the safe return of your baby. *Do not notify the police.* That is a warning, and I won't repeat it after today. *Do not notify the police.*

The note ended without a signature. In its place was a symbol Martin recognized with a terrible sense of *déjà vu*. Oh God, the whole long nightmare is starting again, more frightening than the first time because this time we know what comes next: Scene one, the baby is kidnapped. Scene two, the parents ignore the warning and call the police. Scene three, the baby is found in a shallow grave in the woods.

Martin suddenly realized that Laurie was shivering violently. He put his arm around her and they clung together silently.

Martin wanted to comfort her but he did not know how to begin. There were several subjects he had never been able to discuss with Laurie. The long-ago kidnapping of his older brother was one of them. As he looked into her wide, frightened eyes, he realized with a stab of guilt that he really had no idea what she knew about the tragedy that had locked so much of himself away from her.

"Laurie, do you recognize the little design at the bottom?" he asked, staring at the three triangles, one inside the other, enclosed by a circle. No one had ever known what Ochsner meant by it.

"Yes," Laurie said. "It was the signature on all the ransom notes...Ochsner's, the man who killed your brother...I know. I've read about it for years. I know who wrote this note. I know who has our baby."

"Ochsner's son."

"Ochsner's son," she repeated, dully reciting the fact both of them were still too numb to fully comprehend. "His father was executed when you were only three years old. He must have been about your age."

Yesterday the murderer, Martin thought. Today, the murderer's son. So Laurie *did* know the underlying message of the note: An eye for an eye, a tooth for a tooth; your baby's life for the death of my father and the slow destruction of my mother. And still she didn't cry.

At Martin's insistence, they took off their damp clothing and returned to the kitchen in bathrobes and slippers.

"I want you to sit down, Laurie, and pull that lap robe around you. I'll make some tea."

"Such a strange note. Such a . . . tragic . . ."

"Yes, Laurie. We'll talk about it in a few minutes."

"We've got to decide what to do."

"I know, I know. But first, the tea."

Laurie watched as he went through a ritual she had learned prefaced every important decision. Scalding the old-fashioned hand-painted teapot, a wedding gift from his old nurse in Ireland. Measuring the curly black tea leaves. Stirring the pot as the boiling water poured into it . . .

Laurie knew instinctively that tonight the tea served another purpose. It helped postpone the moment when Martin would have to share his thoughts, for this was always difficult, and sometimes impossible, for him to do. In four years of marriage, Laurie often felt their only true intimacy was physical, as if the act of love was her intense and introverted husband's way of pouring out the feelings he couldn't bring himself to express in words. Whether he was truly like his father, or had merely adopted his father's mannerism, Martin was a passionate loner. The more important the issue, the more important that he come to grips with it alone. He *must* be suffering, Laurie thought. He *must* be terror-stricken. But he can't tell me, so he's taking a very long time to make the tea. While I sit here trying not to feel.

Martin filled two thin china teacups, poured a little milk into each and added a spoonful of honey to his own. As Laurie took the steaming cup from his hands he said, "Would you like something with it?"

She shook her head.

"But you haven't eaten since lunch."

"It doesn't matter. I couldn't eat."

"Well, if you want something . . ."

She moved from her chair to the breakfast table and sat down opposite Martin. "I *do* want something. I want to talk. For God's sake, what are we going to do?"

He pushed his teacup to one side and gripped the edge of the table. "First," he said, his knuckles whitening, "I know what we are *not* going to do. We are not going to notify the police."

"Ah . . . ," sighed Laurie. "Because that's the mistake your father made."

He looked up quickly. "Yes. He never really forgave himself."

Laurie saw that she had startled him, either by knowing what he was thinking or, more likely, by bringing it out in the open. Did he really believe that these past four years she hadn't guessed what had been happening on his side of the barricade? "I understand that," she said patiently. "But I doubt very much that calling the police was the cause of your brother's death. I think the baby was dead before your parents even knew he had been kidnapped."

Martin shook his head. "That's one theory. It was never proved."

"During the trial, the doctor who performed the autopsy . . ." Laurie choked on the ugly word. What had happened to that little boy in 1932 might already have happened to hers. She looked at Martin helplessly, begging him to hear her. But it was his forefinger that held his attention, tapping the table as if to underline the irrevocability of his decision.

"The medical report did *not* establish the exact time of death. Too much time had passed. The body was badly decomposed—" Martin stopped abruptly, recoiling as Laurie had from the terrible implications. Even before he spoke, Laurie knew he would change the subject in order to avoid an argument. They had never argued. Their differences had been set aside, but never settled, because an argument forces both parties to bare their feelings, and Martin could not, and therefore, neither could she.

Now he was looking at her, about to break his silence. "Yes, Marty?" It was strange that at this moment she had used his nickname. He preferred to be called Martin, yet every once in a while "Marty" slipped out.

"I'm very puzzled by the note," he said thoughtfully. "Nothing like his father's. The handwriting, for one thing. Of course, Klaus Ochsner was an Austrian, while his son was born here. Even so, his vocabulary, his way of expressing himself. I think he must have had a good education. But the real puzzle . . ." He paused, his glance moving automatically to the sheet of white paper. "It doesn't say anything about ransom. It doesn't tell us what we have to do to get the baby back." Martin lifted his head for the first time and looked directly at Laurie. *"What does he want me to do!"*

"I don't know. I can't think, except in circles. What do people do, in a case like this? I think we should notify the police."

"He specifically said we should not."

"I've read about cases when the child was returned safely although the police had been called."

"Luck," Martin said grimly. "Those people were gambling with their children's lives." His dark eyes clouded. "My father didn't mean to gamble with my brother's life," he said in a voice that shook with bitterness. "He didn't notice the ransom note until after he had called the police. I absolutely believe that he would never have ignored the kidnapper's warning if he had seen it when he first went into the nursery. That was a deadly error, an error you and I are *not* going to commit."

Once more Martin lapsed into silence, gaze fixed on his tapping finger. Laurie knew that while he was in this mood he simply would not hear her. That she could understand, for she often had trouble listening to him. The inner Martin was such a battleground of hopes, fears, and expectations that she often ignored what he was saying and focused her attention on why he was saying it. Was he doing the same thing now? She decided to go on.

"Martin, we've both read more articles about kidnapping than most experts. We both know that, more often than not, the kidnapper is caught and not by the victim's parents. By the police. The professionals, Martin. They are the ones who can find Leif. Not untrained amateurs, like you and me."

"I don't intend to let you get involved," Martin said firmly. "I will handle this, and I am beginning by respecting the kidnapper's warning. Is that clear, Laurie?"

"Clear?" said Laurie. "Clear? That I am to do nothing at all to find my baby? That you are going to take full responsibility for saving Leif's life? No detectives, no FBI? You don't need them. And you don't need me."

"If you want to put it that way."

"I *don't* want to, Martin. It's *our* baby, Martin. *We* are in danger of losing our child. I have a right to take part in anything we do to get Leif back. The shock and the terror and maybe the grief—they are mine as well. You are not alone, however much you pretend to be. For once in our married life, we are going to share. Whatever is done, we do together."

"Laurie!"

Laurie's eyes widened at the anger behind his shout.

He continued more calmly, "All right. *We* will not notify the police! Please understand me. *We will not notify the police!* My brother would be alive if my father had not broken that one basic rule. The kidnapper will make his demands, and you and I will

do exactly what he says. That's the only way we will get
our child back. That's all we have to decide tonight. It's
very late. You must be exhausted."

"Your mother?"

"That's another reason for not calling the police.
The newspapers would pick it up in no time. Another
Dahlquist kidnapping. Can't you see the headlines?
Mother would see the story in an Italian newspaper
almost as quickly as she would at home. I think it
would kill her."

Laurie wanted to cry out, *I* am the mother! *My* baby
is gone, and I think it will kill me! Long habit silenced
the words. "Your mother will ask where Leif is when
we take her to the airport in the morning."

"I know. I'll have some logical explanation. And
then, thank God, she'll be out of the country for three
months. If something happened to Leif, I think . . ."

Laurie stood up. She had never felt so alone.
Numbly she heard Martin repeat the words that so
effectively excluded her: "Mother has suffered so much
already. I think it would kill her."

Despite the room's temperature, kept at 78 degrees
for the baby, Laurie felt cold to the bone. "You're right,
Martin," she said dully. "It's time to go to bed."

"I'll be along in a minute," he said without looking
up. "You go ahead."

Shivering in her warm robe, Laurie left the room.
And still she hadn't cried.

As soon as she had gone, Martin put both elbows on
the table, dropped his head into his hands, and closed
his eyes. His mind was whirling with dimly
remembered scenes. He could not distinguish between
what he had actually experienced and what he
"recalled" because he had been told about it later. The
more he thought about what was happening now, the
stronger his sensation of being overtaken by the events
of forty years ago.

But he would do it right this time. He would defy the past, and save his child. Until this moment, he had never fully understood his father's sense of guilt. Now, facing an identical dilemma, he felt closer to his father than he ever had before. Leif Dahlquist had not been a complicated man. To recover his firstborn son, he had simply tried to do what was right. He had erred, and the error had been irretrievable. This time, even if the weight of the decision crushed him, Martin swore he would not make the same mistake.

Painfully he remembered the first five or six years of his life when "home" had often been a scary place because of his father's methods of protecting him. There were the armed guards, patrolling the yard with shotguns. The mysterious rules his father made—rules that he knew, from what little contact he had with other children, were peculiar to his own family. He was not to close his bedroom door. He was not to go outside without Siegfried, the German shepherd, as well as a big man who never smiled, called Detective Young. He wasn't going to day school any longer; he was to stay inside the house and have his lessons from a tutor. He could not visit other children, though they could come and play with him. It was all meant to protect him, of course. But, in fact, it was the protectors themselves that had frightened him.

Especially Siegfried. Martin had loved his old cocker spaniel. He did not understand why his father brought home another dog, nor why anyone would want the kind of dog you dare not pet or play with. He had never forgotten the day a friend of his mother's— by some freak oversight unwarned—had attempted to fondle the big shepherd.

"Hello there, doggie," the woman had said, extending a hand to pat Siegfried's head.

The dog lunged, ripping her clothing, sinking sharp teeth into her arm and shoulder. Blood was smeared all over her face and hands and dripping on the shredded scraps of her blouse before a guard grabbed Siegfried's collar and issued the right command.

This was the dog his father said was to stay with Martin at all times. Though Martin had seen it all on the safe side of the living room window, his screams were more terrified than the woman's, and for nights he could not fall asleep until his nurse worked the magic she had invented to calm him down.

Holy water, she called it. When odd sounds and unseen perils kept him awake, she would appear with a special little bottle, and ceremoniously sprinkle a few drops before the open bedroom door. "It's a charm," she assured him, and for a long time he had believed it. "Nothing bad would dare cross that magic line. You are fine now, Marty. Sshhh, go to sleep."

There were memories that Martin still carried with him along with an undischarged load of resentment

against the imprisonment his father had imposed to protect him from the outside world, an outside world he knew was hostile before he was five years old.

Tonight he kept thinking: What price "normal childhood"? His father had made one choice. Who was to say he was wrong? If Martin had guarded his own son as zealously as his father had guarded him, this terrible thing would not have happened. But he had wanted his child to have a normal life. As a result, little Leif was not asleep in his crib upstairs, Laurie was grieving in tearless silence, and he was sitting alone in an empty room, praying desperately for guidance.

Laurie meant to hurry past the nursery. But none of the upstairs lights had been turned off since their frantic search of the house. There was no point in leaving them on. So she went into the baby's room, just far enough to reach the wall switch at the left of the door.

Her eyes moved slowly from one familiar detail to

another, as if this were the last look she would be allowed for a long time. The shelves of toy animals, where a black and white panda bigger than Leif himself presided. The small blue rocking chair, waiting for the baby to grow big enough to sit in it. The bright yellow diaper pail and the padded table where she changed his clothes. And hovering over everything, the faint smell of talcum powder.

Her hand dropped from the light switch and her arm fell heavily to her side as she surrendered to her grief and wept, bitterly and loudly, not even bothering to cover her face. The anguished wailing filled the room and echoed back like the answering cry of all women who have ever lost a child. She was blind with tears, and so helpless against the attack of her released emotion that she did not see Martin run into the room. She only felt him as he put his arms around her, supporting her, drying her face with a freshly laundered diaper.

"Laurie, Laurie," he said over and over. "You're crying. I couldn't understand why you didn't cry before."

"I couldn't, until now."

"You mean you couldn't cry in my presence."

"I don't know. Yes, I suppose so."

"Everyone cries," Martin said. "In different ways."

"You, too, Marty?" Again the nickname, in the rare moment of understanding.

He nodded. "You were right, Laurie. I've begun to realize that, since we talked downstairs. We *are* amateurs. Maybe we do need professional help. No police, though. But if we hire a private detective, we would not be calling the police and we would have some expert help. In the morning, Laurie, we'll talk to a detective agency. If I think they can help more than they can hurt, I'll ask them to take our case."

Laurie clung to him gratefully, resting her head

against his shoulder and closing her eyes. "I'll sleep better now," she murmured. "Thank you, Marty..."

Martin was still holding her when an object on top of the blue chest of drawers came into focus. Leif's special medicine. "Four times daily, after meals."

"This new medication will do the trick, Mr. Dahlquist," the specialist had said. "Just make sure he gets the proper dosage. Four times a day after meals. It's the regularity that counts. You can't skip one dose and make it up with the next. Be sure to keep a good supply on hand, because if he doesn't get what he needs, in two or three days your son is going to be a very sick boy."

Martin had asked, "I want to understand exactly what you mean, Doctor. Without this medicine, the baby will die?"

"Well now, we don't need to consider that possibility because it won't come about as long as he receives his daily dosage of Neostigmine. Listlessness, drooping eyelids, a weak cry—those are the danger signals. They're plain enough and can be corrected. Don't worry, Mr. Dahlquist. Your son has a problem but it can be controlled and basically he's a beautiful healthy child."

That day, Martin had felt reassured. Tonight, gazing at the little blue bottle, Martin felt a new kind of terror. It was now midnight, Sunday, March 13. The baby had already missed one dose.

Five

IN A SMALL but fastidiously neat apartment in the Hotel
Alaska, ex-cop, ex-private eye Jack Howard was about
to plunge into his favorite hobby—collecting
newspaper and magazine articles about old or
notorious crimes. For the first time in many years, he
had new material for his notebooks on the Dahlquist
case.

Three large photo albums, carefully dusted, were
stacked on the old dining table he used as a desk. A tidy
stack of newspapers, a pair of scissors, and a plastic
bottle of Elmer's glue was arranged beside them.
Howard sat down, sighed contentedly, and picked up
Sunday's *News-Record*. He had already clipped the
first five installments of the Dahlquist series. Tonight
he would cut out the final article and get the whole lot
pasted up, dated, and annotated.

He felt a curious pang of guilt as he looked at a
picture of the Dahlquists on the day of the funeral.
Like so many of the articles and pictures that filled his
notebooks, this photograph existed despite the

subjects' sincere wish to escape the public eye. Though he had been in the best possible position to spy on the camera-shy Dahlquists, Jack Howard had never attempted to invade their privacy. And there was something ironic about that. He had the motive: his lifelong interest in the hero and his family. He had the means: he was in the spying business, a pro, and a damned good one, if his competitors could be believed. *And* he had the opportunity: very few people had lived their lives within four miles of the Dahlquist estate. But for him these elements didn't add up to an equation. He hadn't tried to sneak into the cemetery. He hadn't chased the Dahlquist limousine down the road.

He started to apply paste to the back of the clipping showing the mourners but stopped almost immediately. Picking up a magnifying glass, he studied the photograph in detail, struck again by Leif III's incredible resemblance to the baby kidnapped so many years ago.

He opened the oldest of the three notebooks and turned to one of the most prized items of Dahlquist memorabilia—a photograph of the first Leif Dahlquist, taken when he was about two or three. The picture was dated by a certain quaintness in the way he was dressed, but the features and the expression around the mouth and eyes had clearly been passed down the line to his first son and grandson.

Jack Howard frowned, overcome with a sudden uneasiness. The storm outside was reminding him vividly of his strange premonition the night of the 1932 kidnapping—his vision of the Dahlquists' house, its windows blazing with light...

He realized his hands were ice cold. He closed the notebook. There had been three Leif Dahlquists, three beautiful boys with blond curls and large, serious blue eyes. One had been murdered, one had just died, one remained. He tried to ignore his increasing sense of unease.

• • •

When Ricky reached the city limits, the storm was beginning to subside. He said silent thanks, for the Wendell Arms was only twenty minutes away and he had been worrying about carrying the baby from the car to his apartment. The child seemed to be suffering from a head cold. Getting wet or chilled would make it worse.

The baby had been restless almost the entire trip from the Dahlquist farm. Ricky had thought at first that his sleepy whimpers were the result of an obvious sniffle. Now, almost in sight of his apartment, the steady wailing made him wonder if something were wrong, something more than a head cold? Ricky tried to dismiss the thought. Leif Dahlquist III looked as healthy as any baby he had ever seen. With his pink cheeks, clear blue eyes, and shiny curls, he had undoubtedly consumed more vitamins, orange juice, and milk than any two children Ricky had grown up with.

At the end of the boulevard Ricky braked the car and pulled over to the curb. He had forgotten all about his neighbors at the Wendell Arms. Mrs. Dennison, the white-haired cricket whose apartment was next to his, was particularly curious and the chances of bringing a crying baby into the building without being seen were small. He would have to think things through. Initially, he had not planned beyond snatching the baby from the Dahlquist house. Now he realized he could not simply hide in his apartment.

He drove to the end of the block, beyond the range of the streetlight and too far to be seen from a window of the Wendell Arms, and parked the car. The possibility that a stroller might hear the baby's cries dogged him as he ran down the street, unlocked the back door, and loped up the stairs to the second floor. He hurried past Mrs. Dennison's door and into his apartment. In the bedroom he took clean shirts, socks, and underclothing from the bureau drawers. A suitcase wouldn't do, for he might not get out of the building without being seen. He pulled a green and white Pendleton shirt off its hanger and wrapped it around the other clothing. A rolled-up jacket under his arm shouldn't arouse curiosity.

He let himself out of his apartment as quietly as he had gone in and tiptoed past Mrs. Dennison's door, hearing the quiet drone of a television drama. He passed up the elevator in favor of the stairs. He decided to pick up his mail, which meant leaving by the front door. In the hall he unlocked his mailbox, withdrew a half dozen letters, and without glancing at any of them hurried out into the welcome dark.

The beginning of a plan was forming. He would drive to another part of the city where he wasn't likely to run into someone he knew and take a motel room.... But what about food? Of course, that's what was bothering the baby. He was hungry. How stupid of him to leave the apartment without bringing the quart of milk and some eggs and butter.

For a second, Ricky considered going back but that would be taking an unnecessary chance. Although the supermarkets were closed, he was sure to pass an open delicatessen.

Ricky opened the car door, threw the clothing on the back seat, and jumped in. The cries from the cardboard box were weaker, and interspersed with hiccups. The baby was crying himself to sleep.

Intent on finding a grocery store, Ricky made a quick U-turn at the corner and raced back toward the city center. The maneuver took only half a minute, but that was enough for Mrs. Dennison to spot him under the streetlight and wonder why the nice young man in 28 was speeding off into the night instead of going to bed.

● ● ●

The clerk in the Maple Street delicatessen was looking at her watch when the wide glass doors opened and a tall young man burst into the store. He looked worried, and he was obviously in a hurry. "Can I help you?" she asked.

"Yes... Oh, yes, thank you. Milk. Homogenized milk."

"Quart, half gallon, gallon?"

"I..." He hesitated, as if it were a big decision. "I guess... Well, make it a half gallon."

The woman went to the refrigerated dairy cooler and took out a carton. The man was looking from shelf to shelf as if he had forgotten what he had come for. "Is there something else, sir?" she said, hoping to hurry him.

"No... Well, perhaps..." His gaze settled on the baby food section. With a nervous glance at the clerk, he went to the shelf. Box by box, he picked up each variety of baby cereal and carefully studied the label.

"Can I help you?" the woman said again, without bothering to smile. "It's ten minutes after eleven. I'm supposed to close up."

"Oh, yes. I'm sorry." He came back to the counter and placed a box of cereal and a baby's bottle and nipple next to the milk.

"Three sixty-two." He's jumpy about something, the clerk thought as she watched him fumble with his wallet and draw out four bills. Three singles and a ten. She looked at him curiously. "You don't want to give me that, sir. That's a ten."

The man murmured, "Oh yes, sorry." This time he pulled a five from his wallet and handed it to her. She put the milk, the cereal and baby's bottle into a paper bag and turned her back to ring up the sale on the cash register. She was counting out the change when she heard the swish of the front doors opening and closing. "Hey, your change!" But he was already jumping into his car.

She ran around the counter and rushed through the front door, waving the money. She was certain that he saw her before he stepped on the gas and the car leapt forward, wheels spinning and motor roaring. She shrugged, went back into the store, and began the routine of locking up for the night.

But she kept wondering about the man. Years of experience behind a counter had given her a good eye for spotting trouble. And trouble hung over that young man like a cloud, she was sure of that. Well, as her husband liked to say, "Relax, baby. If it's worth worrying about, it'll be in the morning paper." She sighed. If she'd only noticed his license number.

It was his last night in the cell, and Ollie White couldn't relax. For five years he had managed to go to sleep each night by concentrating on the day of his release. But now that the gates were about to open, he felt he couldn't make it through the last few hours.

For the third or fourth time, he got up from his bunk and began to pace his cell. Twelve feet long, ten feet wide. From bars to bunk, from toilet to the desk top hinged to the wall. Lights had been doused as usual at 10 o'clock, but now that the rain had stopped, the small section of the sky Ollie could see through the cell window was a little brighter every time he looked out. As he walked back and forth, the moon broke through the clouds. Tomorrow, Ollie thought fervently, as if God might still do him a favor in spite of the fact that Ollie hadn't thought of Him for years. Let me make it to tomorrow, and you'll never see me in this place again.

Three weeks earlier, Ollie had admitted to the parole board that he had made a bad mistake and solemnly pledged that if they released him, he would never do so again. He had been perfectly sincere in his promise, but the mistake he was talking about was not his crime. It was picking Ricky Cummins as his partner.

At the time, he hadn't seen Ricky in years. Not since they were kids twelve years old, when Ricky and his mother lived in an old house on the other side of Hayes Street. Come to think of it, not since the day they had been making model planes on the Whites' front porch and Ricky overheard Mrs. White gossiping with another woman about the "murderer's son" who lived across the street. By the end of the week, Mrs. Cummins and Ricky had packed up and disappeared, and Ollie's mother had a field day telling everyone how worried she had been, letting Ollie play with a boy whose father died in the electric chair.

It had been a one-in-a-million chance bumping into Ricky in the Mom and Pop corner grocery Ollie was casing for an easy two or three hundred dollars. He needed one other man and his regular partner was in the county jail, singing his heart out about a job he had—fortunately—pulled on his own. Remembering his mother's theories about bad blood, Ollie assumed that the son of a notorious criminal would also set himself against the law. Ollie had been momentarily surprised by Ricky's hot denial when he asked if Ricky had done time, but then decided Ricky's anger simply meant that he had.

That's where he'd made his big mistake—assuming. Thirty minutes after they went into a bar for beer, he was telling Ricky about the grocery job and asking him to help. When Ricky flatly refused to get mixed up in a robbery, Ollie threatened to tell the company Ricky worked for who "Ricky Cummins" was. "And that would be kind of hard on your mother, wouldn't it?" Ollie added as a clincher. "You losing a good job, and all the stuff about the kidnapping coming up all over again?"

Never force a guy to do a job—number one. Number two—never trust a guy who turns you down one minute and the next minute switches over to your side. He'd been pretty dumb, all right, but Ricky had tricked him when he agreed to be the lookout man. Because it was Ricky who sneaked up and tried to grab Ollie's gun when the storekeeper and his wife were filling a canvas sack with the day's receipts. Ollie had whirled around and fired almost directly into Ricky's gut but by that time the storekeeper's wife had run out of the store and was screaming bloody murder for the police. Ollie aimed at her back, but the bullet went into the ceiling, because Ricky, with blood spurting through his shirt, had managed to stand up and tackle him again. Ollie was on the floor, Ricky sitting on top of him, when the squad car came to a screeching halt in front of the store and two patrolmen ran inside.

Whenever Ollie told a friend in the cell block about the job that cost him five years, he omitted Ricky's role, pretending it was the crazy storekeeper's wife who caused the trouble, and saying he could have stopped her if he'd been willing to shoot an old woman. The part that galled Ollie most was that while his court-appointed attorney was plea bargaining with the prosecutor's office, the newspapers picked up the story and make Ricky out to be a hero. The bastard had even gotten a commendation from the police department.

Tomorrow, Ollie thought, tomorrow...He returned to his bunk and stretched out on his back, watching the moonlight fade and reappear as clouds moved across the sky. Tomorrow Ollie would be back on the street. Sooner or later, he'd find Ricky, and when he did, he would pay him back for every hour he had spent in prison.

● ● ●

In Room 17 of the Pines Motel, Ricky Cummins was trying to feed the baby. Babies cry because they are hungry—though he'd had no experience with infants or small children he was sure that was true. Therefore, cereal first, and then a bottle of milk.

He read the directions on the box of instant cereal and then went over them again. Using one of the plastic cups the motel provided along with small envelopes of instant coffee, he measured the proper amount of the dehydrated flakes into the cup and added some of the milk. He felt clumsy, holding the baby, and tried several different positions before he found one that felt right.

For twenty minutes, Ricky coaxed the baby into opening his mouth. At last the cup was empty and he had swallowed a little more than he spit out. But he was still making fretful sounds, still beating the air with tiny fists, and Ricky hoped the milk would quiet him.

He put the baby down and hastily poured milk into the bottle and fitted the nipple over the top. Then with the baby cradled in his left arm, he pressed the nipple gently against the infant's lips. The tiny mouth opened greedily, but after two or three swallows his face puckered in anger and disappointment. He rejected the nipple and began to cry even louder than before. Ricky looked helplessly at the child in his arms. What was he doing wrong? The milk was fresh. The baby had been eager to take the bottle. . . . The feel of it in his hand gave Ricky the answer. The milk was cold.

Along with cups and instant coffee, the motel supplied a small electric pot for boiling water. Ricky hesitated. Put the bottle into a pot of hot water, or pour the milk directly into the pot? He decided in favor of the first because it seemed cleaner.

This time the baby sucked the milk eagerly. Again, after another few swallows, he pushed the nipple out of his mouth and grimaced. However he had downed a little cereal and several ounces of milk. He seemed to be pacified, at least for the moment, and his eyelids were fluttering in the first stage of falling asleep.

But there was something more to putting him to bed than soothing him with warm milk. There were two terrycloth hand towels in the bathroom. Awkwardly but gently, Ricky removed the wet diaper, substituted towels, and pinned them together at each side. In minutes the baby was sound asleep.

Ricky washed the soiled diaper with hot water and bar soap, and hung it over the shower rod to dry. Then he stretched out on the bed, too tired to undress, and was asleep before he could turn off the bedside light.

He knew the dream so well that part of it was his own voice telling him not to be frightened because it was all a dream. He saw himself waking up, saw that he was safe in his bedroom in the Wendell Arms. The nightmare was over. He could go back to sleep. But it wasn't a real waking. He was still inside the dream, and the haunting scene pursued him once again....

He is a child, but he is carrying a child, running through the woods after a shadowy figure he knows to be his father. He is calling after his father—"The baby isn't dead, the baby isn't dead"—but his father doesn't hear. He's screaming it—"The baby isn't dead, the baby isn't dead"—and still he can't get the sound out, and the faceless figure that is his father is getting farther and farther away. Running, he cannot move. Screaming, he cannot release a sound. He falls, drops the baby, and sobbing, lies beside it. The baby's blanket has fallen away from his face. The face is strange, with gaping mouth and hollow eyes. "The baby *is* dead, the baby *is* dead...."

In the motel room, his own cry brought Ricky back to consciousness, but it was a few seconds before he could separate himself from the terrifying image of the dead baby and the live one in the corner of his motel room.

He jumped up, nearly falling in his haste to reach the couch where the baby slept in his improvised crib. He must be all right, Ricky told himself. He wouldn't be sleeping if there were something wrong with him.

For the rest of the night, Ricky sat beside the box, listening to the faint breathing and watching the flicker of eyelashes that signaled this baby, this *real* baby, was alive.

Monday, March 14

Six

ELIZABETH DAHLQUIST PULLED the lap robe over her knees and repressed a shiver. Something was terribly wrong. She knew it in spite of Martin's irritable denials and Laurie's pretense of cheerfulness. From the moment the two of them arrived at The Aerie, there had been a false ring to everything they said and a disjointed quality to everything they did.

Their strained, white faces, their manner of speaking without looking directly into her face, their pointless haste had all combined to alarm her. And now Martin, who disliked fast driving, was speeding toward the airport as if they were an hour late rather than a ridiculous two hours ahead of time. Whatever has happened, Elizabeth thought uneasily, the two of them have agreed to conceal it from me. Somehow that was the most frightening thing of all.

Her immediate thought had been that the baby was ill. The new medication wasn't helping him. She had actually started toward the telephone with the idea of cancelling her trip when they exclaimed simultaneously, "No, no! The baby is fine, just fine."

"Martin, dear, please tell me."

"He's not ill, Mother. Leif is perfectly all right."

Elizabeth turned to Laurie. "Then why didn't you bring him?"

"My mother came just for the day. I knew she would be disappointed if she didn't have the baby to herself."

"Leif is at home, with your mother?"

"Yes," Martin said impatiently. "Look, we can talk in the car."

But they hadn't "talked" at all. Elizabeth was nagged by questions they had not answered. Why would Laurie's mother travel three hundred miles for a one-day visit? Even more out of character—why would she make a trip unexpectedly, as she must have done, since just last night Martin did not know she was coming?

If the baby was well, what *was* wrong? Had they quarreled? Was the tension she felt nothing more than the backlash of an unsolved marital problem? Perhaps Laurie's mother had precipitated a disagreement: Martin wanted to bring Leif, as promised; Laurie had insisted that the child be left with her mother. . . . But that seemed unlikely. No, Leif was not well. Something *had* happened to Leif.

"Laurie? Dear, I really don't want to leave if the baby is ill."

At last she had pressed too hard. Laurie's shrill voice retorted, "Mother Dahlquist, do you really believe that if my baby were ill, I would be here with you driving to the airport?" Instantly her pale face flushed. She mumbled apologies, with what appeared to Elizabeth to be a valiant effort to keep from crying.

"I'm very sorry. . ." Laurie's outburst shocked and frightened Elizabeth more than anything else that had occurred during this strangely discordant morning. She resolved that for the rest of the drive she would not pursue the question. But neither had she accepted their answers.

As Martin turned off the freeway onto the road to the SeaTac terminal, Elizabeth was wondering how she would convince Martin that they should just drop her at the entrance. She knew the suggestion would displease him, for whenever she traveled, Martin insisted on staying with her until the very last moment when she disappeared down the giant tube into the plane. But today she did not want him to come into the terminal at all, not even as far as the PanAm check-in counter.

Martin drove up the ramp to the Departures level and braked the car. "Martin? Laurie dear?" Elizabeth began slowly. "Today, please drop me off at the curb. There's a skycap right there, with a cart. It's too early for conversation. And you have a long drive home. So please don't park the car and come back. Just run along—I'll be fine, I promise you. You've been dears— Laurie, give Leif a hug for me. And write me, will you please?"

Words were still bubbling up when Elizabeth realized that neither Martin nor Laurie had protested. Her voice trailed off. "Well, goodbye..."

"All right, Mother. If that's what you want, I won't insist."

It was difficult to conceal her relief, even harder not to show how shaken she was by his capitulation. She looked from Martin to Laurie, wondering if her own cheerful goodbyes were as transparently false as theirs. No matter, they were allowing her to do as she asked.

Having kissed her, Laurie was back in the car. Martin had signaled the skycap, her luggage was already on its way to the check-in counter... Then suddenly Martin was not returning to the car. His hand was under her elbow and he was guiding her across the lobby.

"The car will be all right for a few minutes," he said. "If not, Laurie can drive it around the circle. I don't want to leave until you've checked in."

She tried to protest, but he ignored her. Her only hope was that a long line of passengers would discourage him. But there was no line at all, only a sleepy attendant who put down his cup of black coffee and tried to be pleasant as he took her luggage and carefully checked off her passport, seat selection, gate number and boarding pass. It was all done. She accepted Martin's last kiss and waved as he ran to his car.

Now... She looked at her wristwatch. Half past six. An hour and a half before departure. Enough time to explain that because of an emergency, she must cancel her reservation and ask that her luggage be returned. She hesitated. The process would be involved, and someone more alert than the man who had checked her in would surely recognize her.

She decided to forget her ticket and her luggage and walked to the far end of the terminal where the airline counters were still unmanned. Glancing frequently at her watch, she let fifteen minutes pass. Then she took the escalator to the lower level and walked briskly to the line of waiting cabs. The driver of the first taxi leapt out to open the door. "Luggage, lady?"

She shook her head.

"No luggage?" he asked, looking toward the baggage claim area.

"No."

"Huh. Where to, please?"

"Black River."

"Black River?" the driver threw over his shoulder. "You know that's a two-hour drive?"

"I do."

"What I mean, I'll have to come back empty. I'll have to charge you for the return trip."

"That's what I expected," Elizabeth said quietly.

"What address in Black River? I don't know that town very well."

"I'll direct you when we get there."

"Okay, okay. Say, it's a great day for a nice long drive. . . ." The cabbie put his car in gear and drove off, whistling.

Jack Howard looked out his window in the Hotel Alaska and noted with satisfaction that Monday morning had brought cloudless skies and a warm sun. On the street below, all traces of Sunday's rainstorm had vanished except for a few puddles. A good day for an early morning walk, Howard decided. He pulled on his favorite sports coat and set out for First Avenue.

Like most people born in the Pacific Northwest, Howard tended to take the mountains, beaches, and forests for granted. First Avenue, the least beautiful street in town, had a special place in his affections because it was a street of people. He felt sympathy for the human detritus that stumbled bleary-eyed from saloon to adult movie house to a free meal at a mission. He set a fifty-cent limit on handouts to the street's frequent panhandlers, but he never turned one down. He respected the Indians stranded on the benches of Pioneer Square. He knew most of the farmers who sold apples, vegetables, eggs, chickens and rabbit meat in the outdoor stalls of the public market; at his age, some of the hucksters were sons of old friends.

The pawnbrokers were Howard's special friends. As a private investigator, he had often depended on their cooperation. His help had been valuable to them, too. No money ever changed hands, except when Howard bought something out of pawn, and this interdependence had resulted in an extraordinary degree of mutual trust. These days he just liked to drop in and visit, but this morning he was too early. The burglar-proof shutters and folding steel doors were still locked in place.

He waved at a group of Japanese sailors from a

Maru docked on the waterfront below the Avenue. He smiled at an old woman with stooped shoulders and skinny legs, dressed in castoffs from a church rummage sale with a faded straw hat perched on top of her head. At the entrance to a narrow alley, he spotted a sleeping drunk, flat on his face on a pile of refuse and old newspapers, probably lying just as he had fallen. Howard picked him up, got a bearlike hold around his body, and half dragged and half carried him for two blocks to the Lutheran mission. His eternal soul probably wouldn't respond to treatment but Sister Imgarde would see that his clothes were deloused and his wasted body momentarily sustained by a hot meal. After saying goodbye to the sister Howard decided he was hungry for a solid breakfast of buckwheat cakes and country sausage. He reversed his course and headed back toward the hotel.

The Hotel Alaska was innocent of such embellishments as a doorman, a bellhop, or a central switchboard. When Howard was still employed by Arcade Investigators, Arcade paid the bills for an answering service hooked up to the private telephone in his apartment. When he retired, Howard insisted that it be removed.

His boss, Warner Kruse, protested. "But how are we going to get in touch with you if we call when you aren't in?"

"Call when I am in."

"Damn it, Jack. I know you. You're such a slick tracer you won't let yourself get traced. We could call you six times in a day and never get through to you."

"Then call the next day. Or don't call. I'm retiring, old boy. I repeat, retiring. Leaving the field to you youngsters. I've handled my last case."

But his last day at Arcade, Howard had agreed to another arrangement. He gave Kruse the telephone number of the Hotel Alaska's manager. The manager would take the message and slip it under Howard's door.

The first year, Kruse had summoned him regularly. Howard had refused every time to be dragged out of retirement even on a temporary basis. The second year, Kruse had admitted defeat and his calls ceased. So this morning it gave Howard a distinct jolt to find a penciled note on the floor under his apartment door, saying "Call Kruse."

Howard chuckled. "Call," hell. He never telephoned when it was possible to go in person. Kruse must really have something stuck in his throat to send this summons after a year's silence. He'd walk. A voice on the telephone never revealed as much as you could pick up watching the speaker's face. Without taking time for the pancakes and sausage, he went down the elevator and set out for Arcade.

At the entrance to the Henry Marsh Building, Howard went through the revolving door like the end man on a relay team and came to a halt before the list of tenants posted on the wall beside the elevators. Arcade had changed locations twice in the two years since he'd been on the payroll. Squinting slightly—he had glasses, but believed that wearing them would make his eyes lazy—he read the alphabetical list. "Arcade Investigators"—ah, there it was.

He grinned at the name "Arcade." That was one of the first lessons Old Man Kruse had taught him. "When you start out in this business, 99 percent of your customers are going to be people who looked up the word 'detective' in the yellow pages. You're more likely to be picked if you're at the head of the line."

Seated in the inner sanctum of Arcade Investigators, Jack Howard leaned back in his leather chair and gave chief detective Warner Kruse a long and appraising look. Kruse was busy, altogether too busy, cutting the tip of a cigar with a slender penknife.

"You still don't use these?" he asked. "Sure you don't want to try one? I get them from Florida."

"That's the only bad habit I haven't acquired." Howard had worked with Kruse for fifteen years. Kruse's father, affectionately known in the agency as the Old Man, had taken the raw material of an eager young ex-cop and molded it into one of the sharpest detectives in the city. That done, the Old Man had both encouraged and goaded his protégé into studying law; when earned, the degree put Howard in a class by himself.

It struck Howard after a year's absence that Warner was looking more and more like the Old Man. "Okay, friend," he said gruffly. "I got your message. Some message. Two words. You didn't even say 'Love.'"

Warner's smile telegraphed a great deal of self-satisfaction. "By God, I finally trapped you, you old coot. How come?"

Howard chuckled. "I don't know. A whim, maybe. Or just my titanic curiosity. I haven't heard from you for a year. So I can't help wondering 'Why now?'"

"You haven't heard from me for a year because I spent the year before that running after you like I was trying to get your autograph."

"Okay, okay. So, why now?"

"Because this is something special." Warner paused, contemplating the end of his cigar. "The only case that's come up in the past two years that I thought you wouldn't turn down."

"That's for me to decide."

"Sure, Jack. Sure. But this one is different. Damn it all, it *isn't* a case. At least, not Arcade's. A young couple came in here very early this morning. I talked to them, the way I always do with new clients. Long enough to find out what sort of a job it is before I make an assignment."

"So far, so good. What did they want?"

"I don't know. Goddamn it, Jack, will you let me tell it *my* way?" And Warner proceeded to tell it his way.

The couple had come in as soon as the agency opened that morning. Warner ushered them into the small lounge he used for interviews. They sat down on the sofa, and he took a chair positioned so as to put him in direct line with the clients' eyes. To avoid his gaze they would have to look at the floor or turn to the side.

He noted that they looked dead tired. The young woman in particular had dark shadows under her eyes and a drawn expression around the mouth. He observed the way they were sitting—their backs ramrod straight. They still hadn't said a word. Noting the woman's anxious glances at her husband, Warner decided they had agreed he was to do the talking and his wife, if she was his wife, was waiting for him to start. He saw a defensiveness in the young man's eyes, a resistance, that probably meant he had been talked into consulting the agency and would be very difficult to work for.

To start things off, Kruse had said, "It might be helpful to know how you came to select Arcade Investigators." Actually, knowing why they had come to Arcade probably wouldn't help anyone but Warner Kruse, who liked to know whether advertising or fee-splitting referrals was contributing the most to his $280,000 a year gross. "Did your lawyer refer you?"

"No."

The young woman spoke for the first time. "We looked in the telephone book, the yellow pages." She threw another quick side glance at her husband.

"Please understand," said Warner, "we *want* to be of service. We have a very fine reputation, not only for the thoroughness of our work but for our discretion. I sense that you are anxious to avoid publicity...."

Bull's-eye, Warner thought as the man's head jerked up
and an expression of sheer panic flashed across his
face. Whatever the problem, the husband obviously
didn't want it to get into the newspapers. "Believe me,
our success as investigators depends on secrecy. If you
retain Arcade, I can assure you that everything told us
in confidence will never go farther than the walls of this
office."

Warner knew instantly that the word "if" was a
mistake. Suggesting that there was any possibility
whatever that Arcade wouldn't be retained was the
wrong way to deal with a prospective client. As if
Warner's thoughts had programmed the other man's
movements, the husband stood up and said stiffly,
"Thank you for your time, Mr. Kruse. At the moment,
we're not in a position to retain an investigator. We
may need help at a later date."

Warner Kruse also rose. It wouldn't do any good to
tell this man that anyone with half an eye could see they
needed help right now. But he nodded agreeably and
extended his hand.

"You said..." The wife was looking up at her
husband, and there were tears in her eyes.

"Sorry, Mr. Kruse. You've been very courteous."
The man turned toward his wife and held out his hand.
Her tears were spilling over now, but she rose and
followed him to the door.

It's to be an orderly retreat, Warner Kruse reflected.
These people have been well brought up. The woman's
tears are definitely out of character. She wouldn't be
doing it now if her husband's decision to walk out
hadn't shocked her into it.

Aware that he had lost a client, Warner was still
curious. No harm in testing their reactions to one last
question. "Excuse me, but have you notified the
police?"

The reaction had been swift. What had begun as a

polite departure became a headlong flight. Without answering the question, the pair bolted across the reception room and pushed the Down button for the elevator. And that had been the end of the interview.

Now, an hour later, Jack Howard said mildly, "An interesting story. Especially interesting because you left something out."

"What was that?" Warner said, getting busy with his cigar and an erratic lighter.

"Oh, for God's sake..." said Howard. "Let's hear your exit line. Their names, of course. I know damn well you asked for their names."

Warner chuckled. "Of course I did. And they gave them. With a little reluctance, but they gave them." He picked up a small looseleaf notebook, and shoved it across the desk. "You want to know why I called you." He gestured toward the open page. "Right there. Those two names. They're the answer to the riddle. Or the beginning of it."

Seven

LAURIE WAS BEYOND CRYING. Most of her tears had
been spent the night before in the empty nursery; the
rest in the investigator's office this morning when she
realized Martin would not ask for help. Now, as they
drove slowly through the rush-hour traffic, she felt she
would never cry again.

Neither of them had spoken since they left the
Henry Marsh Building. Laurie was consumed by her
disappointment and angry because Martin had broken
his promise.

"Marty?" she said finally.

His head turned and their eyes met briefly. It was
long enough to tell her that he was suffering as much as
she was. He was terrified, as she was. It was in his dark
eyes, it was in the grim set of his mouth. She had cried
until she couldn't cry any more. Martin had never been
able to cry at all.

Laurie saw something else in that quick but
revealing glance. Uncertainty, bewilderment. He had
accepted responsibility for their course of action. If his

decision not to notify the police, or his last-minute refusal to employ a private detective, were to result in the death of their child, he would accept the guilt as well.

"Marty, could we talk about it?"

"Yes, Laurie." His voice was husky. "We *must* talk about it."

"What are we going to do now? I don't even know where we're going. This isn't the way home."

"No, it isn't." Now his voice was defiant. "We're going back to The Aerie."

"Back to your mother's!"

Martin nodded. "Back to Mother's."

"But there's no one there," Laurie protested. "Except the caretaker in the garden cottage."

"That's my reason for going."

Laurie heard the familiar note of finality, the announcement that Martin had said all he intended. "Please go on. Please tell me why we're going to The Aerie. Don't shut me out. You don't know how it feels to be shut out..." Her voice broke.

"Don't I?" Martin said quietly. "For the last half hour I've had the feeling that you had left me." One hand grasped the long curls at the nape of her neck and gave them a gentle tug. "Anyway, I'm glad you're back."

Impulsively Laurie slid along the seat, closing the gap between them. As he drove, Martin told her about the cabinet behind his father's desk, and his mother's emotional outburst when he asked about the contents. "It's the package I want to inspect. I'm sure it has something to do with—with what happened to my brother."

"But that's digging up the past, as your mother said."

"Yes," Martin said grimly. "But the past has come alive in spite of us. Klaus Ochsner has been dead for a long time, but something in that package, or perhaps something among my father's old papers, might give us information about what happened to his wife after his execution, or, more to the point, what happened to his son."

Laurie said quietly, "Your mother doesn't want you to open that cabinet. Wouldn't she have hidden the key?"

"I'm sure she has."

"Then?"

"Then I'll break into it. At least, I have a key to the house."

For the rest of the drive they were silent, but with bodies touching in a silent communication as new to them as the terror they felt for their child.

Martin parked at the front entrance to The Aerie. Laurie was out of the car as quickly as he, watching him curiously as he opened the trunk and searched through the tool box. He picked out a ball peen hammer and a tire iron, closed the trunk, and hurried up the walk to the front door. In tense silence he let them in and closed and locked the door. "The caretaker," he explained. "I don't want him to surprise us."

In the library the first thing that caught Martin's eye was the cardboard box of newspaper clippings. So in the end his mother had neither destroyed nor put them away. Now he was grateful. Yesterday he had only scanned them, resisting their power to reopen old wounds. Today he would read them carefully, searching for some small clue to the whereabouts of Klaus Ochsner's son.

His attention moved from the box of clippings to the cabinet behind his father's desk. He placed the hammer and tire iron on the floor and, kneeling, he inspected the brass hinges and the heavy lock. "I hate to damage this. It's beautiful work."

"Perhaps you don't have to," Laurie said. "My first thought was that your mother would hide the key. But now I'm wondering—why would she? Yesterday you didn't go against her wishes. You gave the key back to her."

"I did, but only because I knew she would be gone for three months so that I would have plenty of time to satisfy my curiosity if I really wanted to. She'll have guessed, Laurie. She knows me very well. I'm more Newton than Dahlquist." He got to his feet and with an uncertain smile said, "I'm the small dark one, not the big blond one."

"Stop it, Marty. Stop apologizing because you lived and he died."

"Yes... Well..." Martin shrugged. "It doesn't much matter anyway, does it?" Suddenly his eyes focused on the desk drawer. He opened it, reached into the section at the back from which his mother had taken the key. His fingers touched cold metal. "The key," he said looking at it with an expression of disbelief. "What do you know, Laurie. You were right. She didn't hide it. Apparently I didn't know her as well as I thought I did. Or rather, she doesn't know *me* as well as I thought *she* did."

Smiling, he fitted the key into the lock and opened the cabinet door. Boxes, manila envelopes, file folders, pictures... Everything was there except for the little packet tied with twine and sealed with red wax. The space it had occupied was the only area on the shelf that was not covered with dust.

"She *does* know me," Martin said thoughtfully. "And I know her. Whatever that package contains, I suspect she hid it from my father as well as from me. Something she knew would hurt him. Now she's protecting me. But from what, Laurie? What sort of secret would be so terrible that she hid it from the man she loved, totally and passionately, for almost forty years?"

• • •

Ricky made a second cup of instant coffee. His pulse was fast and the beginning of a severe headache was collecting behind his eyes. He needed sleep, but the nightmare had shocked him into a state of nervous wakefulness. And he had to stay awake. It was a new day. Monday, March 14. He had held the Dahlquist child for over twelve hours and still had no idea as to how to contact the parents or how to care for the baby until he did.

He sipped the bitter liquid and forced himself to concentrate. He would have to take one day at a time. He must start right now, with those things that must be done at once.

He knew what the first of these would be. Call his office before someone there called him. Illness wouldn't be a convincing explanation for his absence if his employer telephoned his apartment and no one answered. It was already half past nine.

Ricky picked up the receiver. A woman's voice said briskly, "Can I help you?" He was about to give her the number when he remembered that the call went through the management's switchboard. He had registered under a hastily contrived false name. If the woman on duty listened in, she would discover that "Harry Thomas" in Number 17 was actually a man named Ricky Cummins. He wasn't sure what she would do about it. Perhaps nothing. But she would be curious, and he could not afford that.

He said, "I'm sorry, operator. I have to look up the number."

"There's a directory in the desk drawer, sir."

"Thank you very much."

He put on his jacket, checked the coins in his pocket, and with a glance at the sleeping baby, went out the door and closed it cautiously behind him. While he was in view of the motel office window, he walked slowly. Around the corner, he broke into a run. In five minutes

he had found a public telephone booth, made his call to
the office, and accepted the receptionist's cheery
command to get well soon. In another five minutes he
was back in the motel room. The baby was still
sleeping.

He sat down on the sofa and forced himself to
review his twin lists of Do's and Don'ts. He must *not*
take the baby to his apartment in the Wendell Arms.
He must *not* depart from routine that involved other
people, such as daily visits to his mother at Sylvan
Home West. He must *not* let his mail pile up at the
Wendell Arms nor leave the daily newspapers to
accumulate where the teenage carrier dropped them at
his apartment door. Both mail and newspapers would
tell everyone in the building that the young man in 28,
the one you could set your clock by, was acting
strangely. He must *not* panic, as he had at the
delicatessen.

On the positive side, he must... He must... Ricky
rested his head against the back of the sofa and closed
his eyes. He *must* hold onto himself. He *must* think
straight, despite his pounding headache.

Slowly decisions emerged. He must find someone
with whom he could hide the baby. And he must get
enough money, so that wherever he had to sleep,
whatever he had to buy, he could pay in cash.

In the Hughes Avenue branch of Puget Sound
Savings and Loan, a teller watched her last customer
stuff the money he had withdrawn into the pocket of
his corduroy sport jacket, button the flap, and hurry
out through the electric door. On the street he hesitated
before apparently making up his mind and hurrying in
the direction of 71st Street.

In the next stall, the teller tapped on the glass
partition and said, "Hey, Cindy! He's not *that* good-
looking."

The teller named Cindy smiled but her eyes were still thoughtful. "Do you know who he is?"

"Sure. I've waited on him lots of times. Cummins, right?"

Cindy nodded. "Ricky Cummins."

"Well, what's bugging you?"

"I know his name, his address, and his balance. That's not the same as knowing who he is."

Her neighbor on the right laughed. "You mean you still haven't asked for his telephone number?"

Cindy was about to answer but a customer was approaching her colleague's stall. In a way, she was glad. The "loyalty oath," as all the girls called it, most certainly prohibited gossip about a depositor's affairs and her observations about Mr. Ricky Cummins of Apartment 28, Wendell Arms would have to be classed as idle speculation. Cindy had never seen a passbook with such regularly scheduled deposits. On the second and the fifteenth of every month. The amounts never changed, except for a slight increase every six months which probably indicated small raises in salary. Moreover, in the five years since Ricky Cummins had opened a savings account with PSS & L, he hadn't made a single withdrawal.

Cindy asked herself why the steadiest depositor in the Hughes Avenue branch would suddenly withdraw $2,000 in tens and twenties? And since she was already allowing herself to get personal, why for the first time had he failed to smile or say hello?

Her friend's voice broke into her thoughts. "Hey, Cindy? Have you gone to sleep? What were you saying about Mr. Cummins?"

Cindy shrugged. "Nothing."

"Oh, so you're going to clam up. Well, the only thing I think of when I wait on Mr. Cummins is that he looks like someone."

"Doesn't everyone?"

At that point, they both had customers, and that was the end of their conversation.

The idea of placing a classified ad in the Seattle *News-Record* came to Ricky unexpectedly. Like other details of his father's crime, it had been filed in the back of his mind and now came forth as if to compel him to try and reenact the famous Dahlquist Case. Steal the great hero's only son. Leave a note threatening the child's life if the police are called. Instruct the baby's parents to make contact through the classified section of a daily newspaper...

Frowning, Ricky opened the desk drawer and took out a sheet of motel stationery. He had plunged blindly into his father's role although he had seen his father no more than a dozen times, could scarcely recall what he looked like, and had never known his true name, until that afternoon at Ollie's house, when he was twelve years old.

He hadn't meant to eavesdrop. He and his seventh-grade classmate, Oliver White, had been assembling model airplanes on the White's dilapidated porch. They were both totally preoccupied when a stout gray-haired woman with small searching eyes puffed up the steps and demanded, "Your mother home, Ollie?"

Ollie barely glanced up. "Uh, huh," he said rudely and turned back to the minuscule wing section in his hand. A half hour later, the woman appeared at the window that opened onto the porch. Ricky looked up, straight into her staring eyes. He turned his head and pretended to be completely absorbed by the model. When he glanced up again, she was gone.

At that point, Ricky had been overcome by a nearly uncontrollable need to urinate. "Hey, I got to pee," he told Ollie as he bolted through the front door into the house.

The kitchen was adjacent to the cubicle Mrs. White

called the "powder room." Ricky relieved himself,
opened the lavatory door, and was on his way back to
the front porch when Mrs. White's nasal voice arrested
him. "No, Tessie, I swear the boy *doesn't* know. And
his mother certainly isn't going to tell him. Would you
if you was her?"

"No, maybe not." The visitor's voice was as gruff as
a man's. "But I'd figure that someday he's going to find
out about his father, and maybe I'd rather be the one to
tell him."

From the first words, Ricky knew the women did
not mean to be overheard. Almost as quickly, he
guessed they were talking about him. For an instant, he
wanted to walk into the kitchen and look Mrs. White
and her fat visitor right in the face and yell, "Don't you
dare talk about my mother and father! My mother *did*
tell me what happened to my father!" The impulse died
quickly and Ricky remained where he was, thinking
"But did she tell me the truth?" She had always cried, or
else she got angry, when he asked questions about his
father.

A moment of silence in the kitchen ended with the
clink of teacups set down on their saucers. Then Mrs.
White's voice rose in protest. "You *sure* that's
Ochsner's widow? After all, it's been a long time since
the trial."

"Look, Tessie, she even kept her own first name. Lisa
Cummins, Lisa Ochsner. I suppose it's hard to give up
all your name. And I never forget a face, Tessie. The
minute she moved in across the street, I knew I'd seen
her before. You remember, Al was always a great one
for scrapbooks. So after I met Mrs. Cummins, I looked
through them and sure enough, there was a
newspaper picture of her and her husband's lawyer
walking down the courthouse steps the day Klaus
Ochsner was convicted.... I tell you, Tessie, that
woman's had a hard life. It's no wonder she's crazy. I'd

go crazy myself if I had to worry that someday my son would find out his father died in the electric chair."

Ricky Cummins's rubber-soled Keds made no sound as he retreated to the front porch, closed the door quietly, and began to throw the parts of his airplane model into the box. "I forgot," he told Ollie in a choked whisper. "I'm supposed to mow the lawn today. I got to go home."

"Oh, hell," Ollie retorted. "You always do what you're supposed to do?"

Ricky looked at him blankly. Grabbing his box, he ran down the steps and across the street to the white frame house where his mother—his mother who was crazy—was taking a nap because she had to report for work at the bakery at two o'clock in the morning.

His mother had answered his questions with an outburst of hysterical curses, mostly in German, at the woman across the street. Ricky was forbidden to visit Ollie and at the end of the week, they moved again, though they had been renting the white house for less than a month. The first day at the new address, Ricky walked two miles to the public library, where he learned from the old newspaper files that Klaus Ochsner, his father, had not died of tuberculosis, as his mother had told him, but in the electric chair.

With her secret known, Ricky's mother seemed obsessed by a need to convince him of his father's innocence. Sometimes she talked quite rationally. About the suppression of evidence that would have supported Klaus Ochsner's not-guilty plea and the manufacture of evidence that proved him guilty. About how the highest police officials in the state had manipulated witnesses in an effort to "solve" the celebrated crime. About circumstantial evidence, and the doubts even the rich and famous Dahlquist family had as to who had kidnapped and murdered their son.

At other times, especially during one of her "bad spells," Ricky's mother talked endlessly about her hatred for the Dahlquists. "They killed him! They killed him! They were so rich they could buy expensive lawyers. Your father died because of *them*!"

His mother's outbursts frightened and repelled Ricky. He did not want to be paralyzed, as she was, by a hopeless obsession. But little by little, he too came to hate the Dahlquists. If it was true, as several of the books he read about the case stated, that Leif Dahlquist himself had doubted that Ochsner was the kidnapper, then the Dahlquists had indeed "killed" his father. And his mother's recurring illness could be blamed on them too. Klaus Ochsner's only son, he grew up with the conviction that he owed it to his mother to strike back. He had never known how until Leif Dahlquist's death.

Composing the classified ad was more difficult than Ricky had expected. After several attempts, he knew why. He was departing from the script. Klaus Ochsner had never placed a classified ad in the newspaper; that had been done by the Dahlquists' intermediary, Professor Marshall, to arrange payment of the ransom.

But he didn't intend to repeat every step in the earlier crime for which, guilty or not guilty, his father had been sentenced to death. It had never occurred to Ricky to demand ransom. He would make the Dahlquists suffer, but he would do it in his own way.

He picked up his pencil and began again. He wrote quickly, and when he was finished he went to the cardboard box and looked down at the child. He was asleep. Ricky touched the baby's hand. It felt cold. He covered the baby with the terrycloth robe and tucked it in at the sides. Then he went out, ran to the public telephone booth in the drugstore around the corner, and called the Classified Ad desk of the Seattle *News-Record*.

Eight

OLLIE WHITE STOOD on the corner of Sixth and Dixon and recalled the old saying that a crook always returns to the scene of his crime. This was the scene, all right, and it looked about the same as it did on that unlucky day when Ricky Cummins had him arrested. Same old Tabernacle of the True Light in the creaky building that had once been the neighborhood movie house. Ming Yee's restaurant, with dusty crêpe-paper streamers masking the rain-spotted windows. The bakery outlet where they sold day-old bread and month-old cookies. The Ladies League thrift shop—"All Garments Washed or Cleaned." The service station . . . Ollie grinned, because that was one he never got busted for.

Cursing the whole world and Ricky in particular, he walked rapidly along Dixon Avenue until he came to the Loggers Cafe with its Paul Bunyan Room. He went inside, walked through the restaurant to the dimly lit cocktail lounge, and chose a table where he could sit facing the door. He ordered a double bourbon and a ham sandwich.

By the time Ollie had swallowed the whiskey his black mood had lifted. He was thinking that he'd done a damn good job tracing Ricky, in spite of the fact that he and his nutty mother had been jumping from place to place just like they did when he and Ricky were kids. He'd started with the apartment house where Ricky and his mother had been living at the time of the grocery store holdup five years before. Dead end, but he had another trump. Six or eight months after his arrest, both Seattle dailies had carried stories about Ricky's commendation for "heroism in the face of grave danger," which Ollie called a dirty double cross. These news items had given an address on Caldwell Street as Ricky's residence. So he checked that out. Also nothing. But he had been holding one more card, and Ollie, sipping bourbon, smiled to himself because he had played it so well.

Maria. Maria Nunez, the girl Ricky was engaged to at the time Ollie was sent up. Through a phone call to her parents, he had learned Maria's married name. (Ha, so Ricky lost out!) They refused to give him her address or telephone number, but that hadn't stopped Ollie. How many Mike Adaskevitches can you have in the greater Seattle area? So, with a pocketful of change and a lot of patience, he had finally located Maria, who didn't know Ricky's address, hadn't seen Ricky for years, but did remember that when they broke up, Ricky was working for some architects who had an office somewhere near Lake Washington.

Ollie ordered a second bourbon. The next step was the yellow pages and another bucket of change, but he was getting the feeling that Ricky was around the next corner so it was time to slow down and think things over. First things first, Ollie thought with a thrill of anticipation. And number one is to get myself a gun. From the moment he started to chase down Ricky, Ollie had figured that the smartest move was to steal a gun registered to someone else. He'd taken the first step while he was in the penitentiary.

He read the Seattle crime news every day. He'd skip from headline to headline, and when he found a lead he'd clip the story. By the time he walked through the sallyport six or eight newspaper fragments were hidden in his shoe. Now they were in his pocket. He pulled them out and lined them up on the table beside his plate. By the time he'd finished the sandwich and another bourbon he had picked the one he figured would be right for him.

The headline read:

COURAGE FOILS
HOLD UP MAN

Beside it, a news photo of Anton Kubek, age fifty-three, the owner of Kubek's Deli & Bakery, standing beside his cash register with a nervous smile on his face and a revolver in his hand. Faced with an armed robber just six weeks earlier, Kubek risked his life by reaching for his own gun. Two shots were fired: one by the gunman, one by the baker. The robber's bullet was wild, Kubek's hit the gunman in the shoulder. The assailant ran from the store but was overtaken ten minutes later, weakened by the loss of blood.

Ollie felt a warm glow as he always did when he was pleased with himself. He had found his man. First Anton Kubek, then Ricky Cummins.

Anton Kubek was rearranging salad bowls and sausage trays in the refrigerated showcase when the little bell over the front door announced that someone was coming into the shop. He slid the glass door into place and stood behind the counter, smiling.

Two people had come in, a man and a woman. At first he assumed they were man and wife, then realized they were not. The woman was elderly. The man was somewhere around forty, though he had the kind of pale skin and small eyes that made it hard to judge. It was a face, Anton Kubek decided from long experience with customers, that hadn't changed in ten years and wouldn't change much for another ten.

The woman was pointing at different platters and asking questions about price. Kubek looked questioningly at the man.

He shook his head. "Take care of her first," he said very politely. "I'm not in any hurry."

When at last the woman had made her purchases and left, the man stepped up to the counter. "I been looking at those cans on the shelf right behind you. No, the next one down. There, that one..."

Anton had picked the can from the shelf and was just beginning to straighten up when he glimpsed the long narrow blade of a knife out of the corner of his eye. His hand was outstretched, reaching for his gun, when he felt the impact of the blade, driven full force into his shoulder by the customer leaning over the counter. Kubek grunted, cried out, and fell.

His wife was the first to find him. Later, when the police arrived, it was his wife who noticed that the robber hadn't stolen any money at all. Nothing had been taken, except her husband's revolver and the box of bullets he kept on the shelf beside it.

Nine

IT WAS INSTINCT rather than knowledge that told Ricky
something more serious than hunger was wrong with
the Dahlquist baby. The baby in his possession was ill.
Without proper treatment, he would get steadily
worse.

The child had stopped his loud, demanding
outbursts. At first Ricky welcomed that as a good sign.
But the energetic protest had dwindled to a weak cry.
He was becoming listless, his eyes were dull and his last
drink of warm milk brought on a spasm of convulsive
vomiting. Ricky was placing all his hopes on the
Dahlquists' reply to his classified ad. But the paper
wouldn't be out until early evening and he had no way
of knowing whether the Dahlquists read the classified
pages or not. And if they did, their response, with
instructions for the baby's care, would not appear until
tomorrow's edition of the paper. It would be thirty
hours at least before he could expect to know what was
wrong with the baby. He couldn't wait that long. He
would have to find someone who had experience with
small children.

With growing anxiety Ricky tried to think of a person who would take care of the child without asking questions. It would be nice if he had a married sister or aunt he could call on. But "Ricky Cummins" did not have relatives. Eric Ochsner might have, but the child by that name had vanished forever with the execution of his father. Perhaps there had been aunts, uncles, and cousins, who might have felt sympathy for the widow and her little son but if so, Lisa Ochsner had cut all ties to them long before Ricky was old enough to know them.

He had only vague memories of an "Uncle Fred" and "Aunt Rhoda," who kept him in their home from the day of Klaus Ochsner's arrest until sometime after his execution. And even if he could find them, he certainly couldn't ask them to take in a baby. No, there was only one person he could turn to even if it was a risk—Annie Freeman.

For almost two years Ricky had been taking her out, finding her a warmhearted but undemanding lover. At their first meeting she had volunteered only the barest facts about herself. That she had been married. That her two children were living with their grandparents in a small town in Minnesota. She hadn't probed for similar information about him. Even after two years she knew little more than his name, his occupation, and his telephone number. Months after they became lovers, Ricky had referred to his mother. Annie neither pressed him for more information nor asked him to explain why he had never spoken of his mother before. Annie accepted him, and made love with him, but Annie never pried.

Ricky checked the back seat. The baby hadn't kicked off his covers and for the moment at least seemed to be sleeping peacefully. Ricky closed the door carefully and took the steps to Annie's front door two at a time.

When she opened up surprise flickered across her face. Monday was *her* day off, yes, but it wasn't Ricky's. The unspoken question disappeared as she smiled, put one hand on his arm, and pulled him into the room. She closed the door firmly, turned, and lifted both arms.

In that warm greeting, free from "Why?" or "How come?," Ricky knew he had been right to come.

Still holding her, he said, "Annie, I've come to ask a favor."

She smiled up at him. "Sure thing. Come on out to the kitchen with me. I'll make some coffee. And some sandwiches."

"No, Annie, thank you. I've got to be on my way." All at once Ricky sensed that it wasn't going to be easy after all. Even if Annie didn't ask questions, he would have to volunteer some reason for having a baby in his possession. Concealing facts about himself was a habit of long standing, but the outright lie he would have to tell Annie stuck in his throat.

"It's twelve-thirty, Rick. Ten to one you haven't had lunch."

"You're right," Ricky said nervously. "But I can't stay."

"You've got to eat somewhere. Why not..." Annie broke off, clearly embarrassed by stepping over the boundary with that forbidden "Why?" "Right you are," she said perkily, and patted his arm. "Now what was that favor?"

"Have I ever mentioned my brother.... My brother...Dick?" Ricky began nervously.

Annie's level gaze told him that of course he hadn't and no one would know that better than he.

Ricky continued doggedly, becoming more apprehensive with every word. "Dick and his wife were in a very bad accident. Auto accident...on the freeway. There were three cars....." An inner voice shouted—

Stop it! You're saying too much! She's already suspicious and you're making it worse! "Both of them are in the hospital. There's no one to take care of their baby. I thought..."

"I'm a working gal, Rick," Annie reminded him. Her eyes hadn't left his face from the moment he started to talk. "I'll do what I can, but tell me, what exactly did you have in mind?"

Her voice was quiet but it penetrated every pretense. "I thought you would know a good baby-sitter. Someone who would take care of him during the day, while you're at work. It's not a small favor I'm asking. I realize that."

Annie shrugged. "It's not a big one, either. The problem is finding the right baby-sitter. It's been awhile since I needed one."

An impulse to get away hit Ricky so hard that he couldn't keep from taking two or three backward steps in the direction of the front door. "I understand. Look, Annie, I shouldn't have bothered you."

"Bothered?" She looked at him curiously. "Rick, what's bothering *you*? Where's the baby now? Out in your car?"

"No, no..." Panic was beginning to sound in his voice. "I'm a little worried. About my brother...and his wife."

"Ricky, I asked you where the baby is."

"With my mother. For the time being."

"And where are your brother and sister-in-law?"

Ricky looked at her mutely. He wasn't thinking fast enough. "My brother?" Ricky said lamely. "I told you. In the hospital."

"*What* hospital?"

The question drove the names of Seattle hospitals out of his mind. Only one name surfaced. "Saint Vincent's," he blurted. "Annie, I've got to go." He started toward the door, realized his error, and turned back quickly. "Goodbye for now," he said as he stopped for the traditional goodbye kiss.

She accepted the kiss without a word. He could feel the weight of her silence as he hurried to the door. Just before it closed behind him, he looked back. She hadn't moved. "See you...," he murmured, though he knew absolutely that he never would again.

He was in too much of a hurry to notice that the front door opened as quickly as he closed it and that Annie followed him to the car. In his haste to start the motor and drive away he didn't see her until she was rapping on the window. He looked up and for a moment stared at a strangely white and angry face. The demanding presence on the other side of the door gestured furiously. The hard mouth opened and shouted, "Roll down the window!" Numbly, Ricky obeyed.

Annie's hands were braced against the car and her enraged face was only inches from his own. Her voice was low and as cold as her eyes. "Before you go, I have something to say. You are never coming back here again. If you telephone, I'll hang up. And if you ever come near my house, I'll call the police."

Her eyes narrowed as they focused on the box in the back seat. "I ought to call the police right now," she said, her mouth twisted into a mocking smile. "So your poor brother's baby is with your mother. Whose baby is *this*, may I ask? Saint Vincent's! Was that the best you could do when you had to come up with the name of a hospital? There's Providence and Swedish and Virginia Mason and Doctors and Seattle General and Saint Cabrini and Group Health. Use one of them the next time you try to get someone to believe your stupid story. Not Saint Vincent's, which is a great big charity junk shop on Lake Union as you damn well ought to know. I can't imagine what you're up to, Rick, and to be honest, I don't *want* to know. But you're a rotten liar and I'm glad to find that out, because now I know that until today you've been telling me the truth. Not the whole truth, of course. But the truth as far as you've gone." She paused, released her grip on the door, and stepped back from the car. "Now get out of here," she said hoarsely. "Get out fast, before I change my mind and yell 'Cop.'"

Ricky was only six blocks from Annie's house when the squad car pulled up beside him. So she *had* yelled "Cop!"

Neither patrolman was looking at him, but he was trapped, in front by the red light which forced him to wait at the intersection and in back by a line of cars. As if he, too, were terrified by the sight of two officers in uniform, the baby burst into loud, despairing cries.

The officer nearest Ricky turned his head and appeared to be staring at the baby. If Ricky had been thinking sensibly, he would have known that from the front window of a car parallel to his own, it was impossible to see down to the back seat. But he wasn't thinking straight, and when the patrolman's gaze shifted to him, Ricky lost his head. Blind to the danger of running over a pedestrian, Ricky put the car in gear and jammed the accelerator to the floor.

The car leapt forward and gained speed. Through the rearview mirror, he saw that by some miracle he hadn't run anyone down. He also saw the squad car had run the red light too and was tailing him with its siren even louder than the wailing of the baby in the back seat.

Officer Dennis exclaimed, "Jesus Christ, Vic! Look at that!"

Vic Kowalski was a veteran. To his excitable rookie partner he growled, "Yeh, kid. I see it. Fifteen minutes before the end of a watch and I've got some turkey who wants to play cat and mouse. This is your first pursuit, kid. I want you to do exactly what I say.

Buckle up. Keep calm. Hit the siren. And report in."

Dennis grabbed the mike and lifted it to his mouth. "X ... X ... This is X-ray 14, in pursuit of a '70 white Plymouth sedan. Heading north on ... Jesus, Vic, he's going to hit that truck!"

Kowalski said, "Just make the report, Dennis."

The rookie nodded and began again. "X-ray 14, in pursuit of '70 white Plymouth sedan. Heading north on Winthrop Boulevard. Just crossing Stuyvesant. License number to follow."

The dispatcher's voice answered. "Roger, X-ray 14. To all units in the vicinity of X-ray 14. X-ray 14 in pursuit of '70 white Plymouth sedan ..."

Vic Kowalski sighed wearily. "Okay, Dennis. I'm going to move up on his tail. You've got good eyes. Try and get his plate number."

"OYT 457," he announced triumphantly to the disembodied voice of the dispatcher. "License number of pursued vehicle is OYT 457."

"Roger, X-ray 14."

"Check the hot sheet," Kowalksi said. "Hey, Dennis, check the hot sheet."

"Dispatcher. X-ray 14, change to TAC 2."

On TAC 2, Kowalski and Dennis could communicate directly with other patrol cars in the area. After only a moment's pause, a new voice entered the scene. "This is X-ray 12. Heading east. Will try to intercept white '70 Plymouth at Winthrop and 128th."

A bleep, and then another new voice: "X-ray 11. X-ray 11 to X-ray 14. We are presently at 140th and Crockett ..."

Officer Kowalski's mental map automatically marked his own position in relation to the other squad cars. He and Dennis were racing north along Winthrop. X-ray 12 was headed toward Winthrop from the west. X-ray 11 was closing in from the east. Boxing the Plymouth, if they didn't get tied up in traffic and managed to keep up their speed without hitting something.

Dennis finished his quick scanning of the department's list of stolen cars. "It's not on the hot sheet, Vic."

"It's not, eh." Kowalski's face was grim. "I'd have given you ten to one that it would be."

Clutching the mike, Dennis reported, "X-ray 14. Still pursuing north on Winthrop. Just crossed 115th. This guy's a madman." His voice rose suddenly to something close to a shout. "He's going to sideswipe! He hit! No, by God, he got by."

With many years of practice behind him, Officer Kowalski could watch the fleeing car, avoid cars and pedestrians, and tell a rookie partner what to do, all with ease and more or less at the same time. But Officer Dennis was getting on his nerves.

"Dispatch requesting X-ray 14 to change to TAC 2..."

The voice of X-ray 12 broke in. "Hey, Vic. This is Lou. I'm sorry, partner, but I've got to drop off pursuit. I'm caught up in traffic. A real snarl."

"Roger..."

"One down," Kowalski muttered. "Two to go."

The voice of X-11 broke in. "To X-ray 14. I'll intercept you at Kelly and Winthrop. Will attempt to set up a roadblock."

"Roger," Dennis answered.

Siren screaming, Kowalski and Dennis raced toward the rendezvous. Blocks ahead they saw that squad car X-ray 11 was in position at a forty-five-degree angle across Winthrop and directly in the path of the Plymouth.

Dennis yelped, "Vic, he's going to run through the block! Jesus, he's trying to run..." Dennis sucked in his breath, expelled it sharply as the collision he had seen coming sent the blocking squad car into a wild spin that ended when the car crashed against a light pole.

Kowalski pulled up beside the wreck and Dennis jumped out. "You guys all right?" he shouted as he ran to check on the men in the damaged car.

The pale face of a fellow officer appeared at the open window. "Couple bruises. Couple cuts. But the car's dead in the water."

Officer Kowalski made a quick appraisal. Even with the screeching siren to make cars pull over and pedestrians scatter, Kowalski knew that to continue the chase would endanger lives and property. He gave the rookie a weary look and held out his hand. "Give me the mike, kid."

"We've still got a chance. With a little speed, we can corner him!"

Kowalski's commanding forefinger beckoned for the mike. "This is X-ray 14. Dropping off pursuit of white '70 Plymouth, license OYT 457, last seen at intersection of Kelly and Winthrop, heading north on Winthrop. Request ambulance and wrecker at this location."

"Roger, X-ray 14 . . ."

Kowalski looked at the frustrated rookie. "Take it easy, Dennis. This isn't a TV show. In the first place, we're going to stay right here until the ambulance arrives. In the second place, we've got the Plymouth's license number. We'll get the guy. Not by chasing him through heavy traffic. But we'll get him." He was out of the car and on his way to talk with the injured policeman when a small detail popped into his mind. He went back to his own car. "Say, Dennis, when we were at that stoplight, just before the Plymouth ran the light, did you hear anything?"

Dennis shook his head. "Don't think so, Vic."

Officer Kowalski frowned. "It just came back to me. Just an impression. Maybe I was hearing things, but when that Plymouth pulled up beside us, I swear I heard a baby crying."

Jack Howard picked up an early edition of the evening *News-Record* and headed for home. The small sheet torn from Warner Kruse's notebook was in his coat pocket. Not that he needed it. The names Warner had scratched down were imprinted indelibly on Howard's memory. The problem was how to investigate for a man who wanted no help. Kruse knew it would be difficult or he wouldn't have been willing to turn over the case.

Back at the hotel Howard dropped the newspaper on the table by the window, sat down, and pulled the slip of paper out of his pocket. The difference between himself and Kruse was that Kruse had identified the young couple from recent newspaper photographs, while Howard knew who they were after one quick look at their phony names. He felt a shiver of excitement as he unfolded the notepaper and studied the two names. John Newton. Betty Newton, his wife. What strange psychological twists take charge when a truthful man tries to tell a lie!

He didn't know from what corner of his subconscious Martin Dahlquist had extracted "John" but the source of his wife's hastily contrived pseudonym was clear as a neon sigh. Betty, a short form of Elizabeth. Newton—Elizabeth Dahlquist's maiden name. There was no doubt at all in Howard's mind that the young man who had visited Arcade Investigators this morning was the son of Leif and Elizabeth Newton Dahlquist.

With a sigh, Howard opened the *News-Record* and began his customary study. His eye was trained to scan and to spot so that no matter how rapidly he passed over items which didn't interest him, his eye always came to a dead halt when he hit something that did.

This afternoon he skimmed quickly until he came to the classified page. The third ad down under Personals registered like an electric shock

> To Worried Parents: Special
> instructions needed. Place
> them in this column. You don't
> want a second K.O.

K.O., K.O.... Howard jumped to his feet and began to pace with an unlighted pipe clamped between his teeth. He might very well be the only *News-Record* reader other than Martin and Laurie Dahlquist to understand the terrible meaning of those initials. He had guessed that the younger Dahlquists were in trouble. Now he knew how desperately they needed help, and how terrified they must be because they did not dare ask for it.

Ten

MARTIN AND LAURIE loaded the trunk of their car with the contents of Leif Dahlquist's private cabinet, and at the last minute decided to bring along the box of recent newspaper and magazine clippings as well. Going through the material in The Aerie's oak-paneled library was out of the question. They had to get home in case the kidnapper telephoned.

Martin spoke once during the hour's drive from The Aerie to Black River. "We've made a mistake, Laurie. A stupid and dangerous mistake. We must never leave home again at the same time."

"Now it's been twenty-four hours since Leif had his medicine," was Laurie's only reply.

Her words hung in the air the rest of the way home. Martin parked by the kitchen door and they began to empty the trunk. Laurie was just carrying in a stack of folders when something on the driveway caught her eye. Small, red . . . She hurried over to it and turned it over with the toe of her shoe. An empty cigarette pack. "Martin!" she said urgently. "Martin, come here."

With a box in his left hand and the key to the back door in his right, Martin looked down at the crumpled red paper. "The milkman?"

"Not on Monday."

"Don't touch it," Martin said hoarsely. "Here, I'll let you in. We'll unload the car and get back to this later." He turned the key and twisted the doorknob. Then his body tensed as he realized that he hadn't unlocked the door. He had locked it.

"Go back to the car," he told Laurie softly. "Get into the back seat. Lock all the doors and lie down on the floor." He waited until she was invisible to anyone going in or out the back door before turning the key once more and opening the door.

He stood absolutely still in the kitchen. The silence was as threatening as the unlocked door. He set the box down on the floor and, with both hands free, took two or three steps in the direction of the nursery. For the first time in his life, Martin wished he had a gun. Leif Dahlquist had always kept two or three in the house and one in the glove compartment of his car. But some of the most frightening experiences in Martin's early years had involved the use of firearms so he had refused to own one.

He advanced again, another two or three steps. This time his ear picked up a faint sound, like a sigh or the rustle of silk curtains lifted by a gust of wind. He walked slowly across the kitchen.

At first he thought the nursery was empty. Then he heard the low sighing sound again. It came from the sofa in front of the fireplace. Martin hurried across the room and looked over the back. A small figure in a camel's hair suit was curled up asleep, her hands clutching one of the baby's blankets. Her lips moved and her eyelids fluttered as she struggled with the images of a bad dream. The sound he had heard was a muffled sob. Her cheek was wet; she had been crying in her sleep.

Martin knelt beside the sofa and gently touched her hand. "Mother," he said softly. "Mother, wake up now. It will be all right, Mother. It will be all right. . . ."

None of them felt the need to explain. Martin and Laurie had attempted to deceive Elizabeth. At the airport Elizabeth had successfully deceived Martin. The cigarette pack? The cab driver had been smoking. He had probably tossed it out as he turned to go back to the city. The unlocked door? Elizabeth had been too disturbed to think of resetting the latch after she came in.

With very few words they agreed on what they must do. First, they must eat, even though they had no appetite. While Martin carried his father's papers from the car to the living room, Laurie prepared soup and sandwiches and a pot of strong black tea.

They ate dutifully, without pleasure. Several times Laurie put down her spoon and sat in tense silence, looking into space. Each time Elizabeth said quietly, "You must eat, Laurie."

"I keep expecting the telephone to ring. He's got to get in touch with us, doesn't he? He must know he's punished us enough by now."

"He'll call, dear. I know he will." Though her face was unnaturally pale and tear spots still showed on her blue silk blouse, Elizabeth's voice was calm.

Martin looked at his mother in admiration. For all her fragility, her delicate features, and large, sad eyes, she had tremendous strength. Once, before he and Laurie had married, Laurie had said, "You'll never be happy in marriage, Marty, because you'll never find a wife who will equal your mother." Laurie hadn't spoken in anger, but with quiet resignation, as if loving him and being compared to his mother were both inevitable. But the two women had always gotten along well, in part, he realized, because his mother's life had been so centered on his father—so dominated by his father, to be honest about it. The birth of her first and only grandchild had brought her out of isolation. The death of her husband had drawn her still closer to her son's family, and that meant closer to Laurie. Had he been comparing them? Martin wondered. His gaze moved from his mother to his wife. Both small, both suffering.

Something about his mother's face reminded him of the scene in the library the night before. But all the papers, boxes, and file folders from his father's cabinet were now spread out on the living room rug. She was too calm, too agreeable to his proposal that the three of them search through the collection. Of course, last night it was natural to object to digging up the past and today there was no choice. Except...

Ah! Martin thought. She's calm because she knows that the small packet she didn't want me to see isn't there. Martin poured tea into his mother's cup. "I just realized that your luggage isn't here. Where did you leave it?"

Elizabeth's smile was rueful. "At the airport. It had been checked through. I didn't try to get it off the plane. I just... left."

"Then for the past two hours your luggage has been sitting at Heathrow. In another hour or two they'll put it in storage, or Lost and Found." He paused, and then added, "We'll call PanAm in the morning."

"No need..." Her eyes, usually so clear and honest, didn't quite meet his. "There are... more important things to do."

Martin looked at her thoughtfully. By trying to conceal the truth, she had pointed to it. She had taken the carefully sealed box with her. It was in her luggage, and whatever secrets it contained, it was now safely locked up in the baggage reclaim area of Heathrow Airport. And that seemed to be where she meant to leave it.

* * *

For an hour an emotional storm had been building. Elizabeth was sitting in the middle of the chintz-covered sofa, with papers she had read stacked on one side and those she hadn't read on the other. Martin was seated at one end of the long coffee table, Laurie at the other. They formed a triangle, and though they had scarcely spoken to each other since they began going through Leif Dahlquist's papers, Martin felt as if their thoughts were jumping from one to another like electric charges. Elizabeth never looked up from whatever document she was reading. Laurie did, and frequently. Whenever Martin lifted his head, she was staring at him or across the room, or out the window. Martin read doggedly, with a rising sense of futility. Even if they did unearth some reference to Klaus Ochsner's son, what good was a forty-year-old clue?

At length Laurie broke the heavily charged silence. "The more I read, the more I'm sure we need help. Professional help."

Elizabeth's dark eyes rested on the younger woman with an expression that was half anxiety, half sympathy. "But the kidnapper's note . . ." She broke off and turned to Martin. "Professional help? Police?"

"No mother. Don't be disturbed. We are not going to notify the police and Laurie knows it."

Laurie shook her head in agitation. "No, no, no! Of course I don't mean the police. I mean a private investigator, who will keep everything confidential. Someone we employ, who won't go to the newspapers. Who won't do anything at all without our approval."

Martin's voice was hoarse with emotion. "For God's sake, Laurie! Don't start again! We've talked about it, we've decided . . ."

"We *haven't* decided not to hire a private detective. You promised me that you would. And then, this morning . . ."

Martin broke in. "That man Kruse recognized us. He might be the most honest man in the city but he's not superhuman. The news that another Dahlquist baby has been kidnapped would be too good to keep."

"We could try another agency, another private investigator."

Martin drew his breath in sharply. In spite of their truce during the ride home to Black River, in spite of their pledges to work together, Laurie had circled back to the unsettled issue. "Why do we have to go all over this again?" he said angrily. "We should have known the man at Arcade would recognize us. With all the publicity during the past few weeks it was inevitable. No, Laurie, we are going to obey the kidnapper's instructions to the letter."

Elizabeth gasped. "Please," she whispered. "Marty..."

Martin turned toward her. "Sorry. But you understand, don't you, Mother? In forty years, Father was never able to convince himself that my brother would have been murdered if he had *not* called the police. His guilt haunted him the rest of his life. You had to live with that, Mother. You know what it did to him, and to you. Tell me, am I wrong? Should we hire a professional?"

Elizabeth's dark eyes shone with tears. "What can I say? This is something you must face together. It distresses me to hear you argue."

Martin nodded. In a tone heavy with accusation, he said, "You didn't argue, did you, Mother. When Father said, 'Call the state police,' you didn't raise your voice. You knew the risk, but you didn't cross him. That's *your* burden of guilt."

Elizabeth covered her face with her hands. "We didn't know. We hadn't seen the note in the nursery when your father called. It was a mistake."

"Exactly. A mistake we aren't going to make."

"Don't argue," Elizabeth pleaded. "Just don't argue."

"I agree. I hate arguments. I'm asking you, Laurie, for the last time. Please cooperate!"

"Cooperate?" Laurie jumped to her feet and ran out of the room. She was back before either Martin or Elizabeth had exchanged a word. The bottle of the baby's medicine was in her hand. "Do you see this, Mother Dahlquist?" She held the bottle in a clenched fist, a foot from Elizabeth's eyes. "Will you please tell your son that it's been over twenty-four hours since the baby got his medicine? Will you tell him . . ." Her voice broke. "Tell him that if his son doesn't get this medicine, he will die."

Elizabeth sat absolutely still, looking down at her hands. Without a word, Martin took the medicine out of Laurie's hand and set it down on the coffee table. In silence, they faced each other, neither able to express the sense of desolation that was simultaneously separating them and binding them together. Martin touched Laurie's cheek. "We've never argued."

"No," she whispered. "Maybe it's good that we are now."

"I know," he said quietly. With his forefinger he lifted her chin and looked directly into her eyes. "Maybe we should learn."

The tears were spilling over but Laurie was smiling. "We got a pretty good start today. I love you, Marty."

"And I love you. But you've never quite believed it, have you, Laurie?"

Exploding into the hushed room like the crack of a rifle, the doorbell rang.

Martin dropped Laurie's hand. "Stay in the living room with Mother." Alone in the hall, he hesitated, and for the second time wished that he had followed his father's advice to keep a hand gun in the house.

The bell rang again. Martin lifted the safety chain, turned the lock, and opened the door.

He saw a man about his own height but with the square build of a middleweight wrestler. The stranger had thick curly brown hair lightly sprinkled with gray, intelligent brown eyes under a bush of heavy eyebrows, and a pug nose. Martin's impression was of a pleasant-looking older man who would easily get lost in a crowd. Nothing striking about him, except the compelling eyes.

"Jack Howard," the stranger said, in a good-natured voice, and patted the rolled-up newspaper protruding from his coat pocket. "I know you're in serious trouble, Mr. Dahlquist. I think I can be of some help."

Eleven

RICKY PARKED IN Sylvan Home West's courtyard and
for several minutes sat in the car trying to collect his
thoughts. From first waking after only three or four
hours of haunted sleep, to the insane chase in which he
had miraculously outrun the police, every moment of
the day seemed unreal. Someone else had stolen the
baby. Someone else had stared helplessly into the
angry face of a woman named Annie Freeman.
Someone else had gone into a supermarket where a
young woman with a baby nestled in her shopping cart
had accepted his mumbled story about a sick wife and
helped him choose cans of strained baby food and
boxes of disposable diapers. The frightened stranger in
Ricky Cummins's skin had been fleeing from
everything—and in particular from thinking about his
mother.

Now once again he was forced to face himself and
who he was. He must visit his mother—Klaus
Ochsner's poor sick widow, and he dreaded it.

Yesterday she would have been under heavy

sedation. Today, she would be in a never-never land between sanity and the grotesque shadows of the past. One moment she would smile weakly and tell him he was all she had in the world and please forgive her for causing trouble. The next she would weep hysterically and pour out denials of his father's guilt. "Klaus never killed a baby! *They* killed him! The whole world loved Leif Dahlquist. The judges and the lawyers and the people—*they* had to kill someone, to show how much they loved their hero. Your father died because of *them....*"

Ricky pitied her. He grieved for her. He loved her. And now he must go in and visit her. She would be expecting him.

Though she was still somewhat drowsy, Ricky's mother recognized him. He sat on the edge of her bed, grasped her hand, and held it firmly between his own. In two days she had aged ten years. The sensible, friendly *Hausfrau* of the last four years was withering before his eyes. Like an overripe boil, bursting and releasing its poisons, Ricky's bitterness against the Dahlquists broke, flooding his mind. He would tell her what he had done. He would *prove* that he was making the Dahlquists suffer, too.

"Mother?"

The gargoyle smile, the spasmodic twitch of her fingers—her response was like a small seizure. "Bübchen," she whispered, "Bübchen..."

"I'm here, Mother."

The hand he was holding went limp. She exhaled in a long, hissing sigh and closed her eyes. "They killed him," she murmured, as if she were talking in her sleep. Her eyelids lifted, frightened eyes fixed on his face. "Klaus?"

"No, Mother. Ricky," he said as his last shred of caution evaporated in his desire to prove that, at long last, he had done something to avenge her wasted life.

"Mother," he whispered hoarsely. "Mother, listen to me." Slowly, repeating when she didn't seem to understand, Ricky told her what he had done.

Lisa Ochsner's screams carried all the way to the nursing station. One of the nurses on the four to midnight shift grabbed her case of sedatives and ran down the hall, almost colliding at the door of Room 11 with Ricky, who exclaimed, "All of a sudden. She began all of a sudden..."

The nurse had spent many years in psychiatric wards of the county hospital. This job at Sylvan House West was like a paid vacation. "Now, now," she murmured, as she forced the patient to lie down and tucked in the covers. "No need to get excited, dear. We'll just have a little something to make us sleep..."

Back at the desk, the nurse wrote a few words on the Cummins chart. "We'd better watch Number Eleven," she said to the aide. "Be sure she doesn't stockpile her pills. I ought to warn her son she's self-destructive." For the first time, she realized that Ricky was neither back there with his mother nor in the waiting room. She turned to the aide. "Did you see a young man, Cleo? Tall, curly brown hair, wearing a sport jacket?"

The aide nodded. "He went racing out the door right after you went in. His face was white as a sheet."

"I don't blame him," said the nurse who had soothed and sedated Number Eleven. "It must be a terrible shock, to see your own mother in that condition."

Howard had often trusted his instinct. Nine out of ten times, its nudging had been right, but he had never staked so much on instinct as he was tonight. And it was working.

Not that the Dahlquists trusted him entirely, not yet. They had allowed him to enter the stronghold, but Leif Dahlquist's widow and son were studying him with ill-disguised suspicion. Elizabeth's distrust was veiled by a transparent curtain of courtesy, but Martin was taking no pains at all to conceal his feeling that he should never have opened the front door. Only Martin's wife seemed pleased to see him.

"You've been brave to let me come in," Howard said, directing himself to Elizabeth. "I understand your position. Let me tell you who I am, and why I'm here. And then if you want me to, I'll leave, and I won't bother you again."

Elizabeth's head inclined in a small bow of consent, though her dark eyes were watchful. Martin spoke for her. "You'd better start by explaining who you are and why you've come."

"Dead right, Mr. Dahlquist. That's exactly what I'd demand, if I were in your shoes." He produced his wallet, withdrew a number of cards and lined them up on the coffee table. Voter registration. Driver's license. Credit cards. His license as a private investigator. City of Seattle police pass that would permit him to go through fire lines and police cordons. "You can buy most of these on the street," he said with a friendly grin, "but it would be pretty hard to get a matched set like these." With that he put down an Arcade Investigators business card with his name printed in the lower left-hand corner.

"I knew it was a mistake to go there," Martin broke out angrily. "For all that man Kruse's talk about confidentiality, he didn't keep our visit to himself." He turned to Howard and said accusingly, "He called *you.*"

"There was a reason for that," Howard said peaceably. "I've worked with Warner Kruse for something like fifteen years. He's honest, and he won't talk to anyone else. In any case, all he knows is that you're in some kind of trouble. He doesn't know what the trouble is."

going to send a couple of officers who have at least read the manual."

Innocence shivered under the impact, but eagerness marched boldly ahead. Howard said, "I'll be glad to do it on my own time. Make it my day off."

The captain's reply was a scowl. Retreating, Jack Howard make the decision that almost ended his career on the force. A day's leave could be arranged without referring the request to the captain. That was the first step. The next was to learn the time and the place, along with other details of Leif Dahlquist's request.

On the day of the conference Howard arrived at The Aerie only to discover Dahlquist talking with the captain and his favorite lieutenant. The captain, white-lipped, ordered him back to the station, but Dahlquist, his eyes filled with understanding, said, "Captain, we can use a third man." And sometime later he must have spoken privately to the captain because the next morning, instead of suspending his insubordinate rookie, the captain just said gruffly, "One more stunt like that and you can look for a job as a piano player." That act made Howard's admiration and affection for Dahlquist permanent.

But one year later, when the terrible kidnapping took place, the captain took the opportunity of satisfying his old grudge and ignored all Howard's requests to be assigned to the case.

Three months passed before the corpse of the Dahlquist baby was discovered, and those months were the most galling of Howard's life. No one from Washington, D.C.'s then infant agency, the FBI, knew the Green Hill country the way he did. No one else was motivated by his sense of obligation to Leif Dahlquist or would have been as selfless in offering his time. Yet Howard was forced to stand aside, mute and respectful, while a disorganized mob of detectives and police officers jockeyed for position on the front page and refused to pool their information. He saw his superiors bungle and then blame it on someone else. He was in the room when the chief of the state police, who had assigned direction of the world-famous case to himself, picked up the ransom note Leif Dahlquist had carefully left untouched, handling it so carelessly that the fingerprints were obliterated.

Howard hadn't resigned right away. He was recently married and the mere hint that he might throw over his job during the worst year of the Great Depression had reduced his new bride to tears. She was frail and he needed the security of a regular paycheck in order to meet her frequent medical expenses. But he promised himself that his life was not going to be spent as a cog in anyone's departmental machine. His father had been content on the force; the son was frustrated and resentful. Right or wrong, Jack Howard was going to become a private detective.

Through tedious hours of night school and correspondence courses, he was spurred on by the memory of the Dahlquist case. In less than two years, he was ready to make the break, and the captain's harrumphing when he handed in his resignation never failed to give him a pleasant glow when he thought about it afterwards.

So, did he have some special understanding about the Dahlquist family? Oh, yes, Mrs. Dahlquist. A sense of gratitude to the hero who saved his job, and who later, without knowing it, had propelled him into a career in which he had been both successful and happy for over forty years.

Jack Howard's voice faded with the end of his story. He looked into the faces of three terrified people. "Your child is missing. I'm here because I think I can help you find him. I'm asking that you let me repay an old debt."

Martin's eyes moved from his wife to his mother and back to Laurie. Then he turned to Howard. "You do understand, Mr. Howard, that we are not going to contact the police."

Howard said solemnly, "You've made that very clear. I understand your reasons, and I'll do what I can within the limitations you are setting. But you've got to realize how difficult the search for your child is going to be. A private investigator normally starts with police contacts and police reports, and then takes it from there. My best sources are inside the police department, though the chief doesn't know it. You say—no police. No inquiry that might come to the attention of the department. Okay. But it's a real handicap. You've got to understand that."

"I do," Martin said. "I accept the responsibility, but we will be grateful for anything you can do to help us. Please sit down."

After Jack Howard memorized the arrangement of the rooms and studied the kidnapper's note, he joined the Dahlquists in sifting through the papers and notebooks Martin had taken from his father's study. Glancing up from time to time, Howard decided that concealing emotion was a Dahlquist tradition which Laurie often failed to live up to. Her feelings showed, and when they started writing the ad for the next day's *News-Record*, her thin wall of reserve began to crack.

"The medicine. Mr. Howard, the baby has to have his medicine...." She said it over and over, tears streaming down her cheeks.

Elizabeth Dahlquist crossed the room and sat beside her. "Yes, Laurie. Yes..." she said softly, covering the younger woman's hands with her own.

Howard put down his pencil. "I think we've got the right wording. I'll call the paper first thing in the morning."

Martin rose. "I'm going to put my wife to bed. Then I'll come down and go through that last box of Father's papers."

Howard said firmly, "I'll check that box. There's nothing more for you to do tonight."

Martin hesitated, as if needing sleep was a weakness he should be able to conquer.

"The best thing you all can do," Howard said, "is to go to bed. You've been under terrific strain. And you've got to get ready for tomorrow."

"Yes," Martin admitted. "You're right, of course. And you'll spend the night, won't you? The downstairs guest room is all ready."

Ten minutes later, the Dahlquists had gone to their rooms on the second floor and Jack Howard was sitting at the breakfast table with a small spiral notebook, a fountain pen, and a large glass of milk.

He opened the notebook to the page on which he had copied the final version of the ad for tomorrow evening's *News-Record*. It was a touchy business, putting something together that would make sense to the kidnapper without being so explicit that a police officer checking the classified section would catch on to what was happening. Howard read it again.

To: Son of K.O. Feed soybean milk only. Medicine also absolutely necessary. By prescription only. Advise where to leave it.

Yes, he thought. That's enough, but not too much.

He flipped the page. It was not too soon to start the "portrait parlé"—the mock-up of the man who had kidnapped the Dahlquist baby. Some cops might laugh at such an old-fashioned technique, but in Howard's experience the old method of fitting together pieces of a psychological puzzle had often led to a solution. Howard's "portrait" went way beyond the pencil sketch the department made of an unidentified criminal by incorporating whatever features the witnesses recalled. Howard knew that habits, quirks, personality traits could lead to the hunted man faster than a frightened witness's recollection of his height, weight, or the color of his eyes. This kidnapper had already dropped some surprising hints about himself.

Howard opened his fountain pen and printed "Portrait—Son of K.O." across the top of the page. Below, he wrote:

(1) Kidnapper has contacted parents twice—note in baby's playpen, classified in Personals. No mention of ransom in either case.

Howard frowned at what he had written. Communication with the family of the kidnapped person is always highly dangerous to the kidnapper. Ochsner's son must know this, and know that therefore he's got to make every contact count. Then why postpone his demand for money?

Howard dropped down a few lines and wrote:

(2) Handwriting—better get a graphologist's comment on this. Seems to indicate that kidnapper has unusual control—that his hand is trained. An artist? Cartographer?

(3) Vocabulary, use of words. Suggests kidnapper is intelligent, well read, generally good at expressing himself.

Howard put down his pen, drained the glass of milk, and pushed his notebook aside. He would go through the last box of Leif Dahlquist's papers, as he had promised Martin, and then would take his own advice and get some sleep.

Howard was in bed and half asleep when the answer to a key question jolted him awake. In his note and in his classified ad, the kidnapper was claiming to be Klaus Ochsner's son. If that was true, Laurie's feeling that she had seen him before was easy to understand: she must have read the abundantly illustrated rehash of the famous Dahlquist Case of 1932, published in Sunday's paper. She had been looking at photographs of Klaus Ochsner only a few hours before her own child was kidnapped.

Accepting the kidnapper's claim to being Klaus Ochsner's son solved another puzzle—the lack of ransom demand. Ochsner's son could have taken the baby solely to revenge his father. Howard's heart began to pound. A kidnapper who demands a ransom may return the child once he's got the money. But the man who steals a child for revenge may believe the only way to achieve his goal is to destroy the baby.

Then why put an ad in the paper asking the parents to tell him how to keep the baby well? What kind of man were they looking for? Howard forced himself to close his eyes and try and sleep.

Tuesday, March 15

Twelve

A BOUQUET OF breakfast odors met Martin and Laurie the next morning as they came downstairs. Perking coffee, pleasantly mingled with broiling bacon. For a moment the familiar early-morning smells produced an illusion of normalcy. The kidnapping of little Leif was illusion; "reality" was starting a new day with a good hot breakfast.

As they entered the living room, the sensation of awakening from a bad dream was even stronger. Last night the floor had been cluttered with untidy piles of papers, scattered notebooks, boxes of newspaper clippings. Today all traces of last night's panicky search had been completely erased. Not a box, not a paper, in sight. Sofa and chair cushions had been plumped up, teacups removed.

"Oh! Who...," murmured Laurie. Martin smiled down at her. "Someone who is almost as neat as my wife." He pulled her arm through his. "Come on. I think we'll find the culprit at the end of the hall."

The kitchen scene was a complete surprise.

Elizabeth Dahlquist was breaking eggs into a mixing bowl. Jack Howard was at the broiler turning the bacon. His mother's face was haggard and the detective badly needed a shave, but they both managed smiles.

"Coffee's made," Howard said. "But I'd better warn you. It's too thick to drink and too thin to plow."

Elizabeth nodded. "It is indeed. But it will wake you up. We'll have breakfast in a few minutes. Doesn't the living room look nice. Mr. Howard did that. The papers are all sorted out and stacked in the..." A mute gesture toward the nursery completed the sentence.

Martin felt a surge of admiration for his mother. The Newton home had maintained a staff of twenty-seven servants. After her marriage to Leif Dahlquist, her parents had "given" four of them to her as a wedding present. As far as Martin could remember, she had cooked breakfast no more than a dozen times in her entire life. On impulse Martin went to her and kissed her cheek.

Laurie stared at Elizabeth with an expression of bleak despair. Martin sat down beside her and squeezed her hand. What could he say to convince Laurie not to measure her own worth against his mother's? Gently he turned her face toward him and kissed her on the mouth. "I'm with you, Laurie," he said quietly. "*With* you, no matter what happens. We'll come out of this. I don't know how, but we will."

It was false courage. Her clear blue eyes told him she knew it as well as he. But an uncertain smile touched the corners of her mouth as she said, "I think I'd like a little more of Mr. Howard's witches' brew."

They had finished breakfast and cleared the table. Jack Howard's spiral notebook lay open before him.

"I make lists," he said amiably, tapping the page with a blunt forefinger. "Of what I know for sure, and what I need to know." His heavy eyebrows drew together. "More than anything else, we've got to find out what name Klaus Ochsner's widow took after her husband's execution."

To Howard's trained eye, Elizabeth Dahlquist's reaction to Ochsner's name couldn't be plainer if she had screamed. The color drained from her face and her dark eyes lost all expression. Martin was staring at her and Howard was willing to bet that their faces concealed far more than simple revulsion at the sound of the Ochsner name. In forty years he had been frustrated countless times by clients who hid things that "aren't important" or "have nothing to do with the case." Ten to one Elizabeth Dahlquist was doing that right now and that Martin knew it and was concerned.

"Is it safe to assume that Mrs. Ochsner changed her name?" Martin finally asked, still watching his mother. "We don't *know* that she did."

Howard said quietly, "Wouldn't you?"

"Yes. Yes, of course." Martin's eyes left his mother and met the older man's level gaze with a degree of frankness Howard hadn't seen before. "'Never assume anything!' That was my father's credo and it was drummed into me from age five or six." He smiled.

"Your father was a scientist. He dealt with absolutes. But we're dealing with human behavior. Specifically, the behavior of an individual about whom we know almost nothing, so we have to make some assumptions." Howard picked up his notebook and held it at arm's length, the only comfortable reading distance since he had decided not to "spoil" his eyes by wearing glasses. "One: we assume that the man we're looking for *is* Klaus Ochsner's son, as he claims to be. Two: we assume that his mother would have changed her name."

"Wouldn't she have had to go to court? Wouldn't there be a record?" asked Martin.

Howard nodded. "If she went to court, yes. But she

might not have done that, for the very reason we wish she had—it would have left an obvious trail. And it wouldn't have been necessary. You can take any name you want as long as you don't use it for fraudulent purposes."

Laurie spoke for the first time since breakfast. "In all those boxes of papers, didn't we find anything about what happened to the Ochsners afterwards?" She paused and looked around the table. They all knew that "afterwards" meant after Klaus Ochsner was put to death; Laurie had learned very early that the word "execution" was never to be said aloud in the Dahlquists' presence. The answer to her question was in their faces. "Isn't that strange?" she said. "During the trial, the name Ochsner was all over the front pages. Isn't it odd that Mr. Dahlquist's notebooks don't tell us anything about the family after 1935?"

"Father might have wanted to forget," Martin said stiffly. "I'm sure Mother does."

"Now?" Laurie cried. "We can't just 'forget.'"

Howard broke in quickly, sensing that Laurie was still on the raw edge of panic. "It is strange, isn't it, but we may still find something in Mr. Dahlquist's papers. Last night was just the first time through. And it is strange that such a notorious name as Ochsner could simply drop out of sight. Though the name hasn't disappeared, of course. Look in the Seattle telephone directory and you'll find nine Ochsners listed. And fourteen Dahlquists." Howard's attention went back to his open notebook. "Let's go on."

He held up one hand and ticked off the fingers with the other. "We know Mrs. Ochsner's first name. Lisa. We know that during her husband's trial she sent the boy to stay with relatives or friends in another state. And we know that the day after Klaus Ochsner was executed, she was confined in the maximum security ward of a mental hospital. There we are. One, two, three, four, five. And there the list ends." He flipped over to another page and nodded in satisfaction at the one short entry. "Late last night I did run across something in Mr. Dahlquist's papers which isn't in any of my scrapbooks, though it was pretty well publicized at the time of Ochsner's arrest: Klaus and Lisa Ochsner's address in 1932. 18345 Grummin Street South. That's where our search begins."

Martin was looking at the slight bulge in Howard's jacket. "Are you carrying a gun, Mr. Howard?"

Howard's hand gave the hidden object an affectionate pat. "I do. A little .38-caliber Smith and Wesson. It's about the only thing I do that's like the private eyes on TV."

"Perhaps I should carry one, too."

"Not on your life," Howard said emphatically. "A gun in the hands of a man who hasn't had either training or experience in how to use it is more dangerous to the man who's carrying it than to anyone else. Anyway, we're not going to find our man by shooting it up." He paused and gave the Dahlquists what he hoped was a reassuring grin. "I'll tell you something. My gun has never been fired anyplace but the shooting range in forty years."

Grummin Street South was not hard to find. It bisected one of Seattle's oldest residential districts. The area had undergone many changes in forty years. Once its two or three hotels had enjoyed the advantage of being within walking distance of the central railroad station. Now they were little more than rooming houses, with coin-operated television in the rooms and old magazines in the lobbies. Many homes had been replaced by warehouses and small factories. Those still standing were sagging with age and the occupants all seemed too old or too poor to escape their joyless surroundings.

Jack Howard pulled his Buick to the curb and signaled the Dahlquists to follow suit. He didn't have to tell them what the problem was. They were parked in front of number 17823 Grummin. One block ahead, at the intersection with 179th, Grummin ceased at a sturdy barrier with a sign warning DEAD END. Just beyond, the concrete canyon of the interstate freeway cut through the district.

"I think Grummin picks up on the other side," Howard said. "But it would have to begin around 189th. It looks like the address we want has been wiped out."

The intensity of their disappointment surprised him. Both Martin and Laurie stared speechlessly at the broken thoroughfare, as if the nonexistence of house number 18345 were a trick or an illusion.

"We aren't stumped yet," Howard said sympathetically. "I should have warned you that there've been a lot of changes in this area." Was it possible that they had expected to pull up at the house the Ochsners occupied in 1932, ring the doorbell, and say "We've come to see Mrs. Lisa Ochsner"? Yes, it was possible and this tendency worried him. His job was to keep them hoping, but at the same time prevent them from having hopes that were too high.

"The situation isn't hopeless," he said, "not by a long shot. We all knew we wouldn't find Mrs. Ochsner here. This is only where we start. We'll split up and go door to door. Cover more territory that way."

His instructions restored their spirits. Martin and Laurie nodded, eager to get on with the search.

"Just ask if they remember the Ochsners, or where Mrs. Ochsner might be now?" Laurie asked, taking a notebook and pencil out of her handbag.

"Yes. Fine. Start with that. But after that you may have to improvise. You'll know what to ask when the time comes."

Martin said earnestly, "I hope so, Mr. Howard. But I'm beginning to realize how badly we needed professional help. We are amateurs. Rank amateurs."

Howard dropped his hand on the young man's shoulder. "Sure you are. But let me tell you something. We haven't got much to go on so far, but don't forget the man we're looking for is an amateur, too."

For an hour they canvassed Grummin on the west side of the freeway. Then they crossed the overpass and began sifting through the east side. At the end of each block, they met and pooled their information. After two hours Laurie said wearily, "It's such a sad place. I've never seen so many old people."

Howard nodded. "Exactly. Which is the reason we may still find an oldtimer who can tell us something about the Ochsners."

A half hour later they found a clue. An elderly man leaning on a cane opened a door and stood blocking the entrance. Even from across the street, Howard observed that he was answering Laurie's questions grudgingly. "Come on, girl," Howard muttered. "Smile. He won't close the door in your face if you're smiling."

When the door closed, Laurie ran down the steps and darted across the street. "I've got something!" she said excitedly. "A man across the street told me that his next door neighbors used to run a family restaurant near here. An Austrian restaurant, where they served schnitzel and white coffee and other Viennese specialties. So I went to the next house. At first the man there, the elderly man you saw with a cane, didn't want to talk about the Ochsners. For a few minutes I thought he was going to slam the door in my face...."

"But you smiled."

"Why yes!" Laurie looked at Howard curiously. "I smiled, and he told me something, probably to get rid of me. He used to know the Ochsners. At one time Lisa

Ochsner worked parttime for him. He hasn't heard anything of her or her son since they moved away, but he did remember this: Lisa had a cousin in Tacoma. She visited the Ochsners several times, and he still remembers her name. Traude. Mrs. Traude Maerchen." The momentary spurt of excitement faded as she looked at the name. "Just Tacoma. No address. It isn't much, is it."

"Yes, you bet it is!" Howard said heartily. He beckoned to Martin. When they were all together, he said, "One of us should go to Tacoma. What's your wish, Mr. Dahlquist?"

Martin turned to Laurie. "You must be very tired."

She shook her head. "Not too tired. And your mother is at home. She'll answer the phone, if . . ." She hesitated and finished in a near whisper. ". . . if there are any messages."

To Howard, Martin said, "A name, one name in a big city. It's going to be hard to locate the cousin, isn't it, even if she is still alive?"

"Yes. But Laurie got her married name. That helps a lot."

"Nevertheless, it's a slim lead. I'm sure looking for her will call for a lot more expertise than Laurie and I have. But we'd both find it easier to go along than to drive back to Black River and wait. Unless there's something we could be doing at home."

"There isn't. Not yet." Howard jerked a thumb in the direction of their parked cars. "Follow me. We'll leave one car at the Shell station and use their phone to call your home and make sure your mother hasn't received a phone call. Then the three of us will make a run to Tacoma and look for Mrs. Traude Maerchen."

Thirteen

EVEN BEFORE HE was fully awake, Ricky knew he had to get rid of his car. The pursuing police officers had undoubtedly reported the make and color, maybe even the license number. With that information, a call to the Department of Motor Vehicles would supply his name and home address. Speeding and reckless driving. Resisting arrest. Leaving the scene of an accident ... Even without the fact that he had broken through a police roadblock and sideswiped a patrol car, these charges were enough to justify a warrant for his arrest. A moment of panic, in which he had imagined that a squad car on routine patrol was searching for him— and now he was a fugitive. The irony was that the police were looking for him because he was a reckless driver, and he was hiding from them because he was a kidnapper.

He had blundered in many ways but continuing to drive the Plymouth would be plain stupid. So he would feed and change the baby, and then go about ditching the car. His plan was far from foolproof, but it would work, if he was lucky.

The baby had swallowed and retained a little cereal. After crying plaintively for a few minutes, he drifted into a restless sleep. Ricky watched him for several minutes, reluctant to leave him alone. But he had no choice. He went out quietly, praying the child would sleep for at least an hour.

He had taken the first step in his plan the night before, when he parked his car some eight or ten blocks from the motel. If an alert patrolman on night duty had spotted a "wanted" license number, the Plymouth would have been towed away, but he was sure the police would not be able to connect Ricky Cummins, 33 Fidalgo Blvd., with Harry Thomas, Room 17, the Pines Motel.

He relaxed a little when he saw the Plymouth standing where he had parked it. No citation under the windshield wiper, and as far as he could determine, no officer keeping watch from a nearby porch. Ricky got into the car and drove away, glancing frequently at the rear-view mirror. After a few minutes he decided he wasn't being followed.

At the Discount City Supermarket, he turned into the block-long parking lot and pulled into a slot where the Plymouth was surrounded by a dozen other cars. The next step was to strip off the license plates and drop them into the nearest litter barrel. He was struggling with a rusted bolt when he recognized that this part of his plan was all wrong. A car with license plates looked "normal." It would be several days, maybe even a week, before a store employee or security officer would bother to report an abandoned car. But a car without license plates would attract attention immediately. Ricky dropped the screwdriver into his pocket and walked to the bus stop on the corner. The Sligo Park bus, Number 23, would take him to automobile row south of town.

● ● ●

Ricky strolled through the used car lot with his hands in his pockets. He must appear to be a casual shopper, only mildly interested in purchasing a car. Stifling his impatience to buy and get out, he passed up several cars that would have served his purpose; settling for the first one he saw was a sure way of being remembered in a place like Harry's Super Buys. After a few minutes, he lingered beside a green '65 Chevie. As he had expected, that brought the salesman plunging over with a wide smile.

"That's a good one," the salesman said approvingly. "Low mileage. Good rubber. And look at the price. Seven seventy-five. Ridiculous, isn't it? It's worth twice that much."

Ricky shrugged. "I don't see the gold bumpers."

"Hey, man, look! These cars are getting popular. They'll be vintage stuff in no time. The price is seven seventy-five."

"How much off for cash?"

The salesman drew down the corners of his mouth. "Like I said, mister. Take it or leave it."

"It's robbery," Ricky said. "But I like that model. I'll take it."

The salesman did not ask to see his driver's license; that had been one reason for buying rather than renting. And he didn't have to present credit cards, as an automobile rental office would have required. The salesman made out the bill of sale to "Irv Martin" without asking for credentials. At Harry's Super Buys, twenty-dollar bills were all the ID he needed.

The transfer of the title was a different story. For this bit of paperwork, Irv Martin would have to have an address. "I might as well fill all that out myself," he said, extending his hand. "I'll do it today. Drop it in the mailbox this afternoon."

"Can't," the salesman said. "Against the law. We have to write up the title transfer ourselves. What was that address, Mr. Martin?"

"It's . . ." He had gone all through this, why was he stumbling now? "The problem is, I'm moving."

"Okay. Fine. Where to?"

"I don't know for sure. I've been looking at a couple of places. Haven't quite made up my mind."

"Then give me the old address. This is Tuesday. We mail these forms in a batch at the end of the week. If you get your new address between now and Friday, give me a jingle. I'll make the change."

"Yes, fine." He had to leave it at that, though it ruined his plan to keep whatever car he bought registered in the name of the former owner. At least it would be for the next six or seven days. He wasn't sure how that would protect him, but it did seem to throw some sort of block in the path of the police department's search for Ricky Cummins. "My address is 1818 Merritt Northwest."

The salesman looked at him. "Merritt Northwest? Where's that? I thought I knew this town."

But to Ricky's vast relief, he wrote it down without further questions. When Ricky drove off, the salesman called after him, "Remember, I didn't say the former owner was a little old lady who never used the car except to drive to the supermarket." The quip seemed to please him very much, for he was still laughing when Ricky pulled out into the street and into the westbound line of traffic.

"Jeesuss," the salesman muttered as the Chevie disappeared. It always amused him to watch someone trying to remember a phony name.

Ricky drove the Chevie into the Pines Motel and parked in front of his room. Before he unlocked the door, he looked around the yard and down the street. Nothing unusual, but he felt jumpy. His nerves were raw and his head ached. He had been lucky to dump one car and obtain another in a little over an hour. The baby must have slept through, for no sound of crying issued from Room 17. He inserted the key and opened the door slowly so as not to wake the child.

A middle-aged woman in cotton housedress and sweater was sitting on the sofa with the baby in her lap. Her left arm cradled him against her body and her right hand held the bottle to his mouth. "I'm the housekeeper," she said pleasantly, nodding toward a stack of sheets and towels. "When I come in to do your room he was crying. So I just did what I always used to do when my own got fussy. First I changed him, and then I warmed some milk. Look at him. He sure likes it. You can see that."

Ricky was about to stumble through some explanation when he realized the woman wasn't asking for one. Perhaps she didn't see anything suspicious in a baby being left alone in the room. He managed to thank the housekeeper, to take the baby from her arms, and to promise that the little love would get plenty of milk always. In his own ears his voice sounded strange.

"I'll just leave the clean linen here," the housekeeper said. "I'll do the room up later, when you're out." At the door, she turned back. "I think your baby might be coming down with something. I'd watch him pretty close, if I was you." She opened the door and paused again. "Well, well. I see you've got a new car, a '65 Chevie. My oldest grandson's a nut on cars. He's taught me to take notice." She blew a kiss to the baby, smiled at Ricky, and closed the door.

A grandmother's sharp eye for cars tipped the balance. Through a crack in the curtain Ricky saw the housekeeper push her cart past every unit between his own and the motel office without stopping to clean any of them. She must be on her way to report the baby. As she disappeared into the manager's apartment, he decided on open flight. He was in the car in seconds with the baby beside him, racing to get away from the motel before the police arrived. His extra clothing, the baby's bottle, diapers and cans of strained food were all left behind. He had nothing but the clothes he was wearing, what remained of two thousand dollars after paying for the car, and the Dahlquist baby, wrapped in a coarse gray motel blanket, and already beginning to cry.

The Maple Leaf Lodge was the best spot Ricky had seen in the half hour since he fled from the Pines. It was located on the opposite side of the city. It had been bypassed by the new highway and stood on a side street two blocks from city traffic. Best of all, the parking area for tenants was behind the building. His car would not be seen from the street and a high wooden fence blocked the view from the alley. It was as safe as any motel he had seen. And he needed a refuge, badly.

He was convinced the Pines housekeeper had looked at his license plates on the way to the manager's office. By now police had read the motel registry and learned that on arrival, Harry Thomas, Room 17, was driving a 1970 Plymouth sedan, license OYT 457, a hot car that was registered to Ricky Cummins, 33 Fidalgo. And they would have also learned that Ricky Cummins, alias Harry Thomas, was now driving a green '65 Chevie, license SJF 007.

What a naive fool he had been to think he was "safe" because the Chevie would be registered as the property of "Irv Martin" who lived at a nonexistent address. That falsehood wouldn't throw them off the trail. On the contrary. It would be evidence of his guilt. They didn't need the registration. All they needed was the license number, and they surely had it by now. He had to get off the street and fast. But he wasn't going to make the mistake that had tripped him up at the Pines. He wasn't going to conceal the baby. He was going to show it off with a logical explanation for its presence.

The Maple Leaf Lodge's office looked like the parlor of an old-fashioned home except for a glass case displaying toothbrushes and safety razors, and a counter with a rack of postcards. A girl was perched on a stool behind the counter, reading. When Ricky opened the door she stood up quickly, as if she were startled. "Welcome to Maple Leaf Lodge," she said, smiling. "It's nice today, isn't it? As if the storm Sunday had washed everything."

The reference to Sunday's storm disconcerted him. Thunder, pelting rain, a baby whimpering in a cardboard box... He approached the counter and forced a smile. "Yes. The city does seem cleaner after a storm." The comment was perfectly sincere. He had spent most of his life in neighborhoods where the air smelled better right after a heavy rain. For the first time he really looked at the girl. Her eyes were dark brown and distinctly slanted. Her hair was straight, shiny black, and hung almost to her waist. Her skin was smooth, the color of coffee with cream. Hawaiian? Korean?

"We've got vacancies for both doubles and singles."

"Things are pretty quiet this time of year?"

Her answer was just what he hoped to hear. "I should say *so*, for the Lodge anyway. You wouldn't care to take four singles and two doubles, would you?"

Ricky laughed so spontaneously that the sound startled him. "Just a single, please. I'm alone except for the baby."

"A baby. Terrific. How old?"

Ricky was writing hastily. This part of his rehearsed plan had to be followed. Dennis O'Connor. 111 Forest Place, Denver, Colorado. '65 Chev, SJF 007.... "He's about four months old." An idea came to him as unexpectedly as his moment of laughter. "It sounds as if you like babies."

An expression of sadness flickered across her face.

"Yes, I do," she said. "I had one." Her eyes and her voice were just as frank in revealing sorrow as they had been to express happiness.

"I'm sorry," Ricky said simply. "I just wondered if you would be free during the day. To help with the baby. He isn't mine, and I don't know much about taking care of him."

"I'd love to! Oh, great!"

"It wouldn't interfere with your job?"

"Job?" She smiled, showing even white teeth. "Oh, I don't work here. Clara and Tip, the owners, are friends. My apartment gets awfully empty sometimes, so I like to come here and help out. I'll take care of your baby whenever you want me to. I can drive here in twenty minutes."

Drive... the girl would take care of the baby. The girl had a car. Ricky looked at her thoughtfully, wondering at his luck and afraid to push it. He had to go back to the Wendell Arms, risky as it was. Letting mail and newspapers collect was an even greater risk, and he needed to replace the clothing he had abandoned at the Pines. The real danger was driving the Chevie. Did he dare ask the girl... Her dark eyes met his without a flicker. She seemed to know he had another question and she was giving him all the time he needed to ask it. To his surprise, the words came easily. "I have an important errand to do, and my car is on the blink. I just got her into your parking lot when she gave up entirely. May I borrow yours, just for an hour or two?"

"Sure," she said, without the faintest overtone of hesitation or doubt. "Here's your room key. Here's the keys to my car. Clara and Tip will be back in about an hour. Then I'll come take care of the baby, and you can take the Gray Ghost. My car. By the way, my name is Marika. Marika Malama."

"You're very trusting, Marika. How do you know I'll come back?"

She laughed. "I'll have the baby," she replied. "How do you know I won't run off with him?"

Ricky left the office feeling as if half the burden of fear and anxiety had been lifted. A small inner voice whispered that the girl who loved babies had, for some reason, lost her own. He ignored the voice, and quickly forgot it as he carried the Dahlquist child into Room 15 and concentrated on a plan to get in and out of the Wendell Arms without being seen.

In a telephone booth at the rear of a Rexall drugstore, Ollie White was running out of nickels and dimes. The listing under "Architects" covered three and a half pages. Maria Nunez had told him that the firm Ricky Cummins worked for at the time they broke their engagement was "somewhere near Lake Washington." That covered a lot of ground, and it wasn't the part of the city Ollie frequented. Cursing the fifteen-cent call and the unwieldy directory and the voices at the other end of the line saying "Mr. Ricky Cummins? Sorry, we don't have any such person here..." Ollie went doggedly down the column, stopping to dial when his forefinger touched an address that might be near the lake. He would soon need more change, and he was just beginning the P's. The druggist was beginning to eye him and any minute now he'd come over and tell him to move on, someone else might want to use the booth.

Pitt, Dobbs, and Webster... Ollie dropped the coins into the slots and dialed. After three rings a gruff male voice said, "Good morning. Pitt, Dobbs, and Webster. This is Mr. Nelson."

Ollie said smoothly, "I'd like to talk to Mr. Cummins. Mr. Ricky Cummins."

"Not in today. Give me your name and number. I'll have him call you back."

Christ! Pay dirt! Ollie almost choked on the rest of his spiel. He had never meant to talk to Ricky. If he hit an office where the voice said, "Mr. Cummins? Just a minute, please," his plan was to hang up. This situation was even better. Ricky wasn't in the office. He could safely ask a few more questions.

"You say he's not in today. How about tomorrow?"

"I doubt it. He's got the flu. He's been home for two days. We really don't expect him back before the end of the week."

"There's a lot of flu going around," Ollie said sympathetically. "Well, I'd better drop by his place. But I've lost his home address. Would you give it to me, please?"

"Sorry." Now Mr. Nelson's voice was a little gruffer than it had been. "We don't give out home telephone numbers or addresses. If you'd care to leave your name, and how he can get in touch with you..."

Ollie broke in. "The trouble is, Mr. Nelson, that I'm only in town for three days. Ricky's an old friend and this is my one chance to look him up. I haven't seen him for five years. So I think you should make an exception."

"Sorry," Mr. Nelson repeated. "It's our policy."

The last of Ollie's pretended politeness crumbled under the pressure of his frustration. "Goddamn you!" he shouted into the phone.

A click, and the line went dead. Mr. Nelson had hung up.

"Damn you, damn you..." Ollie whispered. "You ain't going to do that to me, Mr. Nelson."

The small contemporary building that housed the firm of Pitt, Dobbs, and Webster was ideal for Ollie's purpose. In order to utilize natural light, the architects had designed something like a glass box on stilts. Inside there were partitions, but no interior walls. The occupants were clearly visible from any angle. But for the person who wanted to see without being seen, there was ample cover in the back, where two one-car garages opened onto the alley. Ollie took up a position in one of these. He couldn't watch the front entrance, but that didn't matter. Customers used the front door. Anyone who left by the back door was bound to be an employee, maybe even the Mr. Nelson for whom Ollie was waiting.

Ollie was easily frustrated. Someone was always trying to get the better of him. But when he made up his mind to strike back, he could hang on stubbornly. An hour passed, and the back door never opened. An hour and a half. Two hours. Ollie was churning with impatience, but didn't for a second consider giving up. Sooner or later someone who worked with Ricky Cummins was going to come out to the alley.

At last the back door opened. The man who emerged was carrying his suit coat over one arm— another bit of proof that he was an employee, not a client. Before he closed the door, he called, "This is going to be a three-hour lunch, Betsey." Laughing, he walked down the wide cedar steps and opened the wrought iron gate into the alley. Ollie hit him when he turned his back to close the gate. Not very hard. He didn't want to knock the man out, not right away. Just hard enough to stun and confuse him and drag him into the garage.

A bit of luck—the man was smaller than himself and at least ten years older. Shoving him up against the garage wall, Ollie said, "You don't want to get hurt, buster. Tell me where Ricky Cummins lives."

The man stared as if Ollie were speaking a foreign language. "Who are you?"

Ollie growled, "That doesn't matter. Just tell me where Cummins lives."

"I don't know."

"The hell you don't!" In two quick motions Ollie pulled the unresisting body away from the wall and slammed it back. The man grunted and tried to free his arms. "No, you don't," Ollie said, grinning into the face that was only inches from his own. The man's effort to resist had shown that he wouldn't be able to put up a real fight. Ollie was beginning to feel real good.

"Come on," he coaxed. "Be easy on yourself. Cummins's home address. Let's have it."

The man's mouth fell open, but he shook his head. "No."

Ollie's gun was in an underarm shoulder holster, pressing against his side. He'd figured on using it only if he had to. Now he knew he wouldn't need it, but he pulled it out to scare the man, then put it back. The happy feeling began to spread. He jerked the man forward, released him, and before he fell, swung his right fist in a short, vicious punch to the man's face.

The man slumped to his knees, one hand covering his nose and mouth. Blood ran down his chin and dripped onto his white shirt.

"Okay," Ollie said. "You want to do it the hard way."

Systematically, judging with each blow how much more beating this small middle-aged body could take and still be conscious enough to give him Ricky's address, Ollie swung his fists and repeated his question. And finally, he got what he wanted. "Wendell Arms," the man gasped, closed his eyes, and dropped to the floor.

A half hour later, the back door of Pitt, Dobbs, and Webster opened and the bookkeeper stumbled over the threshold. His blood-smeared, battered face was almost unrecognizable. He had used up most of his strength crawling from the garage to the back door, but before he slipped back into unconsciousness, he gave an accurate description of the man who had attacked him, and instructed one of his colleagues to telephone

Ricky immediately, warning him that a crazy man was on his way to the Wendell Arms.

Ricky was almost ready to leave his apartment when the telephone rang. He started toward it, and stopped. A number of friends had his unlisted number. His mother knew it, as well as the nurses at Sylvan Home West, and of course everyone at the firm. He hesitated, sensing some kind of trap.

The police knew his address. The police would have authority to obtain the unlisted number. Would the police telephone? He didn't know, and that made the insistent ringing even more threatening.

He hurried from room to room, collecting the last few articles he needed. The phone's shrill ring meant danger. It meant get out of here.

In the hall, he forced himself to slow down. The door to Mrs. Dennison's apartment had been closed when he came in, but now it was ajar. Though he had moved around his apartment as quietly as possible, some sounds might have carried through the thin wall. Despite her age, Mrs. Dennison's hearing was almost as keen as her curiosity.

Ricky dropped the key into his pocket, picked up his box of things, and proceeded at a normal pace toward the elevator. As he had suspected, little Mrs. Dennison was just inside her door, peering out. Ricky nodded and murmured, "Hello . . ."

With her eyes fixed on the box, Mrs. Dennison chirped, "Well, I see you're in the moving business, Mr. Cummins."

"No," Ricky said, trying hard for the kind of joking response that would silence her without telling her to mind her own business. "Just taking some books back to the public library."

He had reached the elevator when she called, "Mr.

Cummins? Oh, Mr. Cummins? Isn't that your phone?"

Ricky stammered, "No, no. Not mine. That's coming from twenty-seven." The elevator door opened, he stepped inside, the doors closed. Ricky took a deep breath. He had escaped once more.

Fourteen

MARTIN WANTED TO believe this trip to Tacoma would yield some bit of information about the Ochsners, but when they reached the city, he was overcome by the hopelessness of their quest. Did Howard really believe they could find one old woman, address unknown, in a sprawling industrial city of 150,000?

Howard was driving, with Laurie beside him on the front seat. When they left Grummin Street, she had been excited by her discovery and unusually talkative. Now she seemed subdued. Except for an occasional glance at Jack Howard, she was staring straight ahead, still as a sentry. Martin sensed that, like himself, Laurie was beginning to recognize the odds.

Howard, on the other hand, radiated optimism. Even viewed from the back seat, there was something comforting about his sturdy figure. "I marvel at you, Mr. Howard," Martin said. "Don't you ever get discouraged?"

"Of course. In my line of work you run into plenty of things to get discouraged about. But I don't feel that way about looking for Traude Maerchen."

"That's what I mean. You don't. I do."

"That's just a matter of experience. Very few people have the faintest idea of how many sources of information there are if you really want to find someone. The truth is, almost anyone can be found. But found quickly—that's something else."

In a small, frightened voice, Laurie exclaimed, "We've got to!"

"I know. And you're looking at this big city and wondering where to start. Well, let's talk about it. We start by eliminating sources that aren't likely to have information about an unknown old woman. That knocks out a raft of regional Who's Whos. We'll concentrate on agencies that have something to do with the elderly, beginning with the city of Tacoma's bureau of birth and death records. Then there's the nursing home placement office. The state welfare office. We won't overlook the public library. The old lady might like to read...."

Two hours later, Jack Howard's composure hadn't been dented by a series of dead-end inquiries. "She doesn't have a telephone, and she doesn't drive a car. She's never been arrested. She never worked for the city or for any county agency. She's not on welfare and she hasn't applied for placement in a state-supported nursing home." Howard nodded with satisfaction. "We're doing fine."

"My God, Jack," Martin said. "I can see that shortening the list is a kind of progress. But what, if anything, do we know?"

Laurie spoke up quickly. "Quite a lot. She's alive. She isn't penniless. And she isn't missing. At her age I shouldn't think she would move away from the area where she's lived most of her life. So she must be here, someplace."

Martin shook his head. "There are so many assumptions."

"True," Howard agreed. "But we're eliminating

them, one at a time." He turned to Laurie. "The man you talked to on Grummin Street, Mrs. Dahlquist. Didn't he say Mrs. Maerchen had worked in his restaurant?"

"Yes, I think so. For a little while."

"If she did the same thing in Tacoma, she would have to get a license as a food handler. Next stop, the city license bureau."

But the visit merely added to their list of negatives. If Traude Maerchen had been a cook or waitress, she had worked under a different name or without being properly licensed. At that point, Laurie asked the question that led them to Mrs. Maerchen: "Do you suppose she would be involved with a Senior Citizens project?"

The Rumfield Point Senior Citizens Center occupied an old store on the waterfront. An elderly woman was seated at a desk, picking coins out of a candy box and stacking them in neat piles. On a sofa against the wall, two old men were discussing the benefits of half-fare tickets on the Puget Sound ferry line. A curtain separated the reception area from the back, but the sound of voices and the click of billiard balls showed the recreation hall was in use.

The woman at the desk continued counting her change. When she had finished she penciled a figure on a slip of paper, and then looked up. "Lunch money. I couldn't stop counting or I'd forget and have to start all over again. Nice day, isn't it?"

"It sure is," Howard agreed. "Is Mrs. Maerchen here today? I'm her nephew. I didn't find her at home so I thought she might be down here."

"Traude?" the woman exclaimed. "Traude isn't at home? Why, she should be. Unless they already moved her to the home. She doesn't come here any more, not since her stroke."

Frowning, Howard took his notebook out of his

pocket. "Do you suppose I've got the wrong address?" he asked and began turning pages. "I had to call long distance, and we had a poor connection. I should have hung up and called the operator and asked her to put it through again."

The woman nodded sympathetically. "It's kind of hard to make out what Traude's saying, some of the time. Two four two East Third. Is that what you've got?"

Howard shook his head. "Oh, for Pete's sake. I wrote down *West* Third."

The woman looked puzzled. "West Third? That runs down near the depot. Nothing but warehouses and factories."

"Yes, I know," Howard said genially. "Well, thank you very much." He glanced quickly at the small hand-lettered card that gave the receptionist's name. "You've got a nice place here, Mrs. Johnson."

Mrs. Traude Maerchen was willing to talk, but their questions confused her. Something about poor Lisa. Yes, of course she knew Lisa. Klaus, too. Oh, it was a terrible thing. Poor Lisa would never believe he did it. And she had to send her baby away. For three years, she couldn't keep her baby. Why not? Why not? Of course she knew why, she just couldn't remember right now. Because of Klaus . . . Something about Klaus. Oh, it was a terrible thing. They always wondered about Klaus. Sending Lisa on a trip back home to Austria, when he was so poor and he had to dig graves to make a living. The police came for Klaus. . . . Poor Lisa! Poor Lisa! It was all in the paper, about that poor baby. . . .

She covered her face with her hands, hiding from the staring faces. Strangers, who asked things she didn't understand. She was still huddled into a ball when the nurse signaled and Howard, Laurie, and Martin left the room.

"I know you're disappointed," Howard said when they were back in his car. "But believe me, Mr. Dahlquist, we haven't been wasting time."

"No, I suppose not, considering the fact that the only alternative, at least for Laurie and me, was to sit at home and do nothing. But what has that pathetic old woman told us? What have we learned?"

"At the moment," Howard said affably, "nothing we recognize. But we may have learned something that will add up later."

They spoke very little during the drive back to Seattle. Martin welcomed the silence, for it seemed useless to pretend, as Howard seemed to be doing, that the mumbling of a senile old woman had told them something they didn't already know. He had something else on his mind. The package bound with twine and red sealing wax. He should have told Howard about it right at the beginning, but the instinct to shield one's own from a stranger had overcome common sense.

"Jack..."

"Yes, Mr. Dahlquist?"

Martin hesitated, wondering when he had begun calling the older man by his first name. "Sunday night at my mother's, there was an incident I should have mentioned before. My mother is concealing something. I don't know what it is, but I'm convinced that it has to do with the kidnapping of my brother."

Martin went quickly through the series of events. His mother's emotional outburst when he asked about the package. Her secrecy in removing it from his father's cabinet and packing it in her luggage for her trip to Europe, so as to prevent him from opening it during her absence. And all of it so unlike her.

"Yes, it doesn't sound like Elizabeth Dahlquist," Howard said. "It's obvious that you and your mother are very close. I'm certain that you're the last person in the world she would deliberately attempt to deceive. So the contents of that package must be something she knows would hurt you very much. What a tough decision for a mother to make."

"I know," Martin said quietly. "Mother is the most honest person I've ever known."

"Let me ask you something. Would your mother keep anything secret that might have some bearing on the kidnapping of *your* child?"

"Absolutely not."

"Ah, well . . ." Howard drove for a few moments in thoughtful silence. "In that case, we've answered one important question. If your mother's secret would help us find young Ochsner, she would reveal it. But there's a second question. Is your mother a good judge of the importance of that package? Can we be sure that she would recognize a clue?"

"I don't know," Martin said grimly. "I honestly don't know."

"Of course not. And neither do I, without knowing the contents of the box. My advice is to call PanAm, recover your mother's luggage, hand it over to her, and see what she does. That would force the issue."

"I would hate to do that to my mother."

"That's understandable. And there may be another way to solve the riddle. Let's wait a little. Give your mother a chance to weigh her choices. Meanwhile, call PanAm."

Laurie said softly, "I have a suggestion, Martin. When you phone PanAm, do it in your mother's presence."

Howard took his eyes off the highway long enough to give her an admiring smile. "Very good, Mrs. Dahlquist."

"Laurie, please."

"Thank you, Laurie."

Once more they rode in silence. Martin was

beginning to notice that for the genial gray-haired investigator, periods of silence were inevitably followed by a new thought or observation. After a few minutes, Howard proved he was right.

"Let's get back to Mrs. Maerchen..." With that, Howard recited everything the old woman had said word for word. "Now, her statement 'It was all in the paper, about the poor baby...' You'd assume she was talking about your brother, Martin, and the newspaper stories about Ochsner's trial and execution. But for the moment let's avoid assumption. Maybe she didn't mean the Dahlquist baby. Whenever she referred to the baby, it was in the same breath with 'Poor Lisa.' Could it be Lisa's baby?

"Now, if Mrs. Maerchen was talking about the *Ochsner* child, you've got to look at her reference to 'It was all in the paper' from a different angle. I've got three notebooks filled with clippings about the Dahlquist case. I've read everything in them countless times. There isn't a word about the Ochsner child that would account for Mrs. Maerchen's referring to 'that poor baby.' Maybe 'the paper' means one of those neighborhood weeklies that would feature the kind of local news about its subscribers that they couldn't read anyplace else." He paused, looked at Martin's face in the rear-view mirror. "Are you with me?"

Martin said slowly, "A small newspaper, published in the area where the Ochsners were living in 1932."

"It's worth a try, isn't it?"

"Anything is," Martin said. "Anything at all."

In Unit #23 of the Maple Leaf Lodge, Marika Malama was walking back and forth with the baby in her arms, rocking him and humming. He had taken the bottle eagerly, but minutes later went into a colicky spasm and coughed it up as well as most of the strained fruit and cereal. Now he was unnaturally still, or perhaps the pacing and gentle bouncing was soothing him. She hoped he would fall asleep.

It had been the same with her own baby. Sometimes he cried when she put him down in his crib but he would always fall asleep in her arms. This baby might be coming down with something. She felt his forehead. He wasn't running a fever. If anything, the skin was too cool. She was puzzled. Her baby had been supremely healthy. Not a single cold or touch of colic from birth to the day she had given him up. So a sick baby was new to her. She'd have to talk to Mr. O'Connor.

Ever since his return, he had been sitting at the desk, writing on sheets of motel stationery. As she walked the baby, Marika observed that he must be having a hard time deciding what to say, for he had gone through the same routine three or four times. He would stop writing, frown at the paper, and with an angry gesture, cross it all out. Then he would pick up the classified section of the *News-Record*, read it for a few minutes, throw it down and start writing again. He must be terribly nervous about something; it was a bad time to interrupt him. But she had told him she knew how to care for a baby. It was only fair to admit that if something was wrong with his baby, she wouldn't know what to do about it.

"Mr. O'Connor?"

His head jerked up. His blue eyes looked at her with such a funny startled expression that she almost laughed. "I'm sorry. I didn't mean to scare you." She walked toward him. Like a child hiding something behind his back, he picked up the writing paper, turned it over, and dropped the newspaper on top of it.

Marika felt blood rush to her cheeks. She wasn't the kind of person to read over someone else's shoulder. Then he smiled, and it was such a terrific smile that it disarmed her completely. "I'm sorry," she said again. "I just wanted to ask you..." She stopped and looked down at the baby. "What's his name?"

Something odd happened to Mr. O'Connor's smile. It was still there, but the warmth was gone, "Eric or Ricky."

"I like the name Eric. He's going to grow up and discover Newfoundland." The man responded with a genuine laugh. Whatever had got him so uptight seemed to have passed. Relaxed and laughing, he was one of the best-looking men Marika had ever met.

"I just wanted to ask, has Eric been sick?"

"Sick?"

She'd done it again. That one word seemed to trigger the same panicky reaction he had to her asking the baby's name.

"Yes," he said after a moment's hesitation. "Yes, he had been. Partly it's the milk. I forgot that cow's milk upsets him. I've got to buy some soybean milk, and some more of his medicine. I'm making arrangements .... That is, I'm going to get it as soon as possible. It's a prescription."

"What a relief! I was beginning to worry." Marika wondered whether comforting the baby or sympathizing with the man was arousing such a strong sense of identification. She was drawn to both of them. Careful, Marika, it isn't your baby. It isn't your man. Do you want to go through it all over again?

The man was waiting, bound to her by the unfinished sentence. Marika smiled. "Don't mind me. I get these lapses. They aren't catching."

"You say you were beginning to worry about the baby?"

"Yes, but you explained. He needs his medicine. If you'll give me the prescription, I'll go out and get it filled. There's a good drugstore about three blocks from here."

He got to his feet so quickly that he swept newspaper and stationery off the desk. "No, you can't.

I'm supposed to take the bottle back to the drugstore where it was filled originally. I'll use your car again, if you don't mind."

"No. Of course not." Marika watched curiously as he pulled on his jacket, dropped the newspaper into the wastebasket, folded the sheets of writing paper and stuffed them into his coat pocket. "Better put in some gas," she said as he opened the door. "Regular. Don't believe the fuel gauge. It cheats." He gave a quick nod of assent, and he was gone.

Marika stood in the middle of the room, sifting through impressions that were so elusive and so laden with emotion that they danced away when she tried to put them into words. One bit of logic stepped forward and insisted on being heard. If Mr. O'Connor was getting the baby's medicine from a pharmacy where the prescription had already been filled, the doctor's prescription would be on file, and there would be no reason at all to bring in the empty bottle.

And if he *was* supposed to return the bottle? There was something wrong with that picture, too. She had been in the room for hours. She would have seen a medicine bottle unless it was in one of Mr. O'Connor's coat or trouser pockets. But she had been near him when he put on his coat, and she had a distinct visual memory of well-tailored slacks with no bulges in the pockets and of coat pockets that were flat and therefore empty until he picked up several sheets of motel stationery and put them into the left pocket. So he had left without the bottle. Was he absent-minded? Or was he lying?

At home in Black River, Martin and Laurie were reading an ad in the Personals column of Tuesday's *News-Record.* "To K.O. Jr. Special prescription. We must fill. Need instructions for delivery." Words of their own choosing. Words that gambled on Jack Howard's conviction that the kidnapper was an amateur, guided more by emotion than by hard cold sense.

"There are two ways of getting the medicine into the kidnapper's hands," Howard had said when they debated the wording. "We could ask for an address. When he gives it—and it would probably be the general delivery window of some big post office—we mail a letter with the doctor's prescription form. But this man is bound to be thinking about the risks. Showing up to claim the letter is risky business, and presenting the prescription to a druggist is even more so. The pharmacist says, 'I'll have it for you in ten minutes'— and the kidnapper is afraid part of that ten minutes will be spent checking the prescription with the doctor who wrote it. So he panics, and never tries to claim your letter. And the baby doesn't get his medicine.

"The other way is to deliver the medicine itself. Your ad would say that you yourselves have to get the prescription filled. I think he'll go for that, because it bypasses two dangerous roadblocks. He doesn't have to show up at a general delivery window or a prescription counter. From your point of view, it's good, too. There's more chance of getting the medicine to the baby because you're making it a little bit easier for the kidnapper to pick it up. And that's what you want more than anything else. To keep the baby well."

Martin put his arm around Laurie. "I know what you're thinking. Why are we acting as if the kidnapper will make any effort to get Leif's medicine. Why should he bother to do something he knows is dangerous to himself?"

"Because . . . Oh, Marty, I can't make myself say it."

"Because he's afraid he won't collect a ransom if he can't produce a living child." Martin pulled her closer. "Courage, darling. Jack is sure he'll answer our ad in tomorrow's paper."

"Sunday, Monday, Tuesday," Laurie whispered. "No medicine for three days." Clinging to each other, they sat in silence for a long, long time.

Ollie White decided not to enter the Wendell Arms until after dark. Getting into the building wasn't a problem. Getting out would be, unless the place was a lot more soundproof than apartments Ollie had lived in. He hugged his gun against his side, as he always did when he needed reassurance. Right now, he'd check out names and apartment numbers, nothing more.

The door into the foyer was unlocked, as Ollie knew it would be. The inside door between the foyer and the first-floor hallway was locked. He read the panel of residents. Second Floor. Ricky Cummins, Apartment 28.

The mailbox for Apartment 28 was empty. So Ricky was at home. Ollie would just wait awhile before he dropped in for a visit. He went outside, examined the shrubbery, and selected a spot which would give him cover as well as a good view of both the front entrance and the tenants' parking lot in the rear. He didn't want his bird to fly away.

An hour later Ollie reconsidered the situation. The parade of people coming home from work had ended. Tenants who were out for the evening wouldn't begin to show up for another couple of hours. It was happy hour time, when every TV set in the building was turned up loud for the evening news. Okay, Rick old friend. I'm coming up.

Back in the foyer, Ollie pressed the button for Apartment 28 and waited for Ricky's voice on the intercom. His little speech was ready. "It's Nelson," he would say. "I brought your mail from the office. Some of it was personal, so I thought you'd like to see it." These tinny intercoms garbled everyone's voice. Ricky wouldn't be suspicious because Nelson didn't sound natural.

Ollie buzzed three times and the lack of response

was such a letdown that for a few minutes he didn't know what to do next. So Ricky wasn't at home sick.. But he had picked up his mail. So maybe he was home, and wasn't answering the bell. The meaning of that hit Ollie fast. Someone at Ricky's office had phoned to warn Ricky that a man with a gun was looking for him. Okay, Ricky wasn't in his apartment, or he was, and he was hiding. Either way, Ollie wanted in.

He read the names of the second-floor tenants again. Apartment 29, Mrs. A. B. Dennison. He pressed the bell for 29. In seconds the buzzer sounded unlocking the inner door. An eager type, Mrs. A. B. Dennison, Ollie concluded. Doesn't even bother to ask who's there. Which probably meant she was expecting someone, and would probably be waiting in the hall. Not good. But she had let him in, and that's what counted.

Ollie rode the elevator to the second floor and stepped out, almost into the arms of a small elderly woman in a pink housecoat. "Oh, I, who?" she asked in a squeaky voice, hopping to the side and peering into the elevator. "Did you? See someone? The boy from?"

In chirpy fits and starts, she explained that she had called the delicatessen and they were sending over a quart of buttermilk, a loaf of whole wheat bread, and some apples and when her bell rang she thought it was the delivery boy and so she pressed the buzzer. With that she stopped talking. Bright little eyes told him that now it was his turn.

"I guess I pushed the wrong button," Ollie said. "I wanted Apartment 28. Sorry I bothered you." With a friendly nod, he began to walk down the hall.

Mrs. Dennison danced along at his side. "Mr. Cummins isn't home. Not since day before yesterday. Sunday night. Came in like a whirlwind. Stayed fifteen minutes. Out again. Like that. Carrying clothes. Drove away. I remember because it was the night we had the bad storm." She was right beside him when he stopped at the door to Ricky's apartment. Her head bobbed in a fast series of I-Told-You-So's as Ollie rang the bell without getting a response.

Ollie shrugged. "Well, that's too bad. He must be out. Next time I'll phone before I come."

"He has an unlisted number," Mrs. Dennison announced cheerily.

"Yeah," Ollie said noncommittally, wondering if this pesty old lady was going to follow him back down the hall. She didn't, but she was still watching when he got into the elevator and closed the door.

Those sharp little eyes would notice if the elevator went up instead of down. Ollie pressed the button for the ground floor. He got out, walked quickly to a red exit sign, hoping it would lead to a back stairway as well as a door to the parking lot. It did. He walked up to the third floor. For fifteen minutes he waited on the service stairs, prepared to nod casually and walk down again if a tenant decided to use the stairs. When he judged that he'd waited long enough, he walked down to the second floor. With any luck nosy Mrs. Dennison would be perched in front of her TV and he would be inside Ricky's apartment before anyone else came out into the hall. His fingers tightened around the tools he always carried in case he had to unlock a door without a key. In thirty seconds he opened the door, went in, and locked the door behind him. No one had seen him break in.

The apartment was dark. With his gun drawn, Ollie turned on the living room lights. No one here. He moved swiftly from room to room, checking every corner or closet where Ricky might be hiding. Empty. Whether he had fled because the office had warned him, or was away from home for his own reasons, Ollie didn't know. And though he felt frustrated because his surprise visit had failed, fifteen minutes later, after a second inspection of the living room, Ollie discovered something that made his first plan to get even with Ricky look like a child's game.

His purpose in poking through the drawers of Ricky's desk and the contents of his wastebasket was to find a note or letter that would point him toward a girlfriend's place, where Ricky might be staying. There was nothing interesting in the desk except an address book with so many entries there was no way to spot the one he wanted. He dropped it in his pocket anyway, and turned to the wastebasket. No letters or envelopes with return addresses. In fact, nothing at all, except the Sunday edition of the *News-Record*, folded open to the same article about the Dahlquist case that Ollie had been reading in the prison rec room two days earlier. Someone—it had to be Ricky—had drawn a whole series of the same little doodle on the margin. Only it wasn't just doodling. Ollie's personal interest in the Ochsners had sharpened his memory. Three triangles of different sizes, one inside the other and all surrounded by a circle. The symbol Ricky's father had used on all his ransom notes about the Dahlquist baby. Ricky had been practicing that symbol on the margin of Sunday's newspaper.

Ollie jumped up and hurried back to the bedroom. That wastebasket was empty. He went into the kitchen and opened the cupboard under the sink. A small garbage can. Ollie removed the cover. Coffee grounds. Grapefruit rind. An empty milk carton. With a grimace he picked up the can and dumped the contents upside down in the sink.

In the damp mess at the bottom were a dozen scraps of paper. Ollie lifted one of them, brushed it off carefully, and held it toward the light. Though the ink had run, the handwriting was still legible: "... while you pray for the safe return of your baby. *Do not* ..." One by one he separated the torn scraps from the pile of wet garbage and fitted them together on the drainboard. Some words were crossed out, others written along the margin. This was what Ricky had written first, and then copied on another sheet of paper. "Jesus," Ollie breathed, staring at the message signed with the familiar triangles. It was all there. Ricky's ransom note to the parents of the baby he had kidnapped.

For several minutes Ollie was too excited to think. His old buddy. The great Boy Scout, holier than thou, who wouldn't cooperate in a simple little robbery of a grocery store. Like father, like son, Ollie's mother used to say. Bad blood will out. My boy isn't going to play with nobody whose father died in the electric chair. . . .

The idea came to Ollie like a bright light suddenly turning on inside his mind. This note had to be the first, the one Ricky left wherever it was he grabbed the baby. It didn't say how much ransom or how to deliver it. Ollie's arm squeezed against his holster. It wasn't too late to get into the act. Ollie decided he was either going to get to Ricky and cut himself in on the money by threatening to blow the whole thing, or reach the grieving parents—*and* their money—before Ricky.

Wednesday, March 16

Fifteen

IN THE DOWNTOWN office of the Washington Newspaper Publishers Association, Martin and Laurie were watching Jack Howard greet an old friend. "Say, I finally found a legitimate excuse for coming here and staring at you."

The woman was tall, slender, and beautifully groomed. Her gray eyes surveyed the investigator with obvious affection. "You know I'm always pleased to see you. And your friends," she said, smiling at the Dahlquists.

"Jim and Martha Whitestone," said Howard quickly, using their prepared story. "They're doing a piece on the decline and fall of the neighborhood weekly."

"Great! What can I do to help you? Though I must warn you that Howard takes a different view of weekly newspapers than I do. They are still very much alive, though there have been some changes." She raised an eyebrow at Howard.

Howard laughed. "I submit. But how about the

159

newspaper that used to cover the area southeast of the railroad yards? It was quite an Austrian community when you and I were young, Nellie."

"Yes, it was. And you're right. There was such a newspaper. One of the first neighborhood papers in Seattle. It lasted for years, until the community was cut to pieces by the highway and gradually taken over by small industry. Let me think. Around Grummin Hill. I'll find it, Jack. It's bound to be in our file."

She disappeared into an adjoining room and was back in a few minutes with a file card in her hand. "*The Southside Home News*. Last published in June, 1946. It had been up for sale for some time, but the community was already moribund and no one was foolish enough to buy it. The building was purchased by a cabinetmaker who had it moved to his backyard and used it as his shop. The equipment was too out of date to interest anyone in the printing business. Most of it was simply carted off to the dump. But Frank Garth—you know him, don't you, Jack? Frank bought all the old handset type, and all the engravings, for his collection of antique type and historic news photos. As far as I know, he's still got it in his hobby shop in the U district. The Appletree Press, he calls it."

"What about copies of the paper? The old weeklies kept bound files of back issues. Do you suppose Frank has them, too?"

"I don't know. But I will in a minute, if he's in." Nancy went to the telephone and dialed. As she had promised, it took one minute to discover that Frank Garth had indeed saved the old files of *The Southside Home News* and would be delighted to show them to Mr. and Mrs. Whitestone.

Back on the street, Martin, Laurie, and Howard agreed to separate. Martin and Laurie would visit the printshop. Howard would pursue one or two lines of inquiry he thought might reveal something about

Klaus Ochsner's son. They would meet later in Black River.

Jack Howard was a self-admitted skeptic. When he lectured university students he always emphasized that skepticism is an all-important tool of the trade and no investigator should accept anything without shaking it to see if it rattles. At the same time he told them to be very careful about *not* believing. Doubt everything. Scoff at nothing.

Howard followed his own advice, privately as well as professionally. He didn't believe in astrology but never failed to read his horoscope. And though he wouldn't admit to being completely sold on graphology, he frequently consulted Toby Weiss, a police graphologist. An hour with Toby Weiss couldn't tell him where to find the kidnapper, but it might point him in the right direction.

Though the kidnapper's note to the Dahlquists was in his pocket, Howard couldn't show it to Toby without violating his pledge of secrecy. So on his way to Toby's office, Howard stopped at the Seattle public library, where he made a photocopy of the letter in one of the coin-operated Xerox machines. Then he borrowed a pair of scissors, cut the note into pieces, and discarded every bit that might suggest the content.

In Toby's office, Howard took the remaining pieces out of his pocket and arranged them on the graphologist's desk. "But it was hard...while all around...would never have been...a little bit at a time. Think about it, while you...repeat it after today."

Toby's round face glowed with pleasure. "So you've just come from the public library, eh, Jack?"

Howard shrugged. "I read a lot."

"Yeh. I know." Toby's eyes moved slowly from piece to piece. Then he picked up a magnifying glass and studied them again, more intently than the first time. "You really believe in this stuff?" he asked while he was still peering through the glass.

Howard chuckled. "I do, and I don't. What are you doing, Toby? Playing devil's advocate? You're the believer. *I'm* the skeptic."

"You're a practical man, Jack. You stick with skepticism because you know how to make it work for you." Toby's forefinger tapped the largest fragment. "Okay, let's start with this one. First, the slant of the writing. Next the weight. Notice how he—you didn't say the writer is a man, but ten to one, it is—okay, notice how *he* dots the i's and crosses the t's."

"It's distinctive, isn't it."

"Very. And for that reason, a better than average index to the writer's psychological makeup. I'm sure it's obvious, even to a Pharisee like you, that the writer is a mature adult, with considerable manual dexterity or artistic ability, or both. Let's go a little deeper. What was going on in his mind when he wrote this? What is he likely to do in the future? That's what you want to know, isn't it, Jack?"

"You're damn right," Howard said with feeling.

"It's in the strokes. The angle between the upright parts of the letters and the line they're written on. Look here. . . ." Toby's finger traced a letter H. "The upstroke goes off at a forty-five-degree angle from the downstroke in the same letter. We call that a breakaway. It's a sign of initiative. The more abrupt the breakaway, the stronger the trait. This man of yours has a goal. He has strong drive. And he wants to get on with it." Toby paused, picked up another piece, frowned at it for a moment, and then handed it to Jack. "Look at those T's, both the small T and the capital. Good examples of the tie formation. The downstroke does a loop the loop. That's persistence. . . ."

When he was done Toby summed up his findings:

"A loner . . . determined, but not aggressive in the sense of pushing other people out of the way. He depends on himself to get where he wants to go. Artistic, as I said before. Talented. But very emotional. He must have been under considerable stress when he wrote this letter."

Interesting, Howard reflected, that so much of Toby's analysis strengthened the misty image that had been forming in his own mind. At the door, he said, "Send me a bill, Toby. I mean it."

"Go to hell."

"No, listen. I charge for what I do. If you wanted me to find someone, you'd pay me."

"Man, are you in for a big surprise! All right, Jack. There is one way you can pay me for today."

"What's that?"

"Someday, show me the rest of that note. The part you cut out and threw away."

The girl at the counter of the *News-Record*'s classified advertising department said, "Yes, sir. Did you want to place an ad?"

"Not today." Jack Howard pulled a page of the classified section out of his coat pocket and put it on the counter. He had drawn a circle around the kidnapper's message in the Personals column. "I ran this ad in the Monday paper. I'd like to pay for it."

"I'm sorry, sir. You'll have to go to the accounting department. Oh, wait. The *Monday's* paper. No, they wouldn't have the charge slips yet. They're still here. I'm sorry. I can't take your money, and accounting won't know what you owe." She smiled apologetically. "Sounds silly, doesn't it."

"No problem. I'll pay when I get the bill. But while I'm here I might as well find out how much I owe. Would you show me the charge slip, please?"

"Oh, sure." The girl was clearly eager to counteract

department silliness with a display of service. She
checked the coded symbols at the end of the ad and
wrote them down on a scratch pad. "Just a second,
please." She darted across the office, flipped through a
box of index cards, and hurried back. "It will be three
dollars and forty cents, Mr. Dahlquist."

Howard was glad that he had had forty years'
experience at dissembling. "Yes, thank you. One more
thing. Did I charge it to my home address or my
office?"

Looking at the card, the girl read, "Box 114, Route
Two, Black River?"

"Thank you very much." Howard strolled out of the
office with his hands in his pockets. He had run into
many strange situations, but this was new. The
kidnapper was charging his ads to the father of the
kidnapped child! Just how did *that* fit into his portrait
of Klaus Ochsner's son?

Martin and Laurie, as Jim and Martha Whitestone,
were sitting at a table in the back of the Appletree
Press. They had been warmly greeted by the owner,
Frank Garth, who was delighted to find someone who
acknowledged the social value of the community
newspaper. In his enthusiasm, he had forced them to
inspect banks of antique type and stacks of faded
photographs, but now at last they were alone with two
large packages, marked "SHN 1931" and SHN 1932."
Martin unwrapped "SHN 31" and opened the bound
volume to the *Southside Home News* for January 8,
1931. They began to read, Laurie taking the page on
the left, Martin the page on the right.

They read silently through page after page of
wedding stories, social notes, club news, and what
Frank Garth had referred to as "Mr. and Mrs." The
type was small and the pages were yellow and brittle. It

was dull, repetitious, and as far as they knew, very likely to be a blind alley. Mrs. Maerchen *might* have been talking about the Ochsner baby instead of the kidnapped Dahlquist child. But it was the wildest sort of speculation.

When they had scrutinized every page of every edition printed in 1931, Martin closed the book and removed the faded brown wrapping paper from the bound volume for 1932. "Fifty-two down, fifty-two to go."

Laurie's voice echoed his sense of hopelessness. "And we don't really know what we're looking for. Any reference to the Ochsners, I suppose, but especially to their son."

"If there's nothing in this volume, we'll go on to the one for 1933."

So they began again and continued doggedly from page to page. January 7, nothing. January 14, still nothing. January 21. Martin exclaimed, "Ah! Laurie, read this."

It was a sad story about the death of a child. The little boy had been riding in the front seat of his father's car. The door on his side wasn't locked. The child was standing on the seat, waving playfully at passing cars, when the father swerved suddenly to avoid hitting a dog. The child lost balance and fell against the handle of the unlocked door. The door opened and the child fell out, into the path of a truck. Karl Ochsner, only son of Mr. and Mrs. Klaus Ochsner of 18345 Grummin Street South, was killed instantly.

"How awful," Laurie whispered. "The door wasn't locked. Think how guilty the father must have felt."

"No doubt," Martin said coldly. "Six weeks later, he kidnapped and murdered my brother. If he really loved his own son and suffered because of his death, why would he make another father suffer in the same way?"

"Maybe that's it," Laurie said. "Klaus Ochsner was a poor immigrant, a nobody. Your father was a legend. Destroying his child was a way of striking back, of evening the score."

"And Klaus Ochsner's son is doing the same thing now." Martin shook his head. "I can't... It's hard to talk about. Let's get back to the implications of this news item. The Ochsners had two sons. The first one was killed before the kidnapping. The second was the child Mrs. Ochsner called 'Bübchen.' That's the man we're looking for. The second son, whose older brother was killed. Like me. What a strange parallel."

"Yes," Laurie said thoughtfully. "Now I understand why Mrs. Maerchen kept saying 'Poor Lisa.' Her first son was killed because of her husband's carelessness. Her second son sent away to avoid her husband's trial and execution. And there's something else, Martin, that Mrs. Maerchen told us. Klaus was so poor he even had to dig graves for a living. What cruel punishment, if he dug a grave for his own son."

Martin said curtly, "Don't ask me to sympathize."

"But you do, don't you, Marty? You can't read this report of a child's death and feel nothing."

"Of course I feel. And that's why I don't want to discuss anything but facts that will help us find our son. Here's one we shouldn't overlook. The last line, second paragraph. 'The fatally injured child was rushed to the office of Dr. Jacob Himmelfarb, who examined the victim and pronounced him dead.' If the doctor were still alive..."

Using Frank Garth's phone, Martin called the only Himmelfarb in the Seattle directory's listing for Physicians and Surgeons: Fred Himmelfarb, M.D., with offices in the Wallingford district.

"Dr. Jacob? Oh, he's retired. Has been for years."

"Do you know him?"

There was a chuckle at the other end of the line. "I should. He's my father."

"Then you know where he lives?"

"With me. But don't try to reach him by telephone. He's very hard of hearing. On the phone, he can't hear at all."

"We're collecting material for a feature article about the Grummin Hills area when it was known as 'Little Austria.' Would your father be willing to answer a few questions?"

"Willing? Mr. Whitestone, you'd make his day. Please call on him. Number 57, Clayton Northwest. I'll phone my wife and tell her to expect you."

Dr. Jacob was delighted. He ordered Martin to sit directly in front of him so that he could read Martin's lips. He insisted that Laurie pull her chair close to his so that he could hold her hand. When Martin asked a question he could answer, he was voluble. When he didn't know the answer, he dismissed the question with an autocratic wave of the hand.

"Sure, I remember Lisa Ochsner. You're not going to revive that story, are you? No? That's good. How that woman suffered. The baby? Yes, I examined him. The Ochsners had never been patients of mine but my office was near the scene of the accident. It was a formality. A mere formality. The baby was terribly mangled. I tried to stop his mother from looking at him, but it was no use. She came to see me several times after that. About depression, insomnia, that sort of thing. Nothing physically wrong with her. I was a psychiatrist more than a medical doctor in the case of poor Lisa Ochsner. Well, my prescription for her was to have another baby as fast as possible. Yes, yes. She did, and it was a good thing. She was pretty stable after her second child was born. For a year or so, anyway, until her husband was exposed as a kidnapper and murderer. . . . No, I don't remember that boy's name, the second boy. She called the first one Bübchen, the one that was killed. . . . One thing I never figured out . . . oh, the *police* claimed they knew how he did it, but not me. A few months after little Bübchen died, Klaus sent Lisa back home to Austria. To see her mother, who was a bedridden old lady and failing. Maybe to get her mind off the accident, too. Lisa stayed quite awhile. That's why I didn't deliver the second child. He was born while she was still over there. . . . Where is Mrs. Ochsner now? I haven't the slightest idea. And I can tell you that if you could locate everyone who knew her on Grummin Street, not one of them would know more than I do. When Lisa dropped out of sight, she might as well have gone up in a puff of smoke. . . . Oh, you're welcome. Entirely welcome. Hope I helped you some. Come back, if you want to. Anytime." He stopped abruptly. Without turning his head in the direction of his daughter-in-law, he called out, "Margaret? Margaret? The folks are leaving now. Come say goodbye. See them out." Once more the old man's flow of speech came to a sudden halt. He looked intently into Martin's face, lips pursed and shaggy white eyebrows drawn together. "Mr. Whitestone, I've seen you somewhere before."

Martin said quickly, "I must be a common type. I probably look like someone you met in the past."

Dr. Jacob didn't agree or disagree, but his eyes followed Martin and Laurie until the door closed behind them.

A second message from "K. O." appeared in the *News-Record*'s Personals column on Wednesday, March 16. Martin and Laurie, Elizabeth Dahlquist, and Jack Howard sat around the kitchen table, reading and rereading the kidnapper's instructions for delivering the baby's medicine.

K. O. says 3 P.M. tomorrow. Litter barrel north end public market. Don't miss.

• • •

In the faces of the baby's parents Howard saw both hope and fear. The advertisement seemed to promise that the kidnapper would retrieve the medicine from the litter barrel. On the other hand they didn't dare believe that he would. And neither did the baby's grandmother. Elizabeth was beyond believing in anything except her power to endure.

"I think I know what's troubling you," Howard said. "We should be relieved because the baby will get his medicine by late tomorrow afternoon. But we don't feel that way.

"This man is not like any kidnapper I've ever encountered. He hasn't demanded ransom and now he's risking capture in order to protect the baby's health. And that's what scares us. He seems totally unpredictable, and it's terrifying to have your child in the hands of a man whose next move we cannot possibly anticipate. But perhaps young Ochsner is capable of compassion. Think about his background. Brought up by a mother who never stopped grieving over the death of his older brother. More important, by a mother who never ceased believing her husband was innocent. Right or wrong, the boy was brought up to believe it, too. So he's bitter, very bitter. And revenge would serve another purpose. It would be a way that a child who feels the rejection of being second best would seek the approval of his mother. His note tells it all. He did it for *her*. She planted the seed a long time ago. For years, revenge has been a dream. And then suddenly something happens, to him or to his mother, which creates more emotional stress than he can cope with. And the dream becomes a reality.

"One thing baffles me, though. Why did he charge his ads to you? That's something. . . ."

Howard's sentence was cut off by the ringing of the telephone. Martin jumped to his feet.

"No, Martin!" Howard intercepted the younger

man before he could reach the telephone. "It could be
Ochsner, so your mother must answer. She's the one
who's staying home while the three of us are in and out
of the house, and she must recognize his voice in case
there are other calls later on."

Elizabeth rose and stood beside her chair, eyes fixed
on the telephone. It rang again.

"Please, Mrs. Dahlquist," Howard said urgently.
"You've got to know the kidnapper's voice. You've got
to be able to identify it."

With Martin holding her arm, Elizabeth walked
unsteadily across the room and sat down next to the
telephone. Another ring. This time she picked up the
receiver. "Yes? Hello. Yes. This is Mrs. Dahlquist.... I'm sorry, I can't quite hear you. Would you
speak up a little, please...."

There was a long pause and then Elizabeth said, "I
understand. Yes, your instructions are clear. But I
would like to ask you..." With the receiver still in her
hand, she turned and looked up at Martin. "He hung
up."

Martin took the receiver out of her hand, replaced
it, and led his mother back to the table. Her face was
ashen, but when she spoke, her voice was steady. "It
was the kidnapper. He wants Laurie to go to the
branch post office at 85th and Waldo and ask for a
letter addressed to me care of general delivery. I am to
do that at two o'clock tomorrow afternoon." She
paused. "Martin, may I have a glass of water, please."

Howard said quietly, "Rest a minute, Mrs.
Dahlquist. Then try and tell us exactly what he said. A
lot can be learned about a person from his choice
of words."

Elizabeth nodded. "At first I couldn't make out
what he was saying. I heard his voice, but it was
muffled."

Howard said, "So our man was disguising his voice.

After you asked him to speak up, did his voice change?"

"A little. It was clearer. But it still had a . . . well, an odd spongy quality."

"Right," Howard said. "Please go on, Mrs. Dahlquist. I won't interrupt again."

"His first words were . . ." Her voice broke. With an anguished glance at Laurie, she went on. "He said, 'I've got your baby. If you want to see him again, you do exactly what I tell you.' And then he gave me the instructions about asking for a letter at the post office. After that, he said, 'Now listen to me, and listen to me good. I'm giving you this warning and I'm only going to say it once. Don't call the police. If you do, your kid is going to end up just as dead as that other one. You can go to the bank if you want to, because you're going to need a lot of cash. You read that letter tomorrow afternoon. It'll tell you how much.'" Elizabeth hesitated. "I think that was all, Mr. Howard."

"You did very well, Mrs. Dahlquist. I gather he thought he was talking to the baby's mother."

"Yes, I'm sure he did."

"We'll have to take that into consideration when we plan for tomorrow. One more question. When he hung up, you were about to say something. Would you tell us what it was?"

"I was going to ask, 'Why did you place an ad in the newspaper with instructions about the baby's medicine when you knew you were going to get in touch with me by telephone?' Hasn't that question occurred to you, Mr. Howard?"

"Yes, Mrs. Dahlquist. It certainly has. It's a pertinent question. But I'm glad he hung up. I'm glad you didn't ask it. There is something odd about this call. Initially K. O. seemed worried about the baby's health and didn't mention a ransom. Now he has asked for a ransom and said nothing about the baby's medicine. Stranger yet, he set up one meeting at three P.M. at a public market and another at two at a post office a good forty-five minutes away."

Howard took the note left by the kidnapper out of his pocket and placed it beside the paper on which he had scrawled the kidnapper's telephone conversation. "When you compare the wording of these two messages, something sounds off key. It's hard to believe that the man who wrote so eloquently, and so grammatically, about his mother would have said *listen to me good*, or referred to the child as a *kid*."

"And who has Leif?" burst out Laurie. "He must be ill by now. I can only think the man asking for the medicine actually has my baby."

"I agree," Howard said quietly. "And that may indicate that the man who just telephoned is more dangerous than the kidnapper."

Before he left the telephone booth Ollie White stuck two fingers into his mouth, pulled out a wadded handkerchief, and shoved it into his pocket. He hadn't been so pleased with himself in a long time.

The phone call had been a smart move. It proved that Ricky had the baby, that the parents were willing to follow orders, and above all, that so far the ransom hadn't been paid. So far, so good. The post office arrangement was smart. He knew what the Dahlquists looked like, but the Dahlquists had never seen him. He could watch the General Delivery window without any risk at all.

If Mrs. Dahlquist kept her promise to pick up his letter, it meant Ricky still had the baby and Ricky still hadn't demanded ransom. If she didn't show up, it meant Ricky had beaten him to the punch. Having received one ransom note, the Dahlquists would damn well know that a second one was a phony. In which case, Ollie wouldn't try to get to the Dahlquists. Let Ricky collect, and then get to Ricky.

One big problem remained. He had to hunt Ricky down and get hold of the baby. It was tough, but he had one advantage: he knew what Ricky was doing, but Ricky didn't know what Ollie was up to. And he won't, Ollie thought smugly. Not until it's too late.

Thursday, March 17

Sixteen

ATER A NIGHT'S sleep in his own bed in the Hotel Alaska, Jack Howard awoke refreshed. It was a few minutes after six. A perfect time to go over his notes. He made coffee and pulled out his scrapbooks, certain that the solution to the riddle was hidden in the past.

Studying the long list of everyone who testified at the Ochsner trial, his mind fastened on one he had marked with a small "dec." Professor Henry T. Marshall, the famous "Henny" who had tried to negotiate with Klaus Ochsner for the Dahlquists. After Ochsner's execution, he had made a great many speeches on the subject, usually titled "I Knew K. O."

He had always kept a diary, so when invitations to speak ceased to occupy his time, he used it as material for a book, *A Child Is Missing*. But as Howard knew, it had never been published. The professor had died nearly twenty years ago but Jack was certain he would never have destroyed the manuscript and possibly he had left it to someone in his will.

Howard reread Marshall's obituary. "He is survived

by one daughter, Mrs. Clarence Stockton of Bend, Oregon, and three grandchildren." It was a long shot, but Howard decided to try and reach the family. His first telephone call established the fact that Mrs. Clarence Stockton was not listed in the Bend directory. It was ten o'clock before his second call was completed.

The quavery voice said, "Let me catch my breath. We're not open Thursdays until noon. I just happened to be here, and I heard the phone ringing. What did you say your name was? Mr. Howard? Yes, Mr. Howard. This is the Olympic County Historical Society. Yes, indeed, we have a fine little museum. Yes, and a library, too. History. Mostly local. Professor Marshall? I knew him well. Of course he was much older than I . . ."

She talked on, encouraged by Howard's sympathetic remarks, and eventually told him that Professor Marshall's manuscript had been donated by his daughter and she would be glad to let him read it, as long as he didn't take it out of the building.

Howard left his car in SeaTac airport's parking garage and hurried to the baggage claim area. Someone on the PanAm staff had been efficient in carrying out Martin's instructions. A dollar to the skycap standing guard over the PanAm carousel, a smile and a word of thanks, and Howard was on his way back to the garage, one of Elizabeth's suitcases in each hand.

When he arrived at the Dahlquist home in Black River, Laurie and Martin were out. Elizabeth opened the back door and murmured, "Good morning, Mr. Howard," as Howard walked past her and put the suitcases down near her chair.

"You have them," she said simply. "Thank you very much, Mr. Howard."

"Martin asked me to pick them up at the airport."

"Yes, I know." Her eyes were sad, but either she had

an extraordinary degree of self-control, or she had given up the fight.

"Please sit down, Mr. Howard," she said. "I'd like to talk to you for a few minutes, if you don't mind."

Howard took a chair at the breakfast table. "About your suitcases."

She sighed, rested her head on the back of the chair, and closed her eyes. "Yes. Or I should say, the package you'll find in the smaller case."

"Do you want me to open it?"

"Yes, I do." She reached into the pocket of her tweed suit and handed him two keys on a silver chain. "I think it's the smaller one."

"Have you talked with Martin about this?"

She inclined her head. "This morning. We came to an understanding. I agreed to let you open the package and examine the contents. My son agreed to leave the decision up to you, as to whether he should be told what the contents are."

"You are both placing a great deal of trust in my judgment."

Elizabeth opened her eyes and smiled. "We're not mistaken in that. Please go ahead, Mr. Howard. I've been hiding that box for almost forty years. It's become an albatross. Now that I've been forced—I should say, now that circumstances have forced me to open it, I can't wait to get it over with. Before Martin and Laurie get back from the drugstore. If you will, please."

Howard placed the smaller suitcase on the kitchen table and opened it.

Neither of them spoke during the ten or fifteen minutes Howard spent examining the contents of the little parcel. When he finished, he put everything back, closed the box, and retied the twine. Elizabeth was sitting up very straight, her dark eyes following every move. Awaiting the judgment. Prepared to accept his decision however painful it might be. A gallant and beautiful woman, Howard thought. A *true* aristocrat.

"I'm glad you've allowed me to read this letter, Mrs. Dahlquist. I see it's dated February twenty-eighth. May I ask when you received it?"

"As far as I know, shortly after it was written. But it was lost in the flood of letters we were receiving at that time and I didn't open and read it until sometime in May."

"Ah..." Howard sighed deeply. "Now I understand." After a thoughtful pause he said, "It doesn't provide a clue to the whereabouts of Ochsner's son, but it does corroborate our ideas about his motivation for stealing your grandchild. Understanding that may be more of a 'clue' than we realize now. As to the mitten... I'm not sure that it proves anything, except that it was meant to shock and frighten you."

Howard paused and looked thoughtfully at the woman sitting ramrod straight in an armchair that suddenly seemed to be too big for her. "I'm having trouble with one thing," he said, rubbing his chin. "The question of showing these things to Martin. I'm honored by your request that I make the decision but it won't be an easy one. Please understand. There is no need to show Martin what that parcel contains. It would upset him, without doing anything to help him recover his child. But if the secret is so unimportant that there's no point in revealing it to Martin, what's the point in concealing it? It has stirred up some unhappy memories for you, but it's time to declare a moratorium on guilt. Forty years is long enough, Mrs. Dahlquist. Lance the secret and let the healing process start."

In the silence that followed Howard wondered how to apologize. He didn't get beyond "Mrs. Dahlquist, I hope you'll..." when Elizabeth stood up and said, "Who will talk to Martin? You or I?"

"What do you think?"

"I think the wound won't heal if I avoid talking to my son."

Suddenly Howard felt a curious lump in his throat. "Right, Mrs. Dahlquist," he said hoarsely. "Right."

Elizabeth began to walk away, then paused and turned back. "Mr. Howard, at the risk of being presumptuous, I'd like to ask you a personal question."

Howard grinned. "It can't possibly be as presumptuous as the ones I've been asking you."

"But that's your duty, as an investigator. I have no such excuse. But I won't apologize. We're getting to know each other, aren't we? In the beginning, you were a stranger, but you are remarkably *simpatico*. You aren't a stranger anymore, after only two days. So I am uncomfortable with the gaps in my understanding of you."

"And you want to fill them in." Howard's voice was low and not altogether steady. "I wonder if you realize what a tremendous compliment you're paying me."

"I'm glad you feel that way. You have referred to your wife, as a young woman, and not very strong."

"She died the day after her twenty-sixth birthday."

"You never remarried?"

"The ones I liked always picked somebody else."

"Nonsense," Elizabeth said with an affectionate smile. "All right. You're too modest, but I won't pursue the issue."

The message was written in pencil and covered one side of a sheet of coarse lined paper torn from a grade school tablet. The handwriting was childish and the English was obviously not the sender's native tongue.

Very honored Mrs. Dahlquist!

I write you becaws you are a Woman like me.
I write you Truth. You must to listen me.

They get wrong Man! My man has not kill your Baby! Now they going to kill him! A terrible mistake. You got to stop it. You stop it before too late!

My husband is good and kind. He love babies. He not the one! I tell you, Mrs. Dahlquist. I promise you Truth.
He dint do it.

See what I send you? Your baby's Mitten. That show I know what happen. Klaus not kill your baby! I can prove it.

I beg you. Stop it, Fr. Dahlquist.
Don let them kill my husband.

LISA OCHSNER

Martin put the letter down, picked up the mitten, and turned it over several times. "This is all, Mother?"

Elizabeth nodded. "Yes. The letter and the mitten. Leif's nursemaid knitted the mittens. The mate to this one had already been found." Her voice broke off.

"I know. On the road near the spot where his body was discovered. But how could the mitten prove her husband's innocence?"

"I think she sent the mitten to show that she knew what happened to Leif. She doesn't deny that her husband kidnapped Leif. Only that he killed him."

Martin picked up the letter and read it again. "So there was an accomplice, after all. Klaus may have been executed for a crime he didn't commit. Is that what you thought when you received this letter?"

"Yes."

"Mother, why didn't you speak up? Why did you hide the letter instead of turning it over to the police?"

Elizabeth looked at him squarely. "Because Ochsner had already been executed when I read the letter."

Frowning, Martin read the date at the top of the page: February 28, 1936. "Mother, Ochsner wasn't executed until the third of April."

"That's just it. When I read the letter, there was nothing I could do."

"Except hide it from Father, who often had doubts about Ochsner's guilt."

"Yes. This letter would have reopened all his uncertainty. He would have suffered terribly, knowing that we had suppressed evidence that might have saved a life."

"Which is exactly what you did, Mother. You say you didn't receive this letter until some time after April third, but it was written thirty-three days before April third."

Elizabeth shook her head. "I didn't mean to imply that I hadn't received the letter before the execution. I did. But I didn't open it. We received thousands of letters, as you know. There was nothing on Lisa Ochsner's envelope to suggest that it was more important than any of the others. Believe me, I never allowed a letter to be thrown away without first opening it and reading it. For years your father and I kept hoping that one of the claims would turn out to be true. I had two secretaries who answered letters serious enough to be acknowledged, but I insisted on opening and reading all of them myself. That caused delays. I didn't read Mrs. Ochsner's letter until . . . Oh, Martin! I felt so guilty. When I saw her letter, the man was dead."

"So you accepted all the blame, and hid these things from Father and me for forty years."

"I know. But I kept silent for another reason. Lisa's letter convinced me that Ochsner had an accomplice and that it was the other man who killed and buried the baby. That meant the real killer was still at large. That thought terrified me. If I came forward with something that would cast doubt on the verdict, I was afraid he would be desperate and enraged. What would that man do to *you*, Martin. That's what frightened me. That's the real reason we lived in Europe for so long. We were protecting you. That letter, the mitten . . . I *wanted* the guilty man to think he had gotten off scot-free. I *wanted* him to feel confident. Because I was afraid that if he didn't, he'd try to harm you."

Martin put his arm around his mother and kissed her cheek. "And Father never knew. He was a strong man, Mother. He could have handled it. Sometimes I wonder—which was the stronger one, you or he?"

Martin handed Laurie the letter from Lisa Ochsner. "This may upset you, Laurie, but I think you ought to read it. This is what Mother's been concealing in that little package we were looking for in Father's study."

Laurie read it slowly, read it again, and let it drop into her lap. "Oh, Marty, how *awful*."

"It has been. But I think her feeling now is vast relief at finally getting something which has been bothering her into the open. It's not nearly so frightening."

"Marty, did your mother ask you to show me this letter?"

Martin shook his head. "No, indeed. I hesitated, but then, as I said, I thought it was something you had to know about." To his surprise, Laurie's eyes suddenly filled with tears. He sat down beside her and drew her into his arms. "Why are you crying, Laurie? About Lisa's letter? About Mother's hiding it for so long? Laurie, it all happened a long time ago. If a mistake was made, we can't correct it now. I don't want you to grieve over it."

"It isn't that." Laurie wiped away the tears with the back of her hand. "Tears come in different shapes and sizes. These are the self-centered kind."

"Caused by?"

"Because you voluntarily showed me this pathetic letter. You wouldn't have a year ago, or six months ago, or even last week. You and your mother would have shared the secret and accepted the responsibility and I would never have known about it."

Martin's arm tightened around her shoulders. "If I've left you out of anything, it's always been to protect you."

"I know that. I've always known that. But when you protect me, you make me small. But this time . . ." The blue eyes were bright, the lips curved in a radiant smile. "Thank you, Marty, for including me."

"Oh, Laurie," Martin said. "Laurie, Laurie . . ." For a long time they sat together on the living room sofa and the only sound in the room was the ticking of the blue enameled mantel clock.

Ollie White was standing on the corner of 85th and Waldo well before two o'clock. Not that he expected Mrs. Dahlquist to be early. He had told her that she was to pick up the letter at two sharp, no earlier, no later, and she sounded scared enough to do exactly what he said. But he liked to check things out because Ollie was too smart to overlook the possibility that the Dahlquists had gone to the police in spite of his threat to kill the baby. That was the difference between the pro and the amateur: think of *everything*. Little things, like remembering that the Dahlquists had a sample of Ricky's handwriting, so his letter had to be typed or they'd know that someone besides Ricky had become involved.

He recognized Mrs. Dahlquist instantly. Young, small, curly blond hair. She was a helluva lot prettier than her picture in the *News-Record*. When she went into the post office, Ollie followed her. She stopped inside the door, hesitated, and hurried to the counter with the sign saying GENERAL DELIVERY. Ollie crossed the lobby at a casual pace and lined up behind her, simply a man waiting his turn.

"Excuse me.... Do you have any mail for Mrs. Dahlquist?"

The clerk glanced up briefly. "First name?"

"Mrs. Leif. Laurie."

"One minute." He pulled a handful of letters out of the slot marked "D," and went through them briskly like a dealer counting out cards. "Yup. Here's one."

"Thank you very much." The young woman wheeled around so quickly that Ollie didn't have time to get out of the way. "Oh!" Her face was so close that he could see her freckles. "I'm so sorry. I didn't mean to bump into you."

"It's all right, ma'am."

"Sorry..." she said again and all but ran out to the street.

The postal clerk said, "Yessir?"

"Mail for Denny Sharp." It came out smoothly, no telltale hesitation. That was what practice did for you.

The clerk pulled letters out of the "S" compartment, flipped them onto the counter one at a time. "Not today."

"Is that right," Ollie said. "Well, I'll try tomorrow."

"You can't receive mail by General Delivery for longer than thirty days. Then you've got to rent a box."

"Yeh," Ollie said. "I'll do that."

On the street he looked for Mrs. Dahlquist but she had disappeared. That was good, because he didn't want her to get another look at him. That little scene at the General Delivery window was something he hadn't counted on. He had followed her because he wanted to hear what she said to the clerk. Ollie shrugged. So Mrs. Dahlquist would recognize him if she ever saw him again.

At a quarter to three, Howard and Martin

Dahlquist left their cars in a parking garage south of the public market. At the elevator, Howard said, "We separate right now. Young Ochsner might not come to the market until later, but chances are he's here now. He knows we don't know what he looks like, and all these shoppers milling around make good cover. He'll want to make sure the man who drops the medicine into the litter barrel is Martin Dahlquist and nobody else."

Across the street from the north end of the market, a neon sign saying DRINK OLYMPIA BEER glowed in the fly-specked window of Ken's Market Tavern. Howard stopped in front of the tavern. While he fished in his inside pocket for pipe and tobacco pouch, he stole a glance at his watch. Five before three. Martin was just coming down the street, carrying the package in his hand, keeping it in plain sight. He was walking too fast, and looking at his wristwatch too often. And as he approached the litter barrel, he hesitated several times and then, as if he were diving into cold water, he lunged at the litter barrel and dropped the package into it. Without a backward glance, he continued up the street.

"Be obvious," Howard had advised. "When you've dropped the bottle, leave. Assume you're being followed. Walk to the garage, pay your ticket, drive home. I'll stay in the tavern, all night if necessary."

When Martin disappeared around the corner, Howard went into the tavern, picked up a schooner of draft beer at the bar, and carried it to a table with a good view of the litter barrel. The kidnapper must have had a reason for choosing his pickup spot. Ten to one, because it was familiar territory. So he must have taken the city garbage truck's schedule into consideration, and would know that he had to get the medicine out of the barrel before six A.M.

Two hours passed. Howard's beer had gone flat and he was getting hungry. Across the street the crowds were thinning out. Vendors were buttonholing the strollers and shouting bargain prices. In another hour, whoever made the pick-up couldn't possibly get lost in a crowd. And still nobody had seemed interested in the litter barrel except to throw something into it.

Howard had just signaled the bartender—"Draw me a fresh one, Den"—when an all-too-familiar figure emerged from the alley just north of the market. He had the shuffling, unsteady walk of a drunk. A dirty canvas bag was slung over his shoulder and he was proceeding straight to the litter barrel.

"Damn!" Howard muttered. "No! Not that one, Sammy, you silly bum!" But there was no stopping him. Nothing to do but sit at the window of Ken's and watch one of the most thorough scavengers on the waterfront dive into the barrel with both hands. Sammy plucked a treasure, dropped it into his canvas bag, dipped into the barrel again. A bunch of rotting bananas. Three returnable Coke bottles. A mildewed orange. And then, inevitable, the parcel containing a large bottle of the baby's medicine.

Sammy straightened up and squinted at the package. He held it up to his ear and shook it, a toothless grin spreading across his face as the nature of the loot dawned on him. With his bag in one hand, and the bottle in the other, he abandoned his southbound route and began to stagger back in the direction from which he'd come. Howard had known Sammy for years, and more than once carried him to the nearest dry-out mission. Today Sammy was flying. It wasn't every day of the week that a man would find a full bottle in a trash can.

Howard watched helplessly while Sammy began his slow retreat. Suddenly another figure, taller than Sammy, broke out of a cluster of shoppers and ran after the old man. He overtook him, grabbed his arm, and tried to wrench the package out of his hand.

Sammy was old and sick but he put up a fight. He dropped the canvas bag, jerked his arm free, lowered his head, and butted his attacker in the stomach.

The taller man made another grab for the package. Sammy swung himself around, arms beating the air. But he lost his grip on the package, which sailed across the street, missed the window of Ken's Market Tavern by a foot, and hit a brick wall with such force that even inside, Howard heard the sound of breaking glass.

He jumped up, ran out into the street, and raced after Sammy's assailant. The man turned and ran up the steep hill toward Second Avenue. At Second, Howard had to stop and catch his breath. The other man continued up the hill and, at Third, disappeared around the corner.

Frustrated and angry, Howard returned to Ken's, paid his bill, and walked to the parking garage. He wasn't looking forward to telling the Dahlquists their child wouldn't get his medicine tonight, and that he had been within thirty feet of the kidnapper without getting a look at his face.

Seventeen

OLLIE WHITE OPENED a new pack of cigarettes and sat down to figure his next move. After beating up the man from Ricky's office, he couldn't show his face there again, but he'd learned where Ricky lived and that was worth a lot more than a visit where he worked. When a guy has kidnapped a million-dollar baby, the smart money says he won't show up for work as usual.

Tuesday night at the Wendell Arms, Ollie had missed Ricky. But it figured that he would show up at his apartment at least once a day, if only to keep that mailbox empty. Hundred to one, he'd have the baby with him; a kidnapper is a guy who doesn't dare trust anyone. So Ollie White would wait patiently at the Wendell Arms.

Thursday night his patience paid off. A gray VW slowed down outside and Ollie got a good look at the driver as the car passed under a streetlight.

Ollie waited in his own car until Ricky had gone into the building. Then he drove around the corner, pulled up to the curb just ahead of the gray VW, and jumped out, leaving the motor running.

But luck was against him. There was no baby in Ricky's car, nothing but a bag of groceries on the front seat. Ollie reached through the open window and looked inside the bag. Baby food. The sight made his heart skip.

He closed the grocery bag, ran back to his car, and backed up until he was beyond the range of the corner streetlight. In a few minutes, Ricky appeared, walking rapidly. Without a glance in any direction, he jumped into his car and drove off.

Ollie was laughing to himself as he put his car in gear and began trailing the VW. What a setup! He'd been a piker to peg the ransom at only a hundred thousand. After he grabbed the baby, he'd give the Dahlquists another call.

When Ricky turned into the Maple Leaf Lodge, another car came to a stop, backed up a few feet and followed him into the parking lot. As he was about to open the door, Ricky froze. Something about the blue Ford bothered him. If the driver was another guest, why had he driven past the entrance so that he had to back up before he turned in? And why was he still sitting in the car? The danger was intangible, but it was there.

Ricky got out of the car, carrying the sack of groceries so that it shielded his face. His hand was on the doorknob when he heard a car door slam, hard-soled shoes thudding along the concrete sidewalk, and a man's voice, right behind him. "Okay, Ricky Cummins, you bastard. Open the door and go inside. No noise. No funny business."

Ricky said quietly, "What do you want, Ollie?"

"Oh *my*, 'What do you want, Ollie?' After all these years?" The nasal voice dropped to a hoarse whisper. "I want *in*. Either we do business together, or I take the kid and handle it alone."

Ricky felt the hard muzzle of Ollie's gun pressing

against his side. "Handle what, Ollie?"

"Don't get smart. You won't get no police medals for this one. Because if you call the cops, I'll give them an earful. Just remember that. *I've* got the goods on *you. That's* a switch." The nose of the gun jabbed him for emphasis. "Okay, Rick. Open her up. You don't want to talk about it out here, do you?"

Now that the danger was real and visible, Ricky's head cleared. The motel door was unlocked. The knob turned in his hand. He put his whole body into a sudden forward lunge which threw open the door. Ollie was caught off balance. He tripped over the threshold, staggered backwards into the motel room, and dropped his gun. Cursing, he ducked down to pick it up and in that fraction of a second Ricky was behind him. With a grunt of pain, Ollie stumbled sideways into the parking lot. Ricky jumped into the room, slammed and locked the door.

Marika was huddled in the corner with the baby in her arms. "He wanted to kill you."

Ricky nodded, too winded to speak, and dropped into a chair.

Marika came forward and stood in front of him. "I heard what he said. Eric *is* your baby, isn't he? That man called you Ricky."

"My name is Ricky. But the baby..." Ricky stood up. "Look, Marika, the man out there is armed. He intends to take the baby away from me. He'll shoot me, or you, or both of us if he has to." Ricky went to the window and lifted the shade just enough to see into the parking lot. Finger to his lips, he walked back to Marika and guided her to the far side of the room.

"I couldn't see him, but his car's still there. He's waiting. I wish you could walk out and get into your car and drive home. But that's impossible. You couldn't run fast enough. You'd be the hostage he needs."

Marika's large black eyes looked at him steadily. "There's the telephone. But you don't want to call the police." It was a statement rather than a question.

Ricky shook his head. "Only as a last resort. Someone besides myself would be hurt very badly. I want to prevent that, if I can."

The baby stirred and whimpered. Marika whispered, "Sshh, sshh ..." swinging her arms in a gentle rocking motion. Was the commitment to the baby, or to the man? Or was it her own needs that commited her to them both? "I'll help you, Ricky," she said softly. "I think I know what to do."

In the shadow of the manager's office, Ollie cursed Ricky Cummins. Anger was eating into him like acid. So near, so goddamned near. But he'd get the baby all right. Ricky and the girl couldn't stay in there forever.

Suddenly the windows of Number 15 darkened. A siren sounded faintly in the distance—the angry wail of a police car headed this way. Ollie's body stiffened. Another siren sounded from the opposite direction. By the time Ollie had reached his car the Ford's rear-view mirror picked up the revolving red lights. Without turning on his headlights, Ollie raced out the driveway. He was around the corner and out of sight when the police parked outside the office.

The manager of the Maple Leaf Lodge was perplexed and a little irritated. "But I *am* the manager," she insisted. "And I did not call the police."

"The lady who called reported that an armed man was prowling around the vicinity of the Maple Leaf Lodge. She said she was the manager."

Clara Holden shook her head vigorously. "I don't know who called you, but it wasn't me. And I haven't seen a prowler."

The officer said patiently, "I'm sorry to bother you, ma'am. It might have been a crank."

The manager shrugged. "Well, I suppose you get

those, don't you? Listen, I didn't mean to be smart. If someone is nosing around here I hope you find him. Please look around all you want."

The door opened and a second officer came in. "Nothing out here, Jim. We've really poked into the corners."

"All quiet, eh."

"One old man taking his dog for a walk. Young couple and baby came out of fifteen and drove away in a gray VW."

The manager exclaimed, "Why, that's Marika's . . ."

"Ma'am? The car that just left? It belongs to someone named Marika? Anything unusual about her being here tonight?"

"No, no. She works here sometimes. Baby-sitting for motel guests."

"If she was baby-sitting for the man in Room Fifteen, she might have seen someone she thought was a prowler and called the police."

"I doubt it. She's not the kind to see goblins in the dark."

"Just in case, ma'am. Do you happen to know the license number of her car?"

The manager looked straight into his eyes. "Sorry, officer. I haven't the faintest idea."

"But you do know where she lives? And her telephone number?"

The manager shook her head. "Used to. But she's moved."

When the squad cars had gone, Clara Holden checked her watch, waited forty minutes, and then picked up the telephone.

Marika replaced the receiver and turned to Ricky. "I had to answer. Clara calls me about this time every night. Just to make sure I get home all right." She crossed the room and sat down on the couch next to the sleeping baby. "You couldn't get the medicine."

"They didn't have it. They said they could get it by tomorrow or the day after."

"Ricky, this child needs it *now*."

"I know, I know!" Ricky jumped to his feet and walked to the window.

"Ricky..." Marika followed him and pulled him back to the couch. "Please sit down. I'm going to help you. But first, tell me the truth."

Ricky shook his head. "You don't want to hear it. You're not mixed up in this thing, except for my being here, and I'll leave as soon as I can find another place. It's not your problem, Marika. Don't say you're going to help me, because you can't, without getting tangled up in a very bad situation. Don't get involved."

Marika smiled. "It's too late, Ricky. I already am. Now please, while the baby's sleeping, tell me whose baby this is, and why you are so desperately frightened."

After they had all read the letter Laurie brought back from the post office, Howard took the note from "K. O." out of his pocket and placed the two communications side by side on the breakfast table. "I'm beginning to get some funny vibes about this kidnapper. Something I should have suspected when he telephoned last night." Frowning, Howard turned the pages of his small spiral notebook to the heading "Wednesday, March 16. Telephone conversation with Mrs. Dahlquist." "We've received a total of five messages. Two notes, one telephone call, and two classified ads in the Personals column. This one"— Howard pointed to the second note—"interests me the most."

"Why, Jack? The fact that it's typewritten strikes me as odd," said Martin. "But I'm not sure why."

"I'm not sure, either, but I know one thing: the note left in the playpen gave us a good sample of his handwriting. Why should he bother to use a typewriter for the second note?"

Martin exclaimed, "My God, Jack. Are you suggesting he wrote on a typewriter to prevent us from comparing his handwriting with the writing on the note from K. O.?"

"That's my guess. If it's right, you can see where it leads us."

Martin said dully, "We're dealing with two men, not one."

"It looks that way. The first man kidnapped the baby. He claimed to be Ochsner's son and I'm convinced that he is. The second man wants us to believe *he* is the same person who stole the child and left the note in the playpen. And there are one or two other indications that two men are involved. Take the wording of these messages. The first is eloquent and grammatical. The man who telephoned last night said *Listen to me good* and referred to your child as *the kid.* In the letter he ordered Laurie to pick up at the General Delivery window, he proves he can't spell. Look at this." Howard's forefinger moved across the page. "Mr. Dahlquist—spelled D-A-L-L-G-U-I-S-T. He isn't literate enough to get your name right. Both on the telephone and in his letter, his English is crude.

"Then there's the difference in their demands. We've all been puzzled by the fact that Ochsner's son is concerned about the baby's health and hasn't said a word about ransom. The man who phoned last night demanded a hundred thousand dollars in his letter. He doesn't even mention the baby's health, though we know that after five days without his medicine, little Leif is bound to be showing some serious symptoms. See what I mean?"

Laurie gasped. "The second man is pretending to be the kidnapper and he's pretending to have Leif so that we'll pay him the ransom."

"At this point," Howard said carefully, "it's mostly speculation and there are more questions than answers. For instance, the symbolic Ochsner signature, the all-too-familiar triangles within a circle. It appears on both these letters. Does that mean Ochsner's son and the other man are working together? I think not. Why would K. O. commit a crime that could cost him his life and let another man negotiate details for collecting the ransom?

"On the other hand, if they are *not* partners, what are they? K. O. kidnapped the baby. How did another man enter the scene? From everything we know now, I say he forced his way in. That he is someone who knows Ochsner personally, who discovered what Ochsner had done and decided to cash in."

Elizabeth Dahlquist's face was drained of color. "Mr. Howard, which one has little Leif?"

Howard said thoughtfully, "I'd say the man who tried to get the medicine is the one who has the child."

Martin said angrily, "In other words, the second kidnapper wants to collect the ransom but won't be able to return the baby."

"Not *now*. If he did have the baby, this letter would include definite instructions for the payoff. He must be afraid that you'll pay the ransom to Ochsner's son unless he gives you proof that the child is in his possession. Something the baby is wearing, for example. When he calls again, Mrs. Dahlquist, I think you should ask him to describe the baby's clothing."

"I'll try," Elizabeth said.

"If he refuses to answer, it would seem likely that he hasn't even seen the baby." Howard paused and continued more quickly. "Don't worry, Mrs. Dahlquist. We'll go right on negotiating with him, whatever he says. We'll deal with him just as we are dealing with Ochsner's son—by doing exactly what we are told to do. Laurie, did you place another ad in the *News-Record?*"

"Yes. Saying—'To K. O. We await further instructions.' Waiting, waiting... My child is missing and all I can do is wait."

"I know it's hard," Howard said. "But we're doing a lot more than waiting. We're looking for K. O., and we've made some progress. Tomorrow, please God, we'll make a little more. Let's go over our schedule...." Laurie seemed a little comforted. She wouldn't be, Howard thought grimly, if I confessed that the idea of a second kidnapper scares me silly, because I believe that he is hunting for Ochsner, too, and the baby's life depends on our finding him first.

Friday, March 18

Eighteen

THE OLYMPIC COUNTY HISTORICAL SOCIETY was a small concrete-block structure built and maintained by innumerable rummage sales, quilt raffles, potluck dinners, and bingo games. The society's most devoted members had a foot in the past and had crowded the two-room building with relics of their own family histories. There had never been a curator, since every member past the age of sixty felt qualified to decide what was "historical." No donations had ever been refused.

The elderly woman in charge on Friday morning confessed to sentimental memories of the late Professor Marshall. Jack Howard made no claim to kinship with the professor, but when he asked to see Marshall's diaries and manuscript, she exclaimed, "My cup runneth over! Your uncle was a dear, *dear* friend. Though he was years older than I. Come with me, Mr. Marshall."

Howard considered correcting her and decided against it. "Thank you very much," he said, following her into the back room. "I wish I had known him, too."

The woman led him to a desk surrounded by storage cartons stacked almost to the ceiling. "Now you sit down here, and I'll find Professor Marshall's papers. We do need shelves, don't we? Everything here has been donated, you know. I do wish someone would donate some shelves. . . . Here. Here it is." She set a cardboard box on the desk and blew off the dust. "There you are, Mr. Marshall. I'll leave you alone now. I'm up front, if you should want to call on me."

Howard began with the manuscript of *A Child Is Missing*, searching for references to the Ochsners. There were long passages about Klaus. Professor Marshall had been particularly eloquent in describing their midnight meeting in the cemetery, which he saw in retrospect as the most dramatic episode in the entire Dahlquist case.

He also devoted three pages to personal impressions about Lisa Ochsner's brief appearance in court, from which Howard learned that "Henny" believed the kidnapper's wife was ignorant of her husband's "Damnable crime" until the day of his arrest. From beginning to end, *A Child Is Missing* was sentimental and vague, an old man's last effort to be remembered for his role in a famous case.

As soon as he opened the diaries, Howard realized he should have read them first. Professor Marshall had preached and rambled when he wrote for publication, but daily jottings that were for himself alone were brief and factual. Howard scanned the first volume rapidly. What he needed most was the name Lisa Ochsner adopted after her husband's death. If it was mentioned it would be in the last entries, written late in 1936. He put down the first volume and opened the last one. January, another appeal. February, first anniversary of Ochsner's conviction. March, date of execution. April, all avenues of appeal exhausted. . . .

Toward the end of the volume the professor's

handwriting became more and more irregular and the logical procession of facts gradually disintegrated into often incoherent rambling, in which he saw the Ochsners as "tragic figures" almost on a par with Leif and Elizabeth Dahlquist. He was obsessed by the fact that he, alone, had seen Klaus Ochsner as a human being "with a nice and kindly voice." Pity and guilt were mingled in his references to Lisa and her son, and he spoke of going to her home on Grummin Street, where she "broke down, cried bitterly and said she was going to change her name and disappear and if it weren't for Bübchen she would destroy herself."

The next words were badly spotted with black ink but they gave Howard the information he had been praying for. "... Will the poor woman suffer less as Mrs. Cummins, or more because of the secret she can never reveal to her son? If God is merciful..." The passage ended with this incomplete supplication.

Howard opened his spiral notebook, and wrote, "Mrs. Cummins, probably Mrs. Lisa Cummins," and added the approximate date of Professor Marshall's visit to Grummin Street. Now at last he had a link between the past and the man they were looking for.

Of course Klaus's widow may have changed her name more than once, or changed her first name as well as her last. But that was unlikely. Long experience had taught Howard that discarding a family name produced a sense of loss and a strong desire to retain at least the given name. Moreover, the man who has changed his name instinctively tries to build identity and "family" into the new name and rarely adopts still another pseudonym. So the chance that the Dahlquists were searching for "Lisa Cummins's" son was a good one.

"Cummins?" The policewoman tapped the counter with the end of her pencil. "You wouldn't happen to have a first name, would you, Jack?"

"Don't get flip, Officer Dunning. You're young, beautiful, and smart, but a little deference would be in order. Cummins. Male, Caucasian. Around six feet, brown wavy hair."

She raised her eyebrows. "What a description. It sounds like you've seen him only from the back."

"You're right, as usual. Now go push all the levers on that electronic monster in the other room and come back and tell me if the guy's got a record."

Howard was still trying to get a pipe going when she was back with a piece of paper covered with numerals and bits of shorthand. "I don't know whether this is *your* Cummins, Jack, but this Cummins is in trouble. Monday this week he got a citation for speeding and related violations. There are different ways of spelling the name, by the way. With a G or with one M instead of two. I checked them all. The clan Cummins seems to be unusually law-abiding. There are a few things, nothing serious, and they're pretty old. This one is still warm, so I thought it might be the one you want. Ricky Cummins. Driver of white Plymouth sedan, license OYT 457. Lives in Apartment 28, the Wendell Arms, 33 Fidalgo. Say, you have a law degree, don't you, Jack? Why don't you take the case, if you can find him?"

Howard grinned. "Who said I lost him?" He took the pipe out of his mouth and looked into the barrel as if a clue was hidden in the ashes. "Cummins. Ricky Cummins. Officer Dunning, honey, thank you very much."

"I've got more, Jack. I checked with our public information office and guess what?"

"I'm afraid this one is going to cost me a lunch at the Space Needle."

The policewoman laughed. "I'm afraid of heights. Okay. Here's what I discovered in the PR file under Cummins, R. About five years ago, he got a special commendation from the department for exceptional bravery in the face of grave danger. Our release said an attempt to rob Schneider's grocery on the corner of Sixth and Dixon was aborted by the courage and quick thinking of Ricky Cummins, Apartment B, 611 Caldwell. Though severely wounded, Cummins attacked and overpowered the hold-up man, Ollie White, and held him while the owner's wife summoned the police." She looked up and asked, "That do you any good?"

"Five years ago he was a hero. This week he runs a police blockade. I think my old psych professor would call that aberrant behavior." Howard tapped the bowl of his pipe against his heel. "Do you have any pictures?"

"One. Our photographer took it while Cummins was still in the hospital. I'll bring it out but it doesn't show what Cummins looks like, with just a pair of swollen black eyes and a lot of bandages. Want to see it?"

Howard shook his head. "But one more favor, please. Go back to your rap sheets and this time look up Ollie White."

The policewoman nodded. "Convicted of armed robbery about five years ago, right?" Howard nodded.

When Officer Dunning returned, she was smiling. "Pay dirt. Maximum sentence was twenty years. Minimum sentence set by the parole board was five. Ollie White was released on parole Monday of this week. Five days ago."

Howard's next visit was to Lew Backstrom, parole supervisor for the Seattle region.

"White? Ollie White?" Backstrom grumbled. "Yes, Jack. He's one of ours."

Howard grinned. "And if he had asked for parole to another region, you would have approved."

"Approved! I would have rejoiced. But he insisted on Seattle. It's his home. We had to take him."

"He hasn't got much of a record."

Backstrom grimaced. "It's not long, but it's ugly."

"Has he been in yet? He's supposed to report in forty-eight hours, isn't he?"

"He reported in, all right. All slicked up, full of Yes sir, No sir, You're absolutely right, sir. I wish he belonged to somebody else."

"Anything wrong so far? Is he clean?"

"Jack, for chrissakes, he's been out less than a week. Give him time." Backstrom pressed his lips together and shook his head. "No, nothing wrong. He's staying at a residential hotel near the factory where he supposedly has a job waiting for him. When he was in here Tuesday, he told me he had a line on something better. I gave him permission to look into it before he reported to the other job. He swears he hasn't got a gun. I don't believe him but I can't prove that he does. No financial bind, at least for the moment. Besides his gate money he inherited a little from his mother. She died while he was in jail. He reports one purchase—a secondhand car, and I approved that. So..." He shrugged.

"But you have no reason to suspect that he might be involved in something?"

The parole supervisor hesitated. "Well, no. I see one soft spot. Like the little shadow on the X-ray that shows the dentist there's a cavity. White bought his car at an agency where another parolee, Alfred Potter, has been working for the past two years. With fifteen hundred inmates they didn't have to know each other, but they were in at the same time. But hell, all White did was buy the car from the place where Potter works. I can't make a violation out of that."

Howard opened his notebook. "All right if I take down his residence and the name of the outfit that sold him a car?"

"Why not? Hey, I just thought of something. I've got an extra mug shot." Backstrom opened a desk drawer, fished through the contents, and handed Howard an inch-square black and white photo of a man with small eyes, thin straight hair, and lips that seemed cast in a permanant sneer. "Pretty, isn't he? I'll tell you, Jack. If he's into something, I hope you get to him before I do."

"That dangerous?"

"That dangerous," Backstrom said. "Because he's part shrewd, and part stupid. He's the kind who would fire his gun when it wasn't necessary."

"I hope it won't be," Howard replied, waved his thanks and left. It was ironic, he thought as he waited for the elevator, that his first thought was to warn Cummins that he was in danger!

It was lunchtime and Al Potter had agreed to go out with Ollie for a sandwich and a beer. He was a little nervous about it. He hadn't been one of Ollie's friends in the penitentiary. In fact, Al had tried to steer clear of the guy. Just a feeling. But now there was a common bond. They had done time together and Ollie was just beginning the rough first six months on the street. Al couldn't refuse to be a little friendly. Nevertheless he was on guard. He wouldn't let Ollie talk him into anything.

While they ate Ollie talked about some of their friends and they laughed at jokes on the warden they had both heard a dozen times. Ollie didn't even hint at something out of line. As the half hour passed without a problem, Al felt so relieved that when Ollie did ask a favor he said, "Sure, Ollie, sure."

Ollie showed him the license number of a gray VW. The car had followed him when he left his hotel in the morning. He was afraid it was someone from the parole office, trying to check on him. He wasn't doing anything, but it gave him the jitters. He didn't want to tell the tail to get lost if it was a parole agent. If it wasn't... Well, he'd worry about that later.

Al said, "All you have to do is write a letter to DMV in Olympia. Enclose two bucks and tell them why you need the information. Or make up something, if you don't want to mention your parole officer. You'll get the information from them in three or four days."

Ollie said, "But I can't wait that long. Look, you work for an auto agency. If you phone DMV, they'll give you the facts in ten minutes flat. I'd sure appreciate it, Al."

Al wished Ollie hadn't asked, but it was such a small lie that he agreed to make the call. Fifteen minutes later Ollie knew that the car Ricky Cummins had parked outside Room 15 of the Maple Leaf Lodge was registered under the name of Marika Malama of 1104 Crescent N.W.

Howard hurried from the courthouse to the Hotel Alaska with a list of telephone numbers in his pocket. He thanked the Lord that he had some good news to report to Black River.

Elizabeth Dahlquist answered.

"It's Jack Howard," he said quickly. Every time the telephone rang, he knew she would be expecting the kidnapper, but she sounded calm. "No, Mr. Howard. There hasn't been another call. I'm well, thank you. Yes, truly..."

Howard told her about discovering the key names—Cummins, né Ochsner, and the probable second man, White. "I feel very much encouraged. Now we're not groping in the dark. I'm going to follow up with some more calls and I'll get back to you by three o'clock at the latest."

Howard sat at his desk by the window and reviewed his notes. His first choice was to pursue Mrs. Cummins. He knew that she was very close to her son and that she had been hospitalized after the trial as a psychotic. He would try phoning several Seattle institutions on the chance she might have been readmitted or that they knew her whereabouts. He had decided that the chance of Ricky's being at his own apartment was slight.

The first hospital had no record of a patient named Lisa Ochsner. 1936? Oh well, of course. The facility hadn't been built at that time. Lisa Cummins? No, sorry.

The second call was no more enlightening. Yes, the hospital had been in operation since 1929 but patients' records from the early years had been lost in a fire. Files dating from 1943 were available but there was nothing in them about a Mrs. Lisa Cummins.

The clerks in the first two hospitals were cooperative, but when Howard called the third institution his questions met with terse answers and repeated references to the confidentiality of patients' files. Howard's frustration peaked when the voice announced in clipped tones that a Mrs. Lisa Cummins had been a patient for two years. Discharged four years ago to an accredited nursing home with special accommodations for the mentally ill. Name of the nursing home? Confidential. Home address? Names of next of kin? Confidential.

"Your name means nothing to me, Mr. Howard," the voice stated coldly, "but we can open our files if given the proper authorizations..."

Howard hung up, swearing. Maybe Lisa Ochsner's medical history was a red herring. Then he remembered his discussion with the Dahlquists.

Ricky had lived all his life with the need to avenge his father. Why had he finally decided to act? Howard recalled his own words: "For years, revenge has been a dream. And then suddenly something happens, to him or to his mother, which creates more emotional stress than he can cope with. And the dream becomes a reality." State hospital records showed that Mrs. Cummins's last confinement had ended four years ago. If she had been well since that time, and then suddenly something happened—"Of course!" Howard said out loud. Dahlquist's death. The dramatic headlines. The rehash of the whole trial with pictures of her husband.

Howard picked up the receiver and dialed a number he knew by heart. The county hospital. In the admissions office another old friend was glad to hear his voice. Lisa Cummins. Age 70. Residing at 122 West Hurley. Emergency treatment for burns, sedation, Sunday, March 13. Transferred same day to Sylvan Home West, psychiatric wing.

Elizabeth Dahlquist said, "Yes, Mr. Howard. Yes, I got that. Please go on. . . ." As she listened, she wrote a few words on the scratch pad beside the telephone. "Thank you *very* much. I'll tell them."

She replaced the receiver and turned to Martin and Laurie. "Mr. Howard has found her. The widow. Lisa . . . poor Lisa! I saw her, you know, the day she testified." Elizabeth's voice broke off. She recovered quickly and began to read Howard's message.

"Mrs. Ochsner . . . Mrs. Cummins . . . is a patient at a nursing home called Sylvan Home West. It's north of the city, on the old road to Everett. He's going to drive up. He believes . . ." She paused, one hand shading her eyes, and finished in a whisper. "Mr. Howard believes that her son will never go very far away from his mother."

Martin said, "We're nearer to Everett than he is. He didn't suggest that Laurie and I visit the nursing home?"

"No, Martin. He was obviously in a hurry. Perhaps he didn't think of it, or perhaps he assumed you'd prefer . . ." Elizabeth looked up at her son. "Do you want to go?"

"I certainly do. Laurie, we'll drive up together."

Elizabeth looked troubled. "I got the impression that Mr. Howard had a specific reason for visiting the nursing home alone."

"Did he say so?"

"No."

Martin said impatiently, "I can't stand much more waiting. Laurie and I may not learn a lot at the nursing home but we'll have the satisfaction of trying."

"Please, Martin. If there is a reason..."

Martin leaned over and kissed her cheek. "Good-bye, Mother. Try to rest. We'll be back as soon as possible."

Elizabeth watched in uneasy silence as the two of them pulled on raincoats and hurried out to their car.

Nineteen

RICKY OPENED THE *News-Record* and pulled out the classified section. "Marika?"

Marika came out of the kitchen with a cup of coffee in each hand and sat down beside him. "Is it there?"

"Yes." Ricky accepted the coffee and read "Personals. To K. O. We await further instructions."

Marika's wide slanted black eyes looked at him sadly. "Oh, Ricky. They say *further* instructions. They think the baby has his medicine by now. They don't realize the bottle was broken."

"Maybe not. But I've got a hunch that they do. Mr. Dahlquist left the market as soon as he dropped the package into the litter barrel. I had been watching for at least two hours when the drunk came along and ruined everything, and I'm sure Mr. Dahlquist didn't come back. But there's something else. Someone chased me when I bolted and ran. I didn't dare look back so I never really saw his face but I'm sure he was shorter than Mr. Dahlquist." He turned to Marika. "You see why I didn't want you to get mixed up in this?"

Marika nodded. Her eyes were solemn but there was a softness to her mouth that was almost a smile. "You think the man who chased you had been waiting for you to pick up the medicine. Have the Dahlquists gone to the police?"

"I don't know. I think if the police had been waiting they would have caught me. But if they weren't watching why would anyone run after me?"

"Ah . . ." Marika picked up the paper and reread the Dahlquists' classified ad. "There are two ways to interpret this, Ricky. The baby's parents do not know what happened to the first bottle of medicine. Or they want *you* to believe that they don't know."

"Exactly."

"I think they *do* know." Marika rested her hand on Ricky's arm. "You told me you never intended to hurt the child. You said you were going to return him to his parents, that all you wanted to do was scare them. I think you were saying—You see? I am my father's son. I am not capable of killing a child and that proves my father wasn't either."

"Yes, Marika," Ricky said hoarsely. "It's twisted thinking, but that's it."

"It was a terrible thing to do." Marika's voice was sorrowful but not at all accusing. "Ricky, you always meant to return the baby. If the Dahlquists have called the police, it's going to be difficult."

"They *have* called the police. Marika, that man who ran after me . . . there's no other explanation."

"No. I don't think there is. So I will take the baby home."

Ricky looked into her face. Her eyes were bright, her smile confident. "Incredible," he said. "You mean it, don't you."

"From the heart."

For several minutes Ricky couldn't speak. This young girl with the oriental eyes and small red mouth had stirred feelings he had never experienced. There had always been a kind of insulated airspace between himself and the girls he had loved. Eventually each girl had discovered it and left, but in three days Marika had penetrated his defenses. She was on his side, smiling at the suggestion that she shouldn't be there. "Marika..." He shook his head and tried again. "Marika, you are placing more trust in me than you should."

Marika's eyes danced. "Haven't you got that backwards? You've told me you're a kidnapper. You've tole me your real name. Do you trust anyone else as much?"

"My God, no."

"I didn't think so. Now let's be practical. I will bundle the baby up and drive to Black River. Just give me directions to the Dahlquist house."

"It's not as simple as that." Ricky stood up, walked to the window, and looked out.

Marika said quietly, "There's no one there. I just looked."

"You are not going to leave this building without me." Ricky returned to the sofa. "You said, let's be practical. I agree. First of all, I think the police have been notified. They will be all around the Dahlquist place. They will be anyplace you might arrange to leave the baby."

"I suppose so. But *I* didn't kidnap the baby. I could have found him someplace."

Ricky smiled. "I didn't realize anyone could be more of an amateur than I am. 'Found him someplace'? How would you explain knowing whose child he was?"

"I could take him to the police, and say a woman came up to me in the supermarket and asked me to watch him for a few minutes but she never came back."

Ricky shook his head. "Maybe that's better, but you're not going to try it. Your explanations might be believable, though I doubt it, because I'll bet you're no

good at lying. It wouldn't matter. No one can walk into
a police station with a 'found baby' and get a 'Thank
you very much and goodbye' and walk out. Besides . . ."
Again he went to the front window. "Don't forget Ollie
White. If he saw you and the baby, you'd never get to
the police station. He might not hurt you but he would
take the baby."

"But he doesn't know where we are. He couldn't
have followed us from the Lodge. He'd left before we
did. Ricky, he's never seen me. He wasn't inside your
motel room for more than a few seconds and I was
hiding in the corner behind the sofa."

"Marika, I know he hasn't seen you. He won't
recognize the baby. Say you got to the police station
and the police accepted your story. The story would hit
the papers. Heir to Dahlquist fortune survives a vicious
crime. Kidnapped child returned . . . Ollie White would
read all about it in the papers. In the length of time it
would take him to get to the telephone, the police
would know my name." Ricky thrust his hands into his
pockets and looked down at his feet. When he spoke
his voice was low but decisive. "I don't know what's
going to happen, but I know we stay right here today.
We're safe. The baby's safe. Maybe he'll get better."

"He won't, Ricky. Honestly, he won't."

"We'll get the medicine. I can still place an ad in
Saturday's paper. Or I'll call their home. . . . No, the
police would be listening. They might be able to trace
the call. God, Marika, I can't think. Tomorrow . . ." He
pulled his hands out of his pockets, strode across the
room, and picked up the telephone. "Tomorrow . . . but
today I've got to make two telephone calls. And that's
all I'm going to do. Today."

In his nest of blankets at the end of the sofa, the
baby began to cry. Marika picked him up and cuddled
him with her cheek resting on the top of his head. For a
moment time was standing still. She and the baby and

the tall man with blue eyes were floating between what had happened and what was to come. She began humming a Hawaiian song. Ricky's voice seemed to be coming to her from a great distance.

His first call was to his office. Ricky was beginning to explain his absence when the excited voice of the receptionist cut him off. Marika watched curiously as he murmured, "I see . . ." every now and then. When the woman finished, Ricky recited the explanation he had planned. He was too sick to stay in his apartment alone; he had been staying with friends, and that's why they hadn't been able to reach him by phone. Yes indeed, he would be extremely careful, and he expected to be well enough to return to work on Monday morning.

The second call was to the nursing home to ask about his mother. "About the same? No improvement?" Then he said he hadn't been in to see her because he'd been ill. Would one of the nurses be kind enough to explain? He was very sorry he hadn't been able to visit. . . . There was a pause while Ricky listened, a longer pause after he'd replaced the receiver. Marika watched him anxiously. Finally he spoke. "The nurse said, 'Yes, Mr. Cummins, do try to visit her soon. She hasn't had any visitors all week. Not until just a few minutes ago. They're with her right now.'" He rose and walked back to the window. Looking down in the street, he said several times, "Who could they be? Who knows where she is? *Who are my mother's visitors?*"

Marika hugged the baby, and did not try to answer.

Martin and Laurie introduced themselves at the nursing home as high school classmates of Ricky's. When they entered Lisa's room, she was on her back, with eyes closed. At the sound of Martin's voice, the eyes flew open, the head turned. Instantly her face froze in an expression of blind terror.

"We didn't mean to startle you," Laurie said gently, and recited the rest of their story. It had been years since they'd been back to Seattle. Years since they'd seen Ricky. But they had always corresponded and only the day before yesterday, they received a letter from him urging them to look him up the first time they came to town. . . .

Mrs. Cummins hadn't moved or blinked her eyes. She seemed paralyzed by the sight of them. Smiling reassurance, Laurie went on with the explanation. "So we went to the Wendell Arms, but of course he wasn't at home. We shouldn't have expected that he would be, on a weekday. Unfortunately his letter didn't mention his business address. It did say his mother was ill and if he wasn't home in the evening, we would find him at Sylvan Home West."

Still no response. Now the frightened eyes were fastened on Martin. Laurie whispered, "Marty, would you . . ."

Martin said quietly, "I think we're disturbing you, Mrs. Cummins. I'm sorry. You see, we have only a few hours in Seattle. We'd hate to leave without seeing Ricky, or at least talking to him on the phone. Please tell us where he works. We'll call him there."

Lisa Cummins's staring eyes narrowed and her lips moved, forming words without sounds.

"Mrs. Cummins?" In an effort to hear her, Martin leaned forward. She pulled back like a startled bird, clutched her bedspread and drew it up under her chin. A few words came out between lips that hardly seemed to move.

"Excuse me. The bakery? Whose bakery?"

The pale lips answered. Martin nodded and stepped back from the bed. Together they thanked her, wished her a speedy recovery, and hurried out of the building.

They left for Holstein's at 183rd and Grummin exhilarated by their success. Their plan for what they would do when they got there was half optimism, half hope. The personality portrait Jack Howard had been building gave them reason to believe Ochsner's son was neither cruel nor insane. "Please give us our baby. He is ill. He will die without the proper care...." Surely that appeal would touch a man who had shown so much concern about obtaining the baby's medicine. And he would see that they hadn't brought police, therefore had not ignored his warning.

The address alone convinced them they were speeding toward Ricky Cummins. Grummin and 183rd—the area they had canvassed before, Klaus and Lisa Ochsner's old neighborhood.

When they saw a sign at the end of the block for HOLSTEIN'S BAKERY, they parked and peered apprehensively through the bakery window. A plump girl of eighteen or nineteen was polishing a glass showcase filled with decorated cakes.

They went in. The girl's crisp white smock and scrubbed soap and water complexion were as reassuring as her homely task. She was friendly, and willing to talk, though their questions puzzled her. She was Dottie Holstein, the owner's daughter. She had worked in her father's bakery since she was ten years old. It was a small shop. It wasn't hard to remember the names of all the bakers Father had hired. There had never been an employee by the name of Ricky Cummins. The name Ochsner meant nothing to her either.

Laurie looked up at Martin and could not hold back the tears. The Holstein girl stared with a mixture of sympathy and curiosity. Martin thanked her, put his arm around Laurie, and led her to the car.

"Never mind, Laurie. We were misled, but we couldn't have known."

Laurie murmured, "She tricked us. She knew Ricky doesn't work here. She lied."

"Not exactly," Martin said thoughtfully. "There is a Holstein's Bakery, and there was a Holstein's Bakery forty years ago. I should have remembered. That's the kind of thing Jack Howard wouldn't have forgotten. Holstein's Bakery is where Lisa Ochsner was working when Klaus was arrested for the kidnapping of my brother."

They returned to Sylvan Home West almost as fast as they'd left, eager to plead again for the name of Ricky's employer. Jack Howard's Buick was in the parking lot. Inside Howard was standing talking at the nurses' station.

They both stopped, unsure of the implications the nurse might draw from their knowing him. But he acknowledged them with a friendly wave and joined them in the waiting room.

"You were here earlier this afternoon."

"Yes. For a few minutes."

"Were you asked for your names, or your relationship to Mrs. Cummins?"

"No. There were no questions at all."

"When you talked to Mrs. Cummins, did you introduce yourselves by name?"

"No, Jack. We didn't. And she didn't ask."

"Fine. I wanted to know what names you used, in case they weren't your own." The detective smiled but it was obvious he wasn't pleased.

Martin said uneasily, "Look, Jack, you didn't ask us to meet you here. Perhaps we acted unwisely. We seemed to terrify Mrs. Cummins, and when she finally told me her son's business address, it was a false lead. A bakery. Holstein's Bakery, where *she* had worked when Ricky was a baby."

"Yes, I know." Howard began exploring his pockets. "Damn. Not even one pipe. Six packs of matches and not one single pipe." He sighed. "Yes, I'm sure you did frighten poor Lisa. It wouldn't have mattered what names you used, or how you explained your visit. She recognized you. I'm sure of it. And I'm equally sure that Ricky has told her what he's done. She knew why you were here."

Martin said, "Jack, I'm sorry. Laurie and I will go back and talk to her again. Perhaps we can convince her that we are not going to hurt Ricky. That all we want is our child."

"You can't, Martin," said Howard abruptly. "Lisa Cummins has disappeared."

One important discovery was still to be explored. Ricky Cummins lived in the Wendell Arms. He wouldn't be there with the baby—of that Howard was certain. But they might uncover some important facts.

Late in the afternoon they parked around the corner from the Wendell Arms. By agreement, Martin and Laurie waited in their car while Howard went into the building and made an appraisal. He was back in ten minutes.

"He's not in his apartment. At least he didn't answer when I called on the intercom, though that's not proof he isn't there. The doors of the tenants' mailboxes in the foyer have frosted glass panels. His box is empty."

Laurie exclaimed, "Then he's been picking up his mail!"

"So it would seem."

"Jack..." Laurie paused and gave him a wistful smile. "Now we have a way of giving him a bottle of medicine, haven't we? We could leave it with the apartment manager. And perhaps drop a note into Ricky's mailbox telling him where to pick it up. I think he would, don't you?"

Martin said anxiously, "Laurie, that would be telling him we know where he lives."

Howard nodded. "And that we have discovered his name. He doesn't know either of those things.

Generally speaking, the less he knows we know, the better our chances of finding him."

"But he would have the baby's medicine!" Laurie's head fell back against the seat and she closed her eyes. "I'm sorry. I know I'm no help when I shout or burst into tears."

"Courage, kids," Howard said. "Let's take one thing at a time. Laurie, you don't happen to have a copy of the prescription with you, do you?"

Laurie sat straight and opened her eyes. "Why yes, I do. It's a new drug, so the doctor gave me several slips, in case the pharmacy we usually go to is temporarily out." She opened her handbag and a zippered compartment on the inside and produced three pieces of paper. "Yes. Here they are."

"Good." Howard was looking thoughtfully into the distance. "The health of the baby is our first consideration, right? What have we got to lose by revealing that we've been to the Wendell Arms? The fact that Ricky has picked up his mail safely has probably convinced him that you are heeding his warning against notifying the police. So your knowing where he lives isn't going to increase his risks by a whole lot. He knows what you both look like. He's had a week's experience at staying in the shadow. Actually..." Howard squeezed his lower lip between thumb and forefinger. "He's proved that he really wants the medicine. But he's discovered that it's damned difficult to pick up and he may not be willing to try again. So leave it here."

Martin and Laurie drove off toward the business district and Howard found a spot across the street from the Wendell Arms where he could sit down while he watched the front entrance. He had been worrying about the incident at the public market the day before. His impulse to break cover and chase Ricky Cummins might have been as foolish as the Dahlquists' presenting themselves at the bedside of a woman who was bound to know their faces. His mistake in the market had been to believe he could overtake Ricky.

People came in and out of the Wendell Arms, cars drove into the parking lot at the rear, but it all looked routine until a sports car stopped near Howard's perch on the bulkhead.

A man got out and said to the driver, "Two seconds, Joe."

The driver left the motor running, while the other man sprinted across the lawn and went into the foyer. Howard wasn't wearing his glasses but his distance vision was excellent. The man put something into one of the mailboxes and ran back to the car.

Howard waited a few minutes. Then he, too, ran across the lawn and into the foyer. The mailbox for Apartment 28 had been empty a half hour earlier. It wasn't now.

Martin and Laurie returned with the medicine. "Very good," Howard said. "Now, we've got to assume Ricky might show up to collect his mail or to get something from his apartment. So I'll have to go into the building alone. Ricky would recognize you." Howard left the couple in the car.

Apartment 28. Second floor . . . First, check the apartment. The service entrance at the back of the building was illuminated by one hundred-watt bulb, and could not be seen from the street. Howard took a penknife out of his pocket and went to work.

Inside, he walked up the back stairs to the second floor and moved soundlessly along the carpeted hallway to Number 28. The lock there also responded to his touch. He pushed the door gently and went in.

The apartment was dark. He groped for the hall switch, found it, and as he was closing the door he saw something he hadn't noticed when he was picking the lock. The brass panel around the keyhole was badly scratched; the marks were shiny and probably fresh. Holding the doorknob, Howard pushed the door gently and slowly released the lock. Somebody else had broken into Apartment 28, and Howard had a good hunch who it was. If the evidence hadn't been so sinister he would have been amused to learn that in five years inside the walls, Ollie White hadn't learned to pick a lock without leaving scratches.

Howard's search was rapid but thorough. Everything he found confirmed his belief that Ricky had not been living in his apartment since Sunday. Sunday's paper strewn on the living room floor, but no papers from later in the week. In the refrigerator, an unused half gallon of milk so sour it looked like rennet custard.

He looked over to the sink. Scraps of soggy paper were pieced together on the drainboard. The ink was blurred but the words he could read told Howard this was the same message Ricky had left in the Dahlquist baby's playpen. Torn up, thrown into the kitchen garbage pail after a corrected copy had been made— that was Ricky's work. But pawing through the garbage and putting the fragments together—that had to be Ollie White. Howard thought: now we know what put Ollie on the trail.

Howard went out as quietly as he came in. In the foyer he worked on the mailbox with frequent glances over his shoulder. The lock was tricky, but he had succeeded when he saw a woman approaching. He pushed the mailbox door so that it appeared to be shut. When the woman opened the door, his back was turned. He was a man busy reading the list of occupants to find the apartment number of a friend. The woman opened her mailbox, withdrew some letters, unlocked the inner door and went inside.

Again Howard opened Ricky's box. It contained one envelope, thin enough to see through. He held it up to the light and squinted. It was a paycheck, with a sketch of a building in the upper left-hand corner and the name of a firm superimposed in prominent letters. A paycheck.

Howard read the return address on the envelope with rising excitement and then put the envelope back in the box. Next he took the bottle of medicine out of his pocket. As he had hoped, it wasn't too large. He slid it into the box, closed the door, and stepped outside.

For the benefit of tenants who might be looking out their windows, his pace was casual. After a few steps, something flashed across his peripheral vision—to the left, where at night a dense cluster of shrubs and flowering trees provided cover for someone watching the Wendell Arms. He had considered using it himself while he was keeping watch on the entrance. Slowly and deliberately, Howard went through the familiar routine with the pipe and the match folder. By now he was absolutely sure someone was hiding in the bushes to his left. The whispering sound of branches brushing against a moving body. Two glimpses of a pale sphere that had to be a man's face.

Howard heard twigs snap, saw a huge rhododendron swaying as if someone had fallen against it. Suddenly a man broke out of the tangle of dark foliage. In the split second before he bolted across the street, Howard saw his face.

Run after him? No sir, he'd learned his lesson the day before at the public market. He could have shot him but he couldn't take the chance of killing the only person who could lead them to the child.

Cursing, Howard returned to the car where Martin and Laurie were waiting. He was chagrined at losing his quarry for the second time, but he had at least discovered Ricky's business address: Pitt, Dobbs, and Webster.

Saturday, March 19

Twenty

WHEN JACK HOWARD telephoned the architectural firm of Pitt, Dobbs and Webster, a man's voice advised him curtly that the office was not open for business on Saturday.

"This is urgent. And I promise it won't take long."

"I'm down here to catch up on some work. I'd a helluva lot rather be out on the golf course."

"It's about Ricky Cummins."

There was a pause, and then the voice added briskly, "What was your name again?"

"Howard. Jack Howard. I'm a private investigator."

"Okay, Howard. I'll be expecting you."

On the way Laurie asked, "We're the Whitestones. Jim and Martha. But tell me, Jack, what explanation do we offer for inquiring about Ricky Cummins?"

"I've been debating that point," Howard said. "It depends on how much the man will tell us. If he's just a clerk we won't get much. But I've got a feeling that the guy we're going to talk to is one of the owners. They're the only ones who work on Saturdays."

After a pause, Howard continued, "To answer your question, Laurie, I think the way to get this guy to open up is to tell him the truth. Not the whole truth," he added quickly. "Not your true names, or anything about the kidnapping. But the truth about our relationship. I'm Jack Howard, private investigator, and you're my clients. After that, back to fiction. You are distant relatives of Ricky Cummins. Martin is an attorney involved in the probate of a will through which Ricky will inherit a considerable amount of money. Your letters to him have not been answered, and you have failed to reach him by phone. You need his social security number in connection with death taxes, and other information necessary to probate proceedings. The point is to ask questions he can't answer without looking into the personnel files. Even then he may not be willing to hand Ricky's file over to us. So while he's reading, we're going to practice reading upside down."

The door to Pitt, Dobbs, and Webster was opened by a man wearing blue jeans, sweatshirt, and tennis shoes. "Come in," he said briskly. "I'm Gordon Pitt. Let's sit over here." He led them to a corner of the reception area where three abbreviated sofas in three shades of purple were grouped around a square coffee table with an antique copper top. His manner was friendly but businesslike. It said, Never mind the chitchat. Get on with it. It was an attitude Howard liked because it usually meant his own time wouldn't be wasted, either.

"Mr. Pitt, these are the Whitestones. Jim and Martha. I'm Jack Howard." He opened his wallet and held it out so that Pitt could see his license.

"I've heard of you," Pitt said brusquely. "Friend of mine hired you couple of years ago. I want to know what your interest is in Ricky Cummins."

Howard stuffed his wallet into his inside breast

pocket. "The Whitestones have retained me to help them expedite the probate of an estate," he said in a matter-of-fact tone of voice. "Ricky Cummins is one of the heirs."

"So?" Pitt said. "What's that got to do with our firm?"

"Cummins is employed here."

"Sure, sure. Has been for five years."

"We hoped you would help us locate him."

Pitt's air of limited tolerance vanished. "My God, Howard! You're telling me you can't find him?"

"Not so far. That's why we're here."

"You've tried the Wendell Arms?"

Howard nodded. "We did."

Pitt frowned, studying Howard's face as if he were debating how far he could be trusted. "I don't like it, Howard, I don't like it at all. You know what happened here last Tuesday?"

"Tuesday?" Howard's mind automatically ticked off the events of the past week. Tuesday. Two days after Ricky Cummins kidnapped the Dahlquist baby. One day after Ollie White was released on parole. "Tuesday?" he repeated. "No, sorry."

"Our bookkeeper was severely beaten by a man who waylaid him in the alley. He's still in the hospital. The man didn't take his wallet. He had a gun, but he didn't use it."

"Not a robbery. Did your bookkeeper have enemies? Someone who hated him enough to beat him up?"

Pitt said sourly, "You can't hate a man if you don't know him. The bookkeeper had never seen his attacker."

"He wanted some information."

"Exactly. He wanted Ricky Cummins's home address. And he got it."

"That's bad." Howard opened his wallet again and

pulled out the small photograph he'd picked up at the regional parole office. "That the man?"

Pitt studied the picture. "You understand, I didn't see him myself. No one did, except our bookkeeper. He's described him, to us and to the police. Insofar as a verbal description is reliable, I'd say this is the man. At least it could be the man. Who is he?"

"Oliver White," Howard replied. "Recently paroled from the penitentiary after doing time for armed robbery. He's been carrying a grudge for five years. He thought Cummins was his rap partner, but Cummins blew the whistle."

"By golly—" Pitt jumped to his feet. "I remember that! Rick was wounded. He got a commendation .... Hold on. I'm going to get Ricky's file. There might be something in it that would give you an idea of where to find him."

While Pitt was digging into a cabinet at the other side of the room, Howard said, smiling, "Well, we won't have to worry about reading upside down."

Howard wrote in his notebook as the three of them went through Ricky's file. Education. Marital status. Previous employment. The name of Ricky's bank. His social security number. And then something unusual.

Unlike many small businesses, Pitt, Dobbs, and Webster gave every employee a physical checkup once a year. Ricky's medical history included the fact that he had been a regular donor to the county blood bank for the past five years. A marginal note had been added to one of the dates on the list of his donations. "February 10, 1974. Mother underwent major surgery. R. C. wanted to donate blood. Refused."

Laurie read the terse notation several times, trying to decide what was wrong. Ricky had wanted to donate blood when his mother needed it but, for some reason, it was not acceptable. It must have been something to do with blood types. She went back to the top of the blood bank report. Type A. That was curious. Wasn't "A" a very common type?

They left the architect's office with thanks to Gordon Pitt and a promise to call him when they located Cummins. "I don't get it," Pitt said at the door. "He calls in Monday morning to say he has the flu. Nothing strange about that, especially this time of year. He calls again Thursday, and it's news to him that someone has damned near killed our bookkeeper in order to get his home address. I'd say that it's pretty plain this man you say is Ollie White is more than a loving friend trying to get in touch with an old buddy. Two full days pass, and he still hasn't caught up with Rick? How do you figure that?"

"Maybe Cummins hasn't been living in his own apartment."

Pitt nodded vigorously. "That's it, of course. When he phoned Thursday he told the receptionist we hadn't been able to reach him because he was so sick some friends insisted he stay with them. He also asked Nelson, one of our draftsmen, to drop his paycheck off at the Wendell Arms on his way home from work Friday evening. Then the girl told him about White, and suddenly Rick was in a tearing hurry and cut her off in the middle of the sentence." Pitt raised both hands in an expression of hopeless confusion. "What's going on, Howard? You got any ideas?"

Howard said cryptically, "One or two. One for sure. White's looking for Cummins, and so are we. For different reasons."

As he drove back to Black River, Howard reviewed the various items on his list of leads. Two of the names had such low priority that he hadn't attempted to trace them—the telephone company linemen who discovered the Dahlquist child's corpse in 1932. They had also been the ones to find the yellow mitten that had been identified as one of a pair the Dahlquists' Irish nursemaid had knitted. But it was unlikely that the linemen were still alive.

Even less likely, Howard realized, that if they were alive they would be able to tell him something that would speed the search for Ricky Cummins. But a long shot can pay off, Howard reflected, and time is running out. He would drop Martin and Laurie off at their home and check with Elizabeth to see if she had received another telephone call. If not, he would leave the three Dahlquists alone for a few hours and do a little exploring in an area so painful for them that he wouldn't discuss it unless it paid off. The yellow mittens. One found on a county road only a short distance from the Dahlquist estate. A second in Lisa Ochsner's possession all through the long trial and then, on the eve of her husband's execution, mailed to the baby's mother as proof that Klaus was not the murderer. Two yellow mittens...

The Green Hill Telephone Company was a small independent concern owned by the son of the man who had set the first telephone poles with a horse and buggy in 1907. The main office was in the village of Green Hill within five miles of the Leif Dahlquist estate, The Aerie. As Howard had feared, it was closed on Saturday afternoon, though there was undoubtedly an operator somewhere in the building to handle calls for special assistance.

An accomplished jewel thief had once given Howard a valuable observation: "When a woman is real careful, she never leaves the house without locking the front door and checking the locks on the windows. Then she walks out to the garage and leaves the kitchen door open." A commercial establishment isn't a residence, but Howard hoped the back-door maxim might apply.

He walked to the back of the telephone building. To his surprise, the door was wide open, revealing a corridor with four office doors open as well. He caught the odor of pine-scented disinfectant. The vinyl floor was still wet. Howard called, "Anybody here?"

A woman appeared at the far end of the corridor, pail in one hand, mop in the other. "Nobody but mé and her." Her head bobbed in the direction of an inner office where Howard guessed a telephone operator was working. "Mr. Murchie left some papers for me to pick up," Howard said, referring to the owner. "He told me you'd be cleaning the offices today and you'd let me in."

The woman said, "Well, you got here just in time. I just finished mopping. Two minutes from now you wouldn't have got in."

"Hey," Howard said with feeling. "How lucky can you get?"

The woman's eyes were fixed gloomily on Howard's dusty shoes. "You won't be lucky if you track up my floors. Okay. Come in."

Four open doors. If he didn't know which was Mr. Murchie's office, she would become suspicious and probably decide to stick right with him. She was standing in front of one of the doors, scowling at his footprints. As he approached, she stood aside. It was a perfect signal. Thanking her, Howard went through the door her body had been blocking.

It was Murchie's office, all right, differing from those he had looked into as he came along the corridor not only because of the furnishings but because there were no file cabinets, business machines, or other useful devices. It certainly wasn't the room where he would find personnel records dating back twenty or thirty years. He was going to need time.

He picked up the letters a secretary had left on Mr. Murchie's desk for his signature, and went back to the corridor. The rear entrance was at his right. Immediately to the left of it was a narrow door he hadn't noticed before. A storage closet of some kind, Howard thought, hoping that it wouldn't be locked.

Muted sounds from the left indicated that the cleaning woman was around the corner muttering as she put mop, pail, vacuum cleaner, and other equipment-away.

Howard called, "Hullo?" She popped into view, wearing her coat. He waved the letters. "They were right where he said they'd be. Thanks a lot."

"Yeh," she said indifferently. "Have a good day."

When Howard reached the back door, she was out of sight. He tried the door at the left of the exit. It opened, revealing shelves loaded with office supplies, paper towels, soap and toilet tissue. He gave the door to the outside a shove that made it close with a loud slam, and simultaneously stepped into the supply closet and closed the door. A few minutes later he heard the cleaning woman open the back door and go out.

Now he was alone in the building, except for the special-assistance operator, who was undoubtedly chained to the inner-sanctum electronic equipment as surely as if she were in leg irons. Fantastic, Howard thought. Now for the search...

The names Howard had written in his notebook were Frank Sligo and Peter Downing. He had explored two out of the three offices before he found the one where old records were stored in cardboard boxes on the highest shelves of a closet smelling of mildew and stale air. In time, he came on an old ledger and a box of payroll records where the names of the two men appeared.

Frank Sligo, the older of the two, had still been working for Green Hill when he died. Peter Downing was younger, and was still in Green Hill's employ, but not as a lineman. Five years earlier he had been transferred to the small local radio station owned by the telephone company, where, as far as Howard could tell, he was still working as a night watchman.

The trip to the radio station was a brief one, and the night watchman was already on duty. Whether it was the loneliness of his job, or his natural temperament, Peter Downing was a loquacious man. He scarcely listened to Howard's explanation for being there. When Howard asked him to tell everything he could remember about finding the body of the Dahlquist baby, he launched right into his story.

"Funny you should bring up the same identical subject that's been on my mind all week. Oh, I guess the both of us seen the article in the *News-Record* last Sunday—that's what brought it all back for me, anyway. I tell you, mister, I could paint you a picture of what me and Frank seen even if it was forty years ago. Well, it was in March, you know. A bad stormy March, too. Me and Frank was on duty when a call came in, reporting wires down along Madrona Road. Man who called said he had to drive two miles before he got to a house where a phone was still in service. . . ."

Howard listened, nodding energetically whenever the old man paused.

The way they discovered the baby's body had always seemed peculiar. There they were, charging back and forth along Madrona Road, which in them days wasn't much more than a country lane, not even hardtop, and they couldn't find trouble of any kind. For damn sure the lines weren't down, no place. They were getting disgusted and about ready to report back when Frank saw something lying on the road.

It was a mitten, a small mitten for a child. Frank put it in his pocket, not for any reason except that it didn't seem right to leave it lying there in the mud. They were walking back to the truck when suddenly it hit them. This was the area police had been searching for three months, looking for the Dahlquist baby.

They ran back to the spot where they found the mitten. Frank went into the woods on one side of the road, and Pete the other. Neither of them had got twenty feet off the road when Frank yelled.

"There was the baby. Only halfways covered, mostly with leaves, and so terribly mangled you couldn't make out what he looked like. Not twenty feet from the road...."

At length the watchman finished his story, and for the first time seemed interested in his visitor. "What did you say your name was?"

"Howard. Jack Howard."

"Oh yeah. You said that before. Okay, Jack. Want a cup of coffee? It's Sanka." He grinned. "You know, I don't want nothin' that'll keep me awake."

Howard laughed, as he was expected to do, and declined. "I've got to get back home or the wife will start phoning bars."

"Yeah, they do that sometimes, don't they? I remember one time that..."

Howard broke in quickly. "I've got to take off but before I leave, I want to ask two questions. Okay?"

"Sure, sure. Shoot."

Howard reached into his pocket and took out the yellow hand-knit mitten Elizabeth Dahlquist had received with the letter from Klaus Ochsner's wife. Before he could say anything the former lineman exclaimed, "Shucks, that's it! That's what they used to prove that body was the little Dahlquist kid."

It didn't seem fair to the old man to deprive him of another detail for his story. "Remember, Mr. Downing, there would be two mittens, right? This isn't the one you found on the road. This is the other one." Before the watchman could ask, Yeh, then where did you find *that*?, Howard diverted him with another question.

"It's all ancient history," Howard said, returning the mitten to his pocket. "But while you've been talking, I've been wondering—what was it about finding the baby that struck you as peculiar? You said there was something you never did understand, even after the trial was over. What was that?"

Eyes narrowed, Peter Downing said, "Well, how would it hit you, Jack? A man who didn't give his name calls the company and says a whole bunch of phone lines are lying on the ground. We get there and no lines are down. We find a mitten, right out there beside the road—a bright color so no one going along Madrona could miss seeing it. That piece of woods had been searched by teams of fifty to a hundred men and *no one* found no mitten. Okay, mister. *You* tell *me*. What does that look like to you?"

Howard said, "Like someone wanted the body of the Dahlquist baby to be found."

"You're a smart man, Jack."

Elizabeth Dahlquist was dozing in her chair when the telephone rang. She reached for the receiver and looked across the room where Martin and Laurie were sitting.

"We're right here, Mother." Martin jumped up and took a position beside her chair. Unless the caller's voice was low or muffled he could listen in. He smiled and put his hand on her shoulder. "Mother, you'd better pick it up."

Elizabeth put the receiver to her ear. "Yes? Hello? Excuse me, can you speak up. Yes, that's a little better."

Though he leaned over his mother's shoulder so that his ear was only a few inches from hers, Martin heard only a few words. "More money...want baby alive...two hundred thousand...like I told you..."

The voice stopped abruptly, giving Elizabeth her first opening. "But we haven't that much money ready for delivery. You said one hundred thousand. We will get more. Oh yes, I promise you, we will get more. But we can't today. Or tomorrow. Not until Monday when the banks..."

The voice cut her off. It was louder now, as if the caller were agitated. To make it even clearer, Martin pulled the receiver a half inch from his mother's ear.

"Lady, I know the banks don't open until Monday. I'm keeping the baby until then."

"But we want him home! He isn't well. He needs..."

"Hey!" The voice was brusque. "Hey, your husband there? Maybe he wants to get the kid back more than you do. I want to talk to him."

Trembling, Elizabeth handed the receiver to Martin. "This is Mr. Dahlquist," Martin said. The nasal voice recited its demands: two hundred thousand, not one hundred thousand; any stalling around and it would be a quarter million. Martin remembered Jack Howard's suggestion that the next time this man called, Elizabeth should ask him to describe the clothes Leif was wearing. At the first pause, Martin said, "I will have the money by noon on Monday. It's yours, if you tell me what my son is wearing."

The reply was a string of obscenities. When it subsided, Martin said, "I don't know who you are, but I don't believe you have my child."

Now the moment of hysteria had passed. The caller's voice was low and angry. "Now you listen to me, Mr. Dahlquist. I'm going to give you one chance, and that's all. One more phone call, sometime Monday. That's when I tell you where to bring the money. You follow orders from me, nobody else. You keep the police out of it. Or your kid is going to wind up in Heatherfield Park cemetery right alongside your brother."

A click, and the line went dead. Martin replaced the receiver and went back to Laurie. He held her close with both arms around her until the shuddering spasms that racked her body finally ceased and she dropped her head on his shoulder and began to cry.

Monday, March 21

Twenty-One

A WEEK AND a day since Leif had been kidnapped. Laurie looked out her bedroom window on a storm as violent as the one that had been raging when Ochsner forced his way into the house. The tops of the pine trees whipped back and forth, lashed by a cold wind. Rain laced with sleet beat a staccato rhythm on the windowpanes while overhead dark clouds raced across a slate gray sky. Shivering, Laurie turned her back on the storm and went into her dressing room.

Today there would be another telephone call, and this time the muffled voice would tell them where and how they were to pay the ransom and recover the baby. Martin had already left for the city. He would be back in two or three hours with cash to meet the kidnapper's increased demands. Meanwhile, she could not bear to wait passively for the telephone to ring. Laurie put on boots and a warm dress, and went downstairs with a scarf and fleece-lined trenchcoat over her arm.

Elizabeth Dahlquist was sitting at the breakfast table with a teacup and a slender little book Laurie recognized as the collection of poems she often carried in her handbag. She looked up, concerned. "You're going out?"

"If you don't mind staying here alone. Today, with so much hanging in the balance..." Laurie's voice broke off.

Elizabeth nodded understandingly. "I know. Waiting is especially painful when you don't really know what you're waiting for. No, dear, I don't mind being here alone. I've been feeling so frightened I seem to have reached a point where I hardly feel at all. But you should have something hot before you go."

Laurie poured a cup of tea and drank it hastily without sitting down.

Elizabeth watched her anxiously. "Should I know where you're going?"

"Yes, of course." Laurie pulled on her coat, covered her head with the scarf, and tied it under her chin. "I'm going back to the rest home. Not because I expect to discover anything important. Just to give myself something to do so I won't explode or start crying. If Jack calls, or if Martin comes home before I get back, please tell them that if Mrs. Cummins has returned I won't ask to see her. I'm just going to... Oh Lord, I don't know. Just going to keep moving..." At the back door, Laurie turned around suddenly and went back to the breakfast table. "I'm just beginning to know you," she said quietly. "Whatever happens, you'll show me how to live with it." She leaned down and kissed Elizabeth's cheek, which was soft and smelled faintly of lilac. "I love you, Mother."

Elizabeth looked up into her face. "You have more strength than you know. I'm old and tired. I'm the one who needs someone to lean on. So we'll help each other. Whatever happens, we'll do what we have to do."

As she opened the back door, Laurie waved

goodbye. "Keep safe," Elizabeth said, and then Laurie closed the door and clutching her headscarf, ran across the yard to her car.

The nurse at the Sylvan Home West reception desk greeted Laurie with a motherly "My goodness, child, you look half drowned. Here, give me your coat and scarf. I'll hang them up near the radiator." That done, she returned to her desk. "Well now. I know most of the regular visitors, but I don't believe I've seen you here before."

"My husband and I were here Friday afternoon. Just for a few minutes." Laurie paused. Seeing nothing but friendliness in the nurse's round face, she plunged ahead. "We came to visit Mrs. Lisa Cummins."

"Oh dear, oh dear." The nurse clicked her tongue. "Mrs. Cummins. Poor woman. Are you a relative?"

"Well, yes. Distant relative. My husband and I were in high school with her son Ricky."

The nurse said enthusiastically, "Isn't he a fine man, though. He couldn't treat his mother better. Oh, my..." The nurse's face showed concern. "Did you expect to visit Mrs. Cummins? Haven't you heard?"

Laurie said quickly, "Yes, we know that she ran away. I came by hoping to hear that she's back, or that you've heard where she is."

"No, she hasn't, Mrs. . . . ?"

"Mrs. Whitestone."

The nurse shook her head. "She's not here, Mrs. Whitestone. And we have no idea where she might be. Poor thing. Out someplace, in a storm like this."

"Perhaps she's with Ricky."

"No, no. She isn't with him. He's been calling us three or four times a day, asking if she's here."

Laurie murmured, "Long distance..."

The nurse's eyes opened wide with surprise. "Long distance? Why no. I shouldn't think so. I'm sure Mr.

Cummins wouldn't leave town until the police have found his mother."

"No, of course not. You're right." Laurie hesitated. What more had she expected? They had hoped to find Ricky by finding his mother, but there was nothing to be learned here, unless, perhaps.... Laurie grasped the last small shred of hope. "I've got an idea. I remember that when Mrs. Cummins wasn't well, but didn't need to be hospitalized, she often stayed with some people who had also come over from Austria. I've forgotten the name, but I think I'd recognize it. It would probably be in her medical records."

"Well, now," the nurse responded, eager to be of help. "Let's just have a look. We wouldn't have much medical history if this was the first time she was a patient here, but she's been at Sylvan Home before."

She disappeared into an adjoining room and returned with a file folder. She opened it and began reading silently, a plump forefinger sliding down the page as she skipped through the report looking for a reference to friends with an Austrian name. Occasionally she read a few words out loud, but for the most part she raced from page to page while Laurie tried with an increasing sense of futility to make sense out of information she was forced to read upside down. When the nurse came to the last page, she closed the file, "Well now, that's a shame. There aren't any Austrian names in here and no reference to home medical care."

"I'm disappointed," Laurie said with genuine feeling. Her hastily improvised fabrication about the "people from Austria" had succeeded in producing Lisa Ochsner's medical history, but it had failed her as a means of studying the record. "Thank you very much. You've been very cooperative."

"Glad to," the nurse said.

Like an eleventh-hour reprieve, her curiosity about Ricky's aborted attempt to donate blood for his mother flashed across Laurie's mind. "Oh, one question, please. What is Mrs. Cummins's blood type?"

The nurse was puzzled, but warmed by Laurie's appreciation she reopened the file. "Type O."

"O ..." Laurie repeated. "Well, thank you again."

"I'll get your coat. Oh, wait a minute." A red light was blinking on a panel of lights beside her desk. "Number four. Excuse me, Mrs. Whitestone. I'll be right back."

While the nurse hurried down the corridor, Laurie turned the open file around. When the nurse returned, the folder was just as she had left it.

"Well, now," the nurse said briskly. "Your coat and scarf." She glanced at the rain-washed window. "You're sure you want to go out in this? It might let up after a little while."

Laurie thanked her again, explained that she had an important appointment, and hurried out to her car. Like the "people from Austria," the appointment didn't exist. She was on her way to the nearest public telephone booth where she could call Jack Howard without being overheard. The medical record had proved fruitful after all.

The notation of Lisa Cummins's blood type had been attached to a reference to major surgery she had undergone in 1931. Type of operation: hysterectomy. But on the job application Laurie had seen at Pitt, Dobbs, and Webster, Ricky Cummins's date of birth was January 13, 1933. So Ricky Cummins, born Eric Ochsner, could not be Klaus Ochsner's natural son. Had the Ochsners adopted him? Or was the kidnapper an imposter, pretending to be the son of a man known all over the world as the kidnapper and murderer?

The baby's wailing became weaker and weaker, until at last he fell asleep. Marika put him down gently and covered him with her sweater. When she was sure he was truly asleep, she left the sofa and joined Ricky at the window.

"He's much worse, Ricky," she said. "Better in some ways, since I've been giving him the soybean milk, but in other ways he's definitely losing ground. He doesn't vomit now—I think that was caused by the cow's milk—but he seems to have trouble swallowing. And his eyelids droop, even when he's awake. His arms and legs are kind of..." She shook her head in an expression of helpless concern. "Well, they're kind of floppy. I'm frightened, Ricky. He's getting weaker all the time."

Without taking his eyes off the street outside Ricky said, "Yes, Marika. I guess we both know what we have to do."

"He's sleeping now. Shouldn't we wait until he wakes up?"

"I suppose so." He turned to face her. "Marika, there are some things I want to say. This might be our last chance."

They sat down at the small table by the window. Marika extended her hand and he grasped it. "Thank you," he said quietly. "This makes it easier." With his eyes on their clasped hands, Ricky said, "First, let's go over our plan. We'll go to my apartment and pick up the medicine I saw the man put into my mailbox. From there to a doctor, to make sure there isn't something wrong with the baby besides the fact that he hasn't been getting his medicine. Do you still agree to that?"

Marika nodded. "Yes, Ricky. Though we can't be positive that the bottle you saw contains medicine, or even that it was your box he put it into."

Ricky said grimly, "I *am* positive. That was the same man who chased after me when I ran out of the public market. Maybe he's a detective. Maybe not. In any case, he's acting as an agent for the Dahlquists."

"So he might very well be keeping watch at your apartment. And he will recognize you."

"We agreed that was a chance I'd have to take."

"No, Ricky. I agreed with your general plan, but not with that part of it. He's never seen me. We'll park the car a block or two away and *I'll* get the medicine. If he's watching, he'll have no reason to suspect I'm not just one of the tenants. And when I leave the building, the bottle will be inside my handbag."

Ricky shook his head. "Ollie White might be waiting at the apartment, too."

Marika said earnestly, "Let's assume that he is. He has never seen me either. Ricky, I think Ollie is an obsession with you. Do you realize you've spent the better part of two days watching the street, as if Ollie would pull up to the curb at any minute? But he couldn't possibly know where you are now."

"I know. I know. It's not logical, but I'm afraid."

"Look, Ricky. If by some sort of miracle Ollie knows you and the baby are here in this apartment, we'd have spotted his car."

"Remember . . . I didn't get the license number."

Marika smiled sympathetically. "Ollie's really gotten to you, Ricky. Granted, we don't know the license number. But we do know the car's color and make. In two days I haven't seen one single light blue Ford sedan anywhere in the vicinity of this building. Listen to me . . ."

Marika pressed his hand urgently. "You're so quick to believe the worst. You're so afraid to be hopeful. We *are* safe here. And I'll be perfectly safe when I pick up the medicine at the Wendell Arms. We have two very important things going for us. We know what kind of car Ollie is driving, and he doesn't know where we are. Our plan will work, Ricky. By tonight, the baby will have his medicine, a doctor will have examined him, and he'll be on the way to recovery. Then we can work out some way to return him to his parents."

Ricky looked thoughtfully into her wide dark eyes. He saw no trace of fear or suspicion. Only trust. "Marika, Marika...Are you sure? There is another way."

"You'll take the baby and drive to the nearest police station and no one will ever know you've been hiding in my apartment or even that you know me. Right?"

"Exactly."

"It won't work, Ricky. Because if you do that I'll go to the police station, too."

Ricky released her hand, stood up, and peered down into the street. "I've never in my life felt as desperate, or as *wrong*. And I have never felt as loved. God, Marika, how can you look at me the way you do? It makes me supremely happy, and totally miserable, all at the same time." He wheeled around and faced her. "Take a good look, Marika. Can you love *me*?"

Marika stood in front of him, looking up into his face. In a clear and steady voice she said, "I don't want a better man." And then she was in his arms, clinging to him as desperately as he was clinging to her, and though she could not see his face she knew by the choked sound of his breathing and the dampness against her cheek that he was crying.

At the agency where he had bought the Ford, Ollie White was making another deal, and silently saying a word of thanks to his mother for remembering him in her will. Money is the key to everything, Ollie reflected, as he counted out the hundred and fifty dollars it took to exchange the old blue clunker for a not-so-old sand-colored Mercury.

"You're a good man to do business with," he said, giving Al Potter a conspiratorial wink. "Stick around. The way I'm getting up in the world, I'll be back in a few days asking what you've got in Lincoln Continentals."

"I'm not going anyplace," Al said, feeling a little squeamish about any transaction with Ollie and especially one that seemed to indicate sudden prosperity for Ollie. Al's street-wise mind told him it meant trouble. "I've got a good job here. Not making me wealthy, but it's steady. My boss knows I'm a con and he still trusts me."

Ollie hooted, "Don't tell *me* your story. I'm not your goddamned parole officer."

"What I mean is . . ." Al was defeated by the problem of telling Ollie to back off without making him so angry he would be sure to hound him. "You got a good buy there. A lot more car than the Ford."

Ollie grinned. "You said it, Al. A better car for Ollie, in more ways than you know. So long, old buddy."

"Yeh. So long." Al managed to keep smiling until Ollie had driven out of the lot and disappeared into the flow of traffic.

Laurie was puzzled by Howard's reaction to the facts she had uncovered at Sylvan Home West. He hadn't been in when she telephoned from a booth near the rest home, so during the long drive to Black River she had been anticipating the shocking effect of her news. Martin and his mother reacted as she had expected, but Howard didn't even seem surprised. From the start she got the impression that she was merely confirming something he already knew.

"Terrific!" he said when she had finished. "The blood type hit me, too, when we saw the note in Ricky's file. It reminded me of an old clipping about blood donors in the penitentiary. Klaus Ochsner was one of the first to volunteer. So after our visit Saturday to the architects' office, I phoned an old friend in the warden's office and asked him if they still had records from the thirties. He called back today. Most of the old files had been destroyed, but someone had decided Klaus Ochsner's file was a bit of prison history that shouldn't be thrown away. Now that you've discovered his wife's blood type, Laurie, the whole thing fits together.

"Klaus was Type B. Lisa is Type O. Ricky is Type A. He cannot be their son. But Ricky could be Lisa's son by another man, which raises interesting possibilities. Until Laurie came up with this discovery of her hysterectomy I was thinking along those lines. Now we know I was on the wrong tack. By God, Laurie, you're a better detective than half the private investigators in Seattle. Or have I said that before?"

"But I don't understand what I've found. Did the Ochsners adopt Ricky?"

Howard answered the question with a noncommittal shrug. "It's a possibility. Well, I've got a little errand to do. Martin, I'd like you to come with me, if you don't mind. Laurie, stay close to Mrs. Dahlquist. That phone call could come at any time. She'll need some moral support."

"So will I."

Howard smiled sympathetically. "Of course you will. But you'll get it from supporting her." He turned to Martin. "Ready to go?"

Howard's explanation was brief. "I want to have a look at the cemetery." He seemed so preoccupied that Martin sensed questions would annoy him. Silence suited his own mood, for he was still trying to sort out Laurie's news. To "have a look at the cemetery" made sense. In his second telephone call, the man who claimed he had kidnapped Leif had referred to Heatherfield Park cemetery where his brother was buried. Howard obviously believed there was something to be learned from the grave in Heatherfield Park.

The route Howard was taking was so roundabout that Martin began to wonder if he knew how to get there. When Howard made a distinct wrong turn, Martin exclaimed, "Hey, Jack. We should have taken a right."

Howard said, "It's okay, Martin," and continued driving. A few minutes later, they were approaching the Great Oaks cemetery and Howard was braking the car.

"Jack, listen. My brother wasn't buried here. This is the wrong cemetery."

Howard said grimly, "No, it's the right one." But instead of driving in, he continued, executing a series of turns which eventually brought them to a wooded area at the back of the cemetery. He parked the car. "Excuse my rudeness, Martin. I know you're wondering what the hell we're doing at Great Oaks. Just bear with me a little longer. What I'm looking for is easier to show than to explain."

"No problem, Jack. What do you want me to do?"

"Come with me." Howard got out of the car and opened the trunk, revealing two shovels. He handed one to Martin and without another word led him through the woods to the cemetery grounds. "It's here someplace," he said, surveying the sloping green with its crowded rows of marble and granite monuments. "Look for the name Ochsner."

It was a small mound, with a simple headstone. The inscription had been eroded by rain and wind and partially concealed by green and orange lichens.

"Karl Ochsner. 1930-1932. God's Will Be Done."

Martin's gaze moved from the pitiful headstone to the shovel in his hand. "The Ochsners' first son, killed when he fell out of his father's car," he said. "We're going to open the grave?"

"Yes. I have a permit, by the way, in case the caretaker shows up."

"I wasn't even thinking of that."

"I know how you feel." Howard removed his coat,

picked up his shovel, and drove the blade into the ground. "This isn't a nice job. So let's get it over with."

They dug in silence. When they struck the top of the casket, they continued digging along one side until there was room to stand beside it. The hinges were rusty and the lock was badly corroded. With a sickish dread of what he was about to see, Martin helped Howard lift the cover.

"My God," Martin breathed. "It's empty."

Howard said quietly, "I thought it would be. But I had to be sure."

Twenty-Two

AFTER HOURS OF patient waiting, Ollie White was becoming restless. One after another, the pieces of his scheme had fallen into line, but the big one still remained, and he resented every hour that stood between him and the final payoff. To his way of thinking, his old adversary, Lady Luck, wasn't being fair to him. He'd been smart and therefore deserved better than to have to camp in the Mercury hour after hour, keyed up like a filly at the starting gate for the moment Ricky would leave the girl's apartment.

Her gray VW was standing in front of the building. He had a good view of it from his parking spot on the side street. Marika Malama... what a helluva name. Never having seen the girl whose apartment Ricky was holed up in was a handicap Ollie itched to wipe out. Knowing her name, her address, and the color and make of her car was his reward for playing it smart, but it didn't tell him what she looked like and that he needed to know.

Several women had gone in and out since he started

to watch the building, but no one had used the VW. Eventually, he was certain, Marika Malama would. Ollie hugged the gun against his side and thought how good it would feel to get even with Ricky, once and for all.

It was now growing dark. The wind had subsided but rain continued to splash on the windshield so that visibility from inside the car was dim. Ollie blinked. Two figures had come out of the apartment building and were walking toward the VW. Ollie switched on the ignition and the wiper blades swept away the rain. Jackpot! He'd lucked out. Ricky and the girl, and the girl was carrying a bundle wrapped in a blanket. They had to be headed for a meeting with the Dahlquists. Tonight must be the night. The waiting was almost over.

Two small question marks still bothered Ollie a little. He didn't know how much money Ricky had demanded or where Ricky was going to pick it up. The first didn't matter, because Ollie had already set up the Dahlquists for two hundred thousand dollars and even if they were disturbed by getting two different ransom demands they wouldn't dare ignore either one. Which meant the pot of gold was going to be even sweeter than he'd figured. What the hell. Money didn't mean anything to the Dahlquists.

The answer to Ollie's second question had fallen into his lap. Ricky was headed for the pick-up point. All Ollie had to do was hang back and let the little gray VW lead him to the end of the rainbow.

Ollie started up the Mercury and continued peering through the half circle cleared by the wiper blades. His insides were churning with excitement as he watched Ricky help the girl into the car. He grinned when he saw Ricky look up and down the street before he walked around to the driver's seat. Dumb bastard, Ollie thought. On watch for a light blue Ford. Doesn't see one and thinks he's safe . . .

At first Ollie didn't believe it, but when the VW turned east on Fidalgo Boulevard he knew. Ricky was headed for the Wendell Arms. The first place a cop or detective would keep under surveillance. It didn't make sense at all, unless . . .

Ollie tried to recall the exact wording of the note he had dug out of the garbage and pieced together on the sink at Ricky's apartment. Ricky's first message to the Dahlquists had said plainly that the kidnapper was Klaus Ochsner's son. No mention of the name Cummins. Ricky must be counting on the protection of his assumed name.

But how about me? Ollie thought irritably. He knows damn well that I won't quit until I get him. What kind of crazy is he, coming back to the one spot where he knows I could be waiting for him?

Two blocks short of the Wendell Arms, the VW slowed and turned into a side street. Ollie waited at the corner. Whatever this maneuver was all about, it probably didn't have anything to do with collecting the ransom. That would be the next stop. And since big bargaining power belonged to the man who had the child, Ollie was going to sit tight and stay close to the baby.

Ricky parked the VW and turned off the lights. A few minutes passed and then the door on the right side opened and the girl stepped out. So Ricky was sending the girl into the apartment. . . . The implication of this gave Ollie a nice warm feeling, like swallowing a shot of bourbon in one gulp. So Ricky *was* afraid of him, and the girl was doing his errands because they both believed Ollie would take her for one of the tenants. But Ollie was still one step ahead of them.

The girl walked to the corner of Fidalgo and continued briskly along the boulevard toward the Wendell Arms. A car crawling after her at five miles an hour would be suspicious, so Ollie waited until she was only half a block from the entrance. Then he put the Mercury in gear, drove along the boulevard past the Wendell Arms and took the first side street. He parked the car in the middle of the block, got out quickly, and giving his gun a nervous pat, began walking rapidly back toward the Wendell Arms.

The more he thought about the setup, the better he liked it. Marika Malama had never seen him. He could follow her into the building, he could look her right in the face, and she would just think he lived there. This was a bonus he hadn't anticipated, and it pleased him.

He trailed the girl up the sloping walk to the entrance, let a few seconds pass, then opened the front door and went inside. Marika was checking numbers on the bank of metal mailboxes. Her quick sideways glance recognized his presence but, as Ollie had expected, she took him for a resident, a man waiting politely for her to finish before he picked up his own mail.

He stood behind her, noting the way her long black hair glistened with rain. He felt a surge of eagerness to see her face. She drew a small package and some envelopes out of Box 28, dropped them into a large brown purse, closed and relocked the box. Ollie tensed. She was finally going to turn around . . .

He had been so sure she couldn't know who he was that her expression hit him as if she had dumped a bucket of icewater over his head. Her small mouth was open, as if the stiff lips were trying to scream, and her slanted dark eyes were wide with terror. Suddenly angry, Ollie snarled, "Wipe that look off your face."

She backed up until she was caught between him and the bank of mailboxes.

"I said, knock it off. I don't let girls look at me like that. Especially not some kind of gook."

The lips moved. "You're Ollie White."

So that was it. . . . Ollie's anger subsided as he began to enjoy the fact that she was terrified. "Yes, sweetie," he said, grinning. "And Ollie White is going to take you back to your car."

"I don't have a car. I live here. I just walked home."

Ollie allowed himself a short burst of laughter. "Try again, sweetie. How about a gray VW driven by a man named Ricky Cummins?" He saw her hand dart toward the buzzer marked Manager's Apartment and caught it just in time. He gripped her wrist, jerked her forward, and pinned her arm across her back. "Okay, little girl. You walk along quietly or I'll kill you. Got it? Good. Let's go."

Ollie was pleased about this girl. Scared stiff, but nervy. At the corner she tried to turn right, instead of left toward the VW. Still gutsy, though her whole body was shaking and her hand was ice cold. She made her last try when they were half a block from her car. Without warning she screamed, "Ricky, drive off! Quick, get away!"

Ollie's right hand hit her across the mouth with such force that she would have fallen if his left arm hadn't been supporting her. "There's more, if you try that again. Look, sweetie, he heard you, and he isn't leaving."

After that the girl did what she was told, like a machine, moving when he pushed the button. And Ricky also did what he was told, because when they got to the VW Ollie's revolver was aimed at Marika's head. It was really something, watching them move like a couple of robots. He ordered Marika into the back seat and Ricky to stay at the wheel. Then he got in beside Ricky and pulled the baby out of his arms. "You drive. I'm the baby-sitter from now on. Tackle me, you bastard, and you'll have a sweet time trying to make the Dahlquists pay ransom for a dead kid. Now, push off."

Ricky said quietly, "Where do you want to go?"

Ollie snorted. "With you. Where else?"

"I'm going to the police station."

The calm voice irked Ollie even more than the crazy lie. "Oh, for chrissakes, Ricky. You think I'm some kind of a moron? Get moving. Don't keep the Dahlquists waiting."

"I'm not on my way to meet the Dahlquists, or anyone else."

"Goddamn it!" Ollie's revolver poked furiously into Ricky's side. "Now you listen to me. You're going to get the money and the Dahlquists are going to get their baby, just like you planned. The only difference is that the ransom is going to end up in my pocket instead of yours. That's what you might call a story with a happy ending."

Once more Ricky's answer came so naturally and his voice was so steady that Ollie began to suspect he was telling the truth. "I've never talked to the Dahlquists. I have made no arrangements whatever for returning the baby. And I've never asked them for ransom."

"You're lying." Ollie took a minute to think it over, and finally decided that if there was one man in the whole world crazy enough to kidnap a child without demanding ransom, that guy would be Ricky Cummins. "Okay, so we'll do it the hard way. You're going to drive me to the phone booth on the corner of Pilchuck and Fidalgo. Me and the kid are going to make a call. You and your girlfriend can take off if you want to, but if you do, that would leave me without wheels and without wheels, I would get very mad. So stick around, unless you want to see a million-dollar baby get drowned in your bathtub. You with me?"

"I'm with you," Ricky said. In the back seat, the girl didn't say anything at all.

A few blocks from Great Oaks cemetery, Jack Howard drove into a supermarket lot and parked next to a public telephone booth. "I'll be glad to make the call, Martin. But maybe you'd like to talk to your mother yourself."

"Yes, Jack. I think I would."

"Got enouch change?" It struck Howard that there was something ludicrous about posing such a question to a man who earlier in the day had filled a suitcase with two hundred thousand dollars in unmarked twenty-dollar bills. But Martin said, "I don't have any," and picked a quarter and a dime out of the small mound of coins in Howard's palm. "Come with me, Jack. If Mother has heard from the kidnapper, you'll want to talk to her, too."

Howard waited outside the glass cubicle while Martin dialed. After saying hello, Martin was silent for several minutes, listening intently. At last he said, "Please hold on, Mother, while I talk to Jack."

Martin pushed the folding door to the side. Handing over the receiver, he said, "The man who has telephoned before called again just a few minutes ago. I'm to go to Heatherfield cemetery with the money. I'm to go alone, and wait beside my brother's grave. He also ordered me to face the headstone, with the suitcase of money in back of me, and I'm not to turn around, even when I hear a voice."

"More threats?"

Martin nodded. "Yes. If I don't follow his orders to the letter, he won't return Leif. Before he gives me the baby, he's going to count the money, and if it's a penny less than two hundred thousand..." Martin paused and with great effort recited the kidnapper's words. "He said, 'You shortchange me, Dahlquist, and you'll get your kid, all right. So you can bury your kid right alongside your brother.'"

"Threats like that are standard. He can't carry them out if he doesn't have the baby, and all evidence so far points to the conclusion that he does *not*. Ricky has your son, not Ollie White."

Martin nodded. "I'm sure that's been true up to now. But tonight Ollie said that it would be just too bad if we didn't complete the deal because the baby is sick, very sick. He added some ugly remarks about ... about the way it looks now, the baby will save him the trouble of using his gun."

Howard said thoughtfully, "The baby has been sick all week, but now, for the first time, Ollie White knows it." He looked at his wristwatch. "You're supposed to be at Heatherfield two hours from now. Okay. Let me talk to Laurie. We've got to move."

Martin stepped out of the booth and handed the receiver to Howard. The investigator's instructions were brief. Afterwards he put a hand on Martin's shoulder and walked beside him back to the car.

The wind and the rain had subsided, but a low ceiling of black stormclouds shut out the rising moon. At the rear gate into Heatherfield Park, darkness was total. Ornate lamps lighted the wide entrance at the front of the cemetery, but at the far side, where the gate was seldom used except by the gardeners, there was no illumination of any kind.

It was eleven-thirty when Howard parked near the gate and switched off the headlights. "Thirty minutes."

"Laurie should be here soon."

"Good." Howard opened the glove compartment and its small bulb showed an object about the size of a man's hand lying under a neat stack of maps. It was wrapped in chamois cloth. Howard took it out and carefully removed the chamois. It was a pistol, small, compact, and deadly. "You ever used one of these?" Howard asked.

"Not for years." A wave of revulsion swept over Martin. "But I know how. It was one of Father's lessons."

Howard handed him the pistol as a car turned into

the lane behind the cemetery. Laurie stepped out and walked quickly to Howard's car. No one spoke until she was in the front seat beside Martin and the door was closed. Even then their voices were unnaturally quiet, as if the blanket of darkness was smothering the sound.

Howard looked at his wristwatch. "Our timing is good. You wait right here, Laurie. Don't be frightened."

Laurie whispered, "I'm not. Except for you and Marty."

Howard glanced at Laurie and decided not to try any empty reassurances. "It may be a long wait, but please remember that you are not to step out of this car under any circumstances. If neither Martin nor I get back by one o'clock, drive to the all-night truck stop on Highway 258, the one you passed before you turned in here, and call the police."

Once more Howard pulled back his sleeve and checked the time. "Okay, Martin. I'll get going. That gives me almost twenty minutes before you change to Laurie's car." The Buick's interior lights flashed on briefly as he opened the car door. Laurie and Martin nodded, their faces like white masks.

While he was fishing through a pocketful of keys for one that would open the padlock on the cemetery gate, Howard was checking out every step in his plan. The lock capitulated to the fifth or sixth key he tried. He removed it and opened the wrought iron gate just enough to pass through. He started to replace the padlock, then thought better of it, and left the gate open, dropping the lock into his pocket with the keys. He might have to leave the cemetery later at a dead run.

Martin crept along the lane behind Heatherfield Park in Laurie's car. At the street he turned right, away from the cemetery, switched on his headlights and proceeded at a normal speed for six blocks before he turned right again. Now he was on the highway he would have taken had he driven straight from Black River to Heatherfield Park. In a half mile, the high wrought iron fence that encircled the park's many acres rose to his right. He braked the car and drove slowly, hugging the curb.

When Howard first gave him his instructions, Martin had suffered a moment of sheer panic. The importance of his part in saving his child had awakened doubts about his ability to meet the crisis calmly. Now, miraculously, they were gone. With the wide front entrance to the cemetery just a few yards ahead, his pulse steadied and his head cleared.

"Be obvious," Howard had counseled him. "Head-lights on bright. Slam the door when you get out of the car...." The instructions ran through his head like a recording. Park the car near the front gate. Get out, unlock the trunk....

Martin picked up the suitcase and closed the trunk after two or three noisy attempts to make the lock catch. The main gate was open, as it always was. Holding the suitcase a little away from his body so that even in the dark someone watching would be able to see he was carrying it, he walked through the gate and proceeded slowly along on the lane that bisected the park. He stayed in the middle of the road, where he would be in full sight.

At the point where he had to leave the road to turn toward his brother's grave, Martin paused to get his bearings in the darkness. The grave was in a family plot in the most remote corner of the park. It was virtually surrounded by a screen of flowering shrubs and had to be approached through a stand of juniper and yew. Martin hefted the suitcase from his left to his right hand, and turned onto the path toward the Dahlquist plot. He had about two hundred yards to go.

The soft path hushed the sound of his footsteps. For the first time Martin became aware of noises other than his own. There was a distinct rustling, somewhere behind him. His first impulse was to turn and look, but he controlled it and continued along the path. One hundred yards. Now he knew absolutely that he was being followed, for the sounds at his back were louder. And under the rustling of leaves and the crack of broken twigs, he picked up the sound of a human voice. It was indistinct, wordless, like an exclamation of pain.

He continued doggedly, slowing his pace and straining to hear something that would tell him how close the man behind him had come. Now, fifty yards. The clump of evergreens was just ahead. Suddenly, a new sound drifted through the shadows at his back. It was the thin high wail of a baby crying. Martin froze, paralyzed by the effort to keep his eyes straight ahead.

"Stop right there!"

The command shot out of the shadows like a bullet. It was the voice he had overheard on the telephone issuing orders to his mother, the whining voice of Ollie White.

"My brother's grave is up ahead. Your instructions were..."

"I told you, Dahlquist. This is far enough. Drop that suitcase."

Martin obeyed. His ears seemed to be getting keener, adjusting to the indistinct medley of sounds the way eyes gradually adjust to the dark. Now he was sure that Ollie White wasn't alone. There was a second man, though whatever he and White were saying to each other was lost in the crescendo of the baby's cries. "I dropped the suitcase," Martin called out. "Now give me my son."

An ugly laugh answered him. "Sure, sure. But first we count the money."

"*We*..." The plural confirmed Martin's guess that

Ollie White had come to the cemetery with another man. The puzzle of the two kidnappers was solved. They had thought Ollie White was an interloper. But they had been wrong. He and Ricky were partners. The second man behind him was Klaus Ochsner's son.

Ollie's nasal voice issued another order: "Go get the suitcase."

Martin sensed the approach of another person and felt someone brush against his leg as the suitcase was picked up. He heard rapid breathing, like that of a person who has been running or is badly frightened. The presence at his back withdrew. He heard a faint click as the suitcase was opened. And a few minutes later, a girl's tremulous voice said, "It's all here."

A girl! It was a possibility he had never considered.

But something was out of kilter in the scene he imagined at his back. The girl's part was to pick up the suitcase and count the money. Ollie White's was to be ready with his revolver. *Who was holding the baby?* The answer was plain. The true kidnapper was Klaus Ochsner's son, as they had known from the beginning.

Martin was seized by anger so bitter and so deep that neither his resolve to keep a clear head nor the menace of Ollie's gun could contain it. As if to spur him further, the baby's cries rose, louder and more pitiful than before. Martin's hand gripped his pistol, and he whirled around, right arm lifted toward the sky. He lowered it slowly, steadying it with his left. In a fraction of a second the dim figures came into focus, and he knew that the short man on the left was Ollie White, that the girl was in the middle, and that the tall man on the right with the child in his arms was the man he wanted to kill.

He paused, allowing himself the extra potentially lethal second to take careful aim at Ricky Cummins's head.

From the woods at his right, a voice shouted, "No Martin! No! Don't shoot your brother!"

Stunned, Martin lowered his arm. Ricky Cummins was running toward him, the girl was at his side. Behind them, Ollie White was shouting curses and pointing his revolver at Ricky's back. There was a burst of gunfire. Ollie White took one stumbling step, grunted, and fell. Jack Howard emerged from the darkness and raced toward them, gun in hand.

Martin stood watching as if paralyzed. Ricky Cummins was standing in front of him, offering him the baby. Martin let the pistol drop to the ground and held out his arms. "Brother?" he said uncertainly, looking into a face he had known all his life. The high forehead, the curly hair, the short nose—it was the boyish, open, friendly face of his father. "Brother?" he asked again, just as his eye picked out of the darkness the sudden movement of Ollie White's hand as he aimed his gun at Ricky's back.

Martin shouted, "Watch out, Ricky!" Ricky dropped to the ground. The bullet went over him, imbedding itself in the trunk of a maple tree a few feet to Martin's left. Ollie had propped himself on one elbow. Still screaming curses, he was taking aim again. Ricky jumped up, ran straight at Ollie and threw himself on top of him. He wrenched the revolver from Ollie's hand and threw it across the grass.

Pinned to the ground by the weight of Ricky's body, Ollie mumbled meaningless threats. For a moment he continued to struggle. Then with a final gasp he went limp.

Ricky got to his feet and turned to face the man who had chased him in the public market and again at the Wendell Arms. "He's dead."

"I'll take the credit for that," Howard said. "But he wouldn't be the only one, if you hadn't rushed him." He extended his hand. "My name's Jack Howard. We've met before."

Ricky hesitated, then took the hand. "Did you shout, 'Don't shoot your brother'?"

"I did."

"What did you mean?"

Howard's voice was warm and fatherly. "Later, Ricky. Right now, let's get ourselves sorted out."

They stood in a cluster, Martin with the baby in his arms, Marika close to Ricky and holding his arm, and Howard hovering protectively over them all. They were beyond speech. With Howard lay the solution to a monstrous riddle, but for the moment, surrounded by the tombs of the dead, they were united in an unspoken desire to postpone hearing the answers.

As Howard checked Ollie's pulse and pocketed his revolver, the night grew brighter. Moonlight began to filter through the last thin layer of stormclouds, casting silvery light on the headstones and monuments and on the faces of the silent group huddled together in front of the Dahlquist plot.

Suddenly from somewhere in the dark forest of marble slabs they heard a wordless crying.

As if an invisible force compelled them, they followed the voice along the path, through the grove of juniper and yew to the Dahlquist plot, and finally to the small mound of earth which covered the grave of the little child kidnapped and murdered more than forty years before. Lisa Ochsner, poor Lisa, totally mad, was sitting on the ground beside the grave. Her empty arms were crossed to form a cradle and she was rocking back and forth, keening, over and over, "My baby, my little Karl. Poor little Bübchen . . . Poor little Bübchen . . ."

Epilogue

THE STORM HAD been gathering all day, but at his desk by the window Jack Howard was so absorbed in finishing his record of the Dahlquist case that he scarcely noticed it. While he wrote, billowing blue-black clouds rolled in from the North Pacific, engulfing the ragged peaks and ridges of the Olympic Mountains and advancing menacingly across the dark water of Puget Sound. With the city in its grip, the storm broke. A shaft of lightning pierced the murky sky, followed instantly by a single clap of thunder as sharp as the report of a gun.

A burst of rain clattered noisily at the window, like an impatient voice demanding attention. Howard put down his pen and looked up. Suddenly the storm sounds were evoking the past. He listened with his eyes closed, letting them carry him back to the night of March first, 1932, when another storm had drawn him to the window of his Green Hill dwelling and held him there, bewitched, while the darkness split open and the Dahlquist mansion, The Aerie, stood before him, more distinct, nearer, than the house across the street, and with all its windows blazing with light. . . .

That night the strange vision of The Aerie had filled him with anxiety. But tonight the storm, for all its fury, was not laden with premonitions of disaster. The storm sounds were loud, but to Howard's ear, cheerful, as if rain and wind were joining in a boisterous celebration. And that, he mused, is thoroughly in keeping with what I've been writing today. The second Dahlquist kidnapping was rooted in the tragic past, but except for Lisa Ochsner's pitiful death, it had ended happily. Ricky Cummins' rebirth as the missing Dahlquist son involved some painful adjustments, but the family, now including Marika as well as Ricky, was taking the hurdles as they came. Already, the legal barrier to a happy future had been removed by the judge's decision to defer prosecution. Ricky and Marika were on probation, but in due course the charges would be dropped and the criminal record expunged.

Howard sighed deeply. His diary had now been updated. He had ended by describing Klaus Ochsner's bizarre scheme for replacing the child he had lost with the Dahlquists' son. Then why this eerie feeling that he had more to say? He turned back a few pages and began to read.

Klaus Ochsner was motivated by psychopathic hatred of a heroic figure, a man who was rich, famous, adored by millions—everything he was not. His crime was also an act of atonement. He believed he had caused his son Karl's horrible death on the highway. This guilt, coupled with the fact that Lisa could not bear another child, drove him to his desperate plan.

The ladder under the nursery window, the stealthy climb and flight with the sleepy baby— that's an old story, but not *all* the story. The next move took place the following morning, when Klaus drove Lisa and little Leif Dahlquist to the home of friends a hundred miles from Seattle, the elderly "Aunt Rhoda" and "Uncle Fred" whom Ricky still remembers vaguely. They, too, were immigrants, cousins of Lisa's mother, and they were easily convinced that Lisa and the child had to be hidden because of some tangle with the mysterious immigration laws. Back on Grummin Street, Klaus told the neighbors Lisa had received a cablegram from her sister saying their mother was gravely ill and that he had put her on the first train to New York where she would board a ship to Hamburg.

The next step, after the police had given up their search for the Dahlquist child, was to be Lisa's return with the baby supposedly born while she was in Austria. Then Klaus, Lisa, and their son Eric would relocate in a new community under a different name.

Of course the search didn't wane, and after a few weeks Klaus realized that even though hidden at "Auntie's," Lisa and the child were in constant danger as long as the manhunt continued. So he improvised another plan.

What a macabre, yet tragic ruse it was! The grisly exhuming of his own son from the grave at Great Oaks cemetery, a grave that Klaus himself had dug. Exchanging Karl's clothing for the Dahlquist baby's garments. Carrying Karl's corpse to a wooded area near the Dahlquist estate and leaving him in a shallow grave only a few feet from the road and directly under a telephone and power pole. And finally, calling the telephone company to complain about lines being down.

The hoax succeeded because it corroborated rather than contradicted facts already established.

The broken ladder outside the second-floor nursery at The Aerie had convinced investigators that the kidnapper had taken a bad fall while he was descending with the baby in his arms. The autopsy disclosed that the child had died of "a fractured skull caused by external violence." Who would have dreamed that the fatal injury had been the result of falling against the side of a truck rather than falling to the ground or being murdered by the kidnapper shortly thereafter? The degree of decomposition was another factor. Medical examiners stated that the child had been dead for two months at least, and probably longer. The Dahlquist child had been kidnapped two and a half months earlier. If anyone had doubts—for instance, a sample of the corpse's hair was never analyzed—they were overcome by compelling visual proof: the mutilated and decayed body was dressed in the Dahlquist baby's clothing.

As Klaus had anticipated, the manhunt ended abruptly. When the body was "found," positively identified by Leif Dahlquist himself and laid to rest in the Dahlquist family plot in Heatherfield Park, the identity of "Eric Ochsner" was buried with him. At last Lisa and the child were safe.

And so was Klaus, until the ransom money led to his arrest. At that point, Lisa left the child with "Auntie" and reappeared on Grummin Street, having supposedly hurried back from Austria. They both knew Klaus was in grave danger—as a man guilty of kidnapping, innocent of murder, but charged with both—yet both Klaus and Lisa remained silent.

Klaus's silence was the act of a madman, whose distorted self-image was of himself as a hero. He simply did not believe he would ever be put to death and he convinced Lisa as well. This demented sense of invulnerability continued right up to a few days before he was led into the death chamber. By then, Lisa had gone over the edge into true insanity. For three months prior to the execution and for a year or more afterwards, she was in the maximum security ward of a state mental hospital. Klaus had waited too long to speak for himself, and too long to call on Lisa to speak for him.

Howard picked up his pen, still feeling compelled to write some sort of finale. After a few minutes he gave up, closed his diary, capped his pen and switched off the desk lamp. He was exhausted, emotionally as well as physically. He looked at his watch. Three-thirty, much too early to think about dinner. He'd rest for a while and then go back to his diary.

He lay down on the couch. Rain was still drumming on the windows, but less insistently, and the sky was clearing. Later in the afternoon he might go out for a long walk. . . .

Howard was drowsing when a small sound brought him wide awake. He lay very still, eyes open, waiting for the disturbing nose to repeat itself. Night had fallen—but that was impossible! He hadn't had time to fall asleep, and when he left his desk it had been daylight. And this strange "night" had brought an unnatural darkness, so opaque there weren't any shadows. The sky was equally black; inside and outside darkness fused so that the windows separating the two had disappeared.

He sat up cautiously, eyes moving slowly from left to right in a futile attempt to force some familiar object to come into focus. Seconds ticked by, and then he knew what had awakened him. It was the sound of breathing. There was someone else in the room.

"Who is it?" he asked. "Who are you?"

The breathing drew closer. It was a little above him, as if someone taller than he were leaning over the sofa. But he felt no anxiety, no fear. Rather he was strangely pleased, even excited, by the intruder's presence in his living room.

Now the breathing grew fainter, moving slowly from the sofa to the windows. Howard pressed the button on the table lamp beside the sofa—though even as he did so he somehow knew the light would not go on. He jumped up and stood in the middle of the living room, so encased in darkness that he was beginning to lose his bearings, when a pale area of light began forming around the old oak table at the window. It was like moonlight, but the source seemed to be inside the room. Howard tried to approach it, but he couldn't. His feet seemed rooted to the floor.

Misty patterns were forming in the pool of light, swirling around each other like parts of a whole trying to find each other. As Howard strained to make out what they were, the fluid light mass settled into a visible whole and the whole came into focus. There was a tall, thin man sitting at the old oak table reading Howard's diary, his face obscured in shadow.

Howard was overcome by a desire to say something important to this dream figure, as if this were a matter of some urgency, a chance he might never have again. The figure was turning the pages of the diary with the graceful dreamlike quality of action filmed at slow motion. Gripped by the need to find that one and only message quickly, Howard tried desperately to clear his mind. As if he sensed Howard's need, the man looked up.

It was an old face—and a young one. Now Howard knew who he was. It was Leif Dahlquist, and suddenly Howard knew what to say.

"He's going to be all right, sir. It isn't going to be easy, but he'll make it."

The man's face broke into a boyish smile. The figure nodded, picked up the diary's worn leather cover and slowly closed the book.

Howard opened his eyes, raised himself to a sitting position and automatically looked at his watch. Quarter to four! So he couldn't have been asleep, and yet his mind was full of dream images as real as if they were projected on a screen. This room engulfed in total, impenetrable darkness? But the late afternoon light was streaming across his desk and it was undeniably real. The memory of a visitation, of a loving presence sitting in a pool of light? A dream he wanted to believe, but already fading because he could not believe in it enough.

His eyes moved around the room and saw that each familiar object was just what it had been, was now, and always would be. Until he focused on the old oak table by the window.

The desk lamp was burning. "Reality" was in knowing he had turned off the light. But "dream" was reality, too, though it might be as hard to hold as a rainbow.

Howard went to his desk. A feeling of great elation came over him. The diary was now complete. Its message had been communicated to the person to whom, from the very beginning, he had unconsciously directed it.

Howard picked up the worn leather volume, and holding it with both hands, he stood at the window until the last pale daylight disappeared behind the mountains and night settled peacefully over Puget Sound.

IN 1942 THE U.S. RATIONED GASOLINE

The basic ration for passenger cars

A

MILEAGE RATION

"A" DRIVERS MUST DISPLAY THIS STICKER

That was wartime and the spirit of sacrifice was in the air. No one liked it, but everyone went along. Today we need a wartime spirit to solve our energy problems. A spirit of thrift in our use of all fuels, especially gasoline. We Americans pump over 200 million gallons of gasoline into our automobiles each day. That is nearly one-third the nation's total daily oil consumption and more than half of the oil we import every day . . . at a cost of some $40 billion a year. So conserving gasoline is more than a way to save money at the pump and help solve the nation's balance of payments; it also can tackle a major portion of the nation's energy problem. And that is something we all have a stake in doing . . . with the wartime spirit, but without the devastation of war or the inconvenience of rationing.

ENERGY CONSERVATION -
IT'S YOUR CHANCE TO SAVE, AMERICA

Department of Energy, Washington, D.C.